1

Introduction

The end of the world. Those words conjure up different things to different people and today it seems like the end of the world is on the minds of a lot of people. The possibility of all life on earth being wiped out seems more and more likely reality with each passing decade in a world that is increasingly unstable and uncertain. It is now pretty much a mainstream topic of discussion that is no longer relegated to the fringes of mere speculation.

From a very young age I have always had a very strong fascination with the whole concept of the complete destruction of the world by any and all means. I guess I was always just cheerful person. Pretty much every time a new Apocalypse prophecy came about I was one of the first people to hear about it. So many Apocalypse dates came and went throughout the years that I have completely lost count. And with so many different causes of Apocalypse tooP People certainly didn't lack any imagination when it came to ways the world could be completely destroyed. Whether it was from religious or secular viewpoints, everyone has their own vision of how the world could likely end and I personally considered each and every one as a possibility. Frankly I am pretty amazed we made it this far without destroying ourselves, but as I said I'm a very cheerful person. But on some of my darker days I sometimes think maybe the world won't end after all! But that won't stop me from thinking about it.

Over the years I have built up a very large number of story ideas and novel ideas on apocalyptic and post-apocalyptic themes, probably hundreds, if not more, of every different variety of Apocalypse you can imagine, and I imagined them all in detail. About a decade ago I embarked on a quest to write 1000 page nuclear war epic that I am still working on. But I thought in the meantime maybe I should take a break from that and just pick a few of those couple of hundred shorter stories to write. So here I managed to pick out 15 of them that I feel give a wide variety of different types of Apocalypse from causes as diverse as nuclear war, religious phenomenon, alien invasion, zombies, biological warfare, asteroids, GammaRay bursts, electromagnetic pulse, technology gone awry and some without any real logical explanation whatsoever.

So I hope you will enjoy these 15 tales from the end of the world and hopefully there will be many more volumes to follow, because when it comes to the end of the world the possibilities are endless.

One Big Happy Family

"Honey, are you almost ready?" shouted Barbara.

"Ready for what??" grumbled Harold as he stared intently at the computer screen.

"Remember, tonight we made reservations at that fancy new restaurant."

"We will go another night. Tonight is not good. I have to do work on the shelter tonight. World events are not looking good. Did you hear about this new situation in the Middle East?"

"There's a new situation in the Middle East all the time. You know what I call it when I hear that there is trouble in the Middle East? I call it a weekday."

"This is really serious this time. We are talking about the threat of imminent nuclear war."

"Last week it was a pandemic super plague you were worried about, after that report of tainted beef somewhere in Southeast Asia broke. The week before that you swore before Almighty God that an asteroid was definitely on its way."

"This is different Barbara. Troops are massing along the borders and missiles are being moved. I really think that this can wait until another night. Going out to eat is not a priority when we are on the brink of World War III."

"Do you even remember what today is?"

"The Eve of destruction?" Harold said in full seriousness.

"It is the Eve of destruction for you if you don't remember."

"Remember what?" Harold asked as he continued to stare hypnotized at the computer screen.

"It is our 17th anniversary!"

"17th anniversary of what?" Harold said, as he continued to read the news story in front of him, almost completely oblivious to his wife's shouting.

"Harold!"

"We'll go out to eat next week, if global events –"

"Screw global events, next week isn't our anniversary! I swear you care so much more about preparing for the end of the world that you don't even pay attention to what is right in front of you."

"Dammit Barbara, I am trying to make sure this family survives. If we don't prepare properly there might not even be a next week for us."

She folded her arms and then slammed down the screen of Harold's laptop. "If you aren't going to go to dinner tonight, then there won't be a next week for us. I'm sick of all this bullshit Harold. The world isn't going to end. And even if it were, what is there to live for for you? All you do is spend your time fixating on what may happen and you never even spend any time with your family. You talk about protecting and saving us, and you don't even spend any time talking to us or getting to know us. You know more about what is going on on the other side of the world than you do what is going on in your own house."

"It's called keeping informed Barbara, maybe you should try it sometime."

"I'm not going to have this argument with you. If you're not going to go out to dinner with me I'll just go with Audrey. I thought it would be nice to spend my anniversary going out with my husband, but if you're not going to come, I'm not going to let the reservation go to waste. So what is it going to be?"

Harold looked up at his wife, her eyes glaring down at him and he knew that she meant business. "Okay," he said as he leaned back in his chair. "I just need a little while to shower and get ready. You and Audrey go ahead and order. I think that I will have the lobster, you can put in my order ahead of time and I should be there by the time the entrée arrives."

Barbara looked him over with an intimidating stare. "Well, you certainly shouldn't go out looking like you do. But I swear to you Harold, you had better be there. I will forgive you for forgetting that today was our anniversary, and we can still have a nice meal, but if you don't show up for dinner it's over."

"Scouts honor," said Harold as he held up his hand. "And I made Eagle Scout, so you know you can trust me."

"Alright," said Barbara with a sigh. "You get ready and I'll meet you there in a half-hour. I'm going to keep my phone on and I'll be calling you if you are even a minute late, even just one single minute," she said as she waved her finger for emphasis. "Come on Audrey, your father will be with us shortly," she said as she yelled up to her daughter.

As Barbara and Audrey left, Harold went up, got undressed and started to shower. As he stared vacantly into the showerhead he couldn't help but thinking about the troop movements in Iran and North Korea. Why didn't his wife understand? He was just thinking about her safety. She never was very interested in world events, and was always dismissive of the possibility that the apocalypse was around the corner. Sure, there had been many false apocalypses. He had been wrong and jumped to conclusions on many occasions, but didn't she realize it was always best to be prepared? It is always better to be safe than sorry.

Harold finished his shower as quick as he possibly could and dried himself off. As he began to get dressed, he decided to put on the TV to see if there were any news updates on the situation in the Middle East. He turned on the TV and began to put on his pants. He looked at the television screen and saw the emergency broadcast symbol. "This is not a test," the announcer's voice said. "I repeat, this is not a test."

As soon as Harold heard that he missed putting his leg into his pants and fell backwards right onto his ass. He then sat there staring up at the television screen.

"The Chinese and the North Koreans have refused the president's demands to withdraw their troops from South Korea and the Middle East. The United States is now in a state of active war and our satellites are tracking a series of missiles that have been launched and are expected to reach our airspace within a short time. If you have a shelter, you should go to it now. If you do not have a shelter you should seek shelter underground and wait for further instructions from local government."

Harold didn't need to hear anymore. As soon as he heard that, he wasted no time in getting dressed as quickly as possible and then immediately called his wife.

"Barbara," he yelled into the phone. "God dammit answer."

"Yes dear, what is it?"

"Why didn't you answer right away?"

"It takes me a minute to get my phone out. Besides, I'm driving, so I really shouldn't be talking on the phone. That's dangerous. Let me pull over."

"The hell with that! There's something much more dangerous going on."

"What is it dear? You sound worried. Did something happen? Are you okay?"

"No, I'm not. You have to come home right away."

"Why, what's wrong?"

"I was right Barbara."

"What are you talking about?"

"This is it. Missiles are heading towards the United States right now as we speak."

"Not this again Harold."

"I'm not lying. If you'd put on a God damn radio and listen to the news sometimes instead of listening to your CDs, maybe you would have some idea of what was going on in the world."

"I'm tired of all this apocalypse crap. I'm going to the restaurant, and if you want us to have a marriage tomorrow, you'll make sure to be there."

He heard the sound of her phone disconnecting. "Barbara, are you there? Answer me!" He tried dialing again but she didn't answer. "Pick up dammit! Jesus Christ, now what am I going to do?"

Harold threw the phone against the wall in frustration, disturbingly enough hitting their wedding portrait and causing it to come crashing to the ground and shattering into a million pieces.

Before he even had time to process that, he heard a loud rumbling off in the distance. As he was listening to the distant sound he saw a flash as the windows shattered and he was knocked to the floor. A second later all of the power got knocked out.

"Holy shit," Harold muttered as he slowly got up, "this is it. I have to get to the shelter."

Harold ran as fast as he could into the basement where the door to the shelter was encased in concrete. He unlocked the door, ran inside and pulled it shut as the walls continued to shake around him. He then heard an even louder rumbling that he thought might shake the shelter to pieces. "It's the blast wave," he whispered under his breath as he put his hand on his chest and felt his heart racing. "I just made it. The explosion must have been some distance away."

He flicked on the emergency power and sat down in the leather easy chair. He began breathing in sequence to try and calm himself down. After a few minutes of doing these breathing exercises he had managed to regain his composure and began to assess the situation.

The first thing he did was walk around the room and check to make sure that everything was in place. It was only now that he realized just how much money he had probably sunk into the shelter. He spared no expense. There were cots for him, his wife and daughter, the easy chair, a small couch, a computer and desk, television and three radios, and shelves full of books and DVDs, most of which were about how to survive disasters or rebuild after them.

Next he went to check the back room. He had enough food and water and other nonperishable items to survive for three months, which he guessed would now last nine months, since it was meant to supply three people but now only had to support one.

That was when it first hit him – his family was gone. His wife of 17 years and his 12-year-old daughter were gone forever. His eyes began to water, but he quickly wiped away the tears. This was no time to be overcome with grief. He didn't even know for certain that they didn't make it. There is a chance they were still alive, however slim.

He thought about that for some time. He didn't know how far away the blast was, but it was close enough to shatter windows. The EMP had quickly wiped out the power, but luckily the shelter was shielded from all EMP damage and could withstand a multiple megaton blast. He was well protected from radiation.

Unfortunately, he had no way of knowing just where the bomb's ground zero was and how close his wife and daughter were to where it struck. These were questions that could easily drive him mad, so he did his best to try to focus on the situation at hand.

He continued to check his supplies and make sure the generators were working. Once he was done checking his supplies, he went into the small bathroom at the very back of the shelter, leaned over the toilet and began to throw up.

Once he had finished vomiting, he went to the sink and rinsed his mouth out. He then took a long look at his face in the mirror. He could see that his hair was still wet from his shower, which might be the last one he would have for quite a while. Although he had a water recycling system installed into the shelter, he had to conserve water, which meant he would have to limit himself to simply washing his face.

That was when the thought suddenly occurred to him. If only he had spent a little more money he probably could've also put in a shower. That was when he started to laugh hysterically. He reached into his pocket, looked at the $65 he had in there, ripped it up and threw it into the air like confetti. It was basically worthless now. If only he had spent more money when he could, then he would have more amenities right now. His wife would frequently complain about all the money he spent on the shelter, and now here he was alive in the shelter and money was completely worthless. The shelter was a wise investment.

His wife. Now he had put her back into his mind, along with his daughter. He looked through his wallet to see a picture of them together as a family as he continued to laugh, his laughter soon turning to heaving sobs. He fell backwards onto one of the Army cots, threw his wallet to the floor and sobbed himself to sleep.

He awoke the next morning at 10:45 AM. He had guessed that the missile attack came at around 7 PM the night before. He had managed to sleep very deeply, yet he still felt tired and exhausted, his eyes crusted over and red. His mouth was very dry and he decided to have a glass of water. He was also hungry, as he missed dinner last night, but thinking about dinner just reminded him of Barbara and Audrey, so he dismissed the idea of eating. He had to conserve food, so he wasn't going to bother eating anything if he felt he was just going to make himself sick again.

After pacing around for a while, he decided to set up the radio to listen for any broadcasts. He didn't get any signal. The surface was silent. The radiation counter that he had installed showed that it was not safe to go outside and probably wouldn't be for quite some time. As a person who spent his life monitoring the news almost constantly, now he had to deal with the fact that there would be no news at all.

He had to take his mind off of his family, so he decided that he would try some light reading. But all of the books on his shelves were practical books, rather than books meant to entertain. He hadn't read very much for entertainment. He was one of those people that read primarily the news and practical books on how to survive. There was hardly anything the least bit entertaining on his shelves. It was times like these that he wished he was a regular reader for pleasure.

Giving up on trying to read, he took out a couple of board games that he had. He had checkers, chess and Othello, board games his daughter enjoyed playing, but that were meant for multiple players. He had stocked those games down here in the assumption that his family would be with him.

Trying to force thoughts of his family out of his mind, he looked in the drawer to see what else he had to entertain himself. All he had was Uno and two packs of standard playing cards – one regular deck, and one a nudie deck. The nudie deck was for him to play in private, which he now thought rather funny since it was unlikely he would be able to have much privacy in that shelter if his family had been with him.

His family. Now he had once again reminded himself of the very thing he was trying to put out of his thoughts. He began to tear up a bit, but soon wiped his eyes on his sleeve and sat back down in his easy chair to work on his breathing exercises in order to calm down and clear his mind.

Once he had finally calmed himself down, he went over to the closet and pulled out a small table, a TV tray, and began to play solitaire. He figured he might as well use the nudie deck. No one was going to disturb his privacy here.

As he looked at all the beautiful naked women on his playing cards, he began to play with himself just a slight little bit. He couldn't remember the last time that he had had sexual relations with his wife. Their marriage had been going downhill for a while. He tried to ignore those issues for the longest time, but now that he finally had time to reflect on it, he couldn't even recall the last time he was intimate with his wife. He had always been faithful to his wife, as between his job at the hardware store and all the time he spent on his shelter, he really didn't have any time for an affair. He would never have considered it. The thought of being disloyal to Barbara had never even occurred to him and he had always remained faithful to her, unless you count looking at pornography as cheating. But every married man looks at porn, that wasn't the same thing as having an affair, even though many women might think differently.

But Barbara was not one of them.

Now that he thought about it, he actually had an amazingly tolerant wife. She had managed to put up with all his weird preoccupations, even though she often complained at the time and money that he spent on survivalism, and his constant fixation on the Apocalypse.

The Apocalypse. He couldn't help but laugh. After everything that had happened, in the end he was right. Little satisfaction that brings. He had put everything, every spare dime, and all of his spare time in preparing for this so that his family could survive it, and now here he was, alone.

He started to tear up again and, in frustration, pushed over his TV tray and knocked his playing cards onto the floor and kicked the wall in anger. "God dammit Barbara," he shouted, "if only you had listened to me. Why didn't you listen to me? Why?!" He pounded his fists against the wall as he began to sob hysterically once again.

He sat around for several hours, and finally he could wait no more and decided he had to eat something. He didn't have much of an appetite, in spite of not having eaten all day, but he managed to force down a couple of mouthfuls of saltines, washed down with a beer. He didn't want to use up all of his alcohol, but dammit he needed it to get through today.

After he finished his beer, he took out a small notebook. He had never been the type to keep a journal before, but he thought that now is a good time to start, if only to keep track of his supplies and try to maintain his sanity. He took out a pen and wrote his first entry.

August 9: Check for radio signals. No signals. Played solitaire. Masturbated. Saltines for dinner. Got drunk.

He laughed at that final entry. He then laughed again at the irony. August 9, the anniversary of the day we bombed Nagasaki. Maybe there is such a thing as karma.

Once he had completed writing in his journal, he took the notebook and put it under his bed and stared blankly at his ceiling. He turned off the lights.

That was the end of the first day.

September 9

Harold had passed the last month with a daily routine that bordered on obsessive-compulsive. He would sleep late every morning until about 10 AM. He would check for any signs of radio broadcasts and then he would jog in place, do push-ups and pull-ups for about an hour before having a combination of breakfast and lunch. Then he would play solitaire with his nudie deck for 3 to 6 hours, usually finding some time to masturbate in the process to help relieve the boredom. After that he would exercise for another hour, have dinner, check for radio broadcasts once more and then read his survival manuals until he was too tired to continue. He would usually go to sleep by 10 or 11 PM. He kept track of all this in his Journal, which he frequently read, only to realize the emptiness of the life that he had worked so hard to preserve.

In assessing his situation, he often felt that he slept too much, but then there wasn't much else to do. He would occasionally watch some of his survival DVDs until it got to the point where he could recite them line for line and figured that he'd better just conserve power.

The only thing that broke up the monotony of his daily routine was that occasionally his extended periods of sleep would result in interesting dreams. One of the few non-survival-based books in a shelter was a book that a friend had given him that he had never read before about lucid dreaming. He read it from cover to cover several times and soon had learned how to program and take control of his dreams, which he would then record in his Journal.

His dreams. That was pretty much the only place where his family was still alive. Once in a while he would dream that his wife and daughter were still alive, and a couple of times he even had a sexual dream about Barbara, but then he would always wake up crying at the false reality of it. At first it was a welcome relief from the loneliness, but the very unreality of it soon just drove him into deeper despair, and in his frustration he began to rip up the book on lucid dreaming, not that he hadn't already basically memorized it.

He went to look at himself in the mirror. He had grown a long beard as he hadn't bothered with shaving. He justified this to himself by saying he was doing it to conserve supplies, but mostly he just didn't care. It's not like anyone was going to see him in his sorry state.

There had been no sign of life from the outside world and his radios continued to be silent. But he did notice one thing that changed. The radiation counter had shown that radiation levels had reached a safe level. He could go outside.

Looking through his closet, he realized he left himself with a limited wardrobe. He eventually decided on wearing a heavy plaid overcoat and his hunter's cap. Holstered at his side was a small pistol for self-defense.

He slowly opened the door to the shelter and walked into his basement. He noticed that it was unseasonably cold, even with his heavy overcoat. Looking around nothing looked too out of place, considering everything that had happened. He noticed there wasn't any wildlife present in his home.

As he checked out the upper floors of his house he could see that everything was basically intact, except for his windows, which had been blown out in the attack. He noticed that his wedding portrait still sat in pieces on the floor. He dug through the broken glass, took the photograph of he and his wife, folded it up and put it in his pocket for safekeeping.

He took out his Geiger counter which showed that the levels of radiation were still safe, although he didn't see any signs of life anywhere. In looking out the window he could see that the sky was very dark and there appeared to be snow on the ground, even though it was only September.

"Nuclear winter," he said to himself, before turning his back to the outside.

First things first. He went through the house looking for any valuables that he didn't have time to grab before the attack. The family photo albums had managed to survive, aside from being a little bit damp from the cold. He took them back down to the shelter. For the last month his only photograph of his family had been the family picture in his wallet. Why hadn't he kept all of their valuables in the shelter?

Actually, he remembered now. His wife said that it was morbid to think that every time they wanted to look at their precious family memories that they would have to go down to that dreaded shelter. But it looks like they had managed to survive on their own. In fact, it looked like most of the family's valuables had been left alone. No looters had disturbed his home, not that he had much that was worth stealing.

In looking through his house, he found that none of the electronic equipment seemed to be in functioning order, no doubt due to the EMP burst. So that was all basically garbage. He did manage to find a couple of more objects of sentimental value. He took his wife's jewelry out of the drawers and brought that back down to the shelter, along with his daughter's doll collection. The prize of her doll collection was a very special doll that was made to look exactly like her. It was so lifelike he almost thought for a moment that it was his actual daughter, and he began to cry again.

He spent most of the rest of the day taking objects of value and moving them into the shelter. There wasn't much that could keep him occupied, but he had managed to find a bunch of old paperbacks and magazines, mostly girly stuff that belonged to his wife and daughter, but it was better than nothing.

At the end of the day he considered going outside, but felt that he wasn't ready. But out of morbid curiosity he couldn't help but step outside for a brief moment.

He looked up to see the sky was completely darkened by a thick cloud cover and everything was covered in snow for as far as the eye could see. It was freezing cold and he could see his breath in front of him. Everything was silent and that sound of silence was deafening to him. No, further exploration could wait.

The next two weeks Harold managed to occupy himself with all of the valuable treasures that he had discovered above. The women's magazines weren't of any interest to him, but he soon found that 50 Shades of Gray was more tolerable when there was nothing else to read. Still, he wished that his wife had had better taste in books. And it left him to wonder what type of things interested her that she wasn't telling him about.

Maybe you never really know the people around you and never even think about it until they are gone and it is too late. Now those burning questions will forever go unanswered.

Harold began to look through the photo albums once more. He found that he often went through all of them two or three times in a single day, as memories were now the only thing he had left of his family.

"Remember this day," he said as he pointed to a picture of himself with Audrey and Barbara on the beach. He looked to the doll that bore the striking resemblance to his daughter Audrey, but she said nothing. Harold laughed. "Of course you don't remember it, you're just a doll."

Harold continued laughing and turned the page to Audrey's 10th birthday party. He drew the Audrey doll closer to him and put his arm around her. "Look how happy you were on that day. I can still remember it vividly. You had wanted a circus party and we hired a clown to come perform for all your friends and he ended up dancing with your mother and everyone was laughing and having so much fun." Harold wiped away a tear. "And that was the day we had this doll of you made. You were so shocked to see it that you almost fainted."

Harold looked carefully at the picture, turned to the doll and dropped the photo album at his feet causing it to slam shut as he began to sob and shake the doll. "And now, now you're all I have left of her. Just a lifeless image. You'll never grow up, never grow older, never have a daughter of your own, and all because you and your mother had to go out for that God damned dinner!"

He threw the doll aside and began knocking stuff over in frustration and kicking the wall in anger until he badly hurt his foot. "God fucking dammit," he shouted as he sat down and began to rub his injured foot. He continued to rub his foot and fought back more tears. He then looked up at the clock to see it was 10:30 PM and figured that it was time he should go to bed.

"Sorry for all my swearing darling," he said as he picked up the Audrey doll and placed it down on the cot next to his and covered it with a blanket up to her chin. "But it is way past both of our bedtimes. I'm not going to let you stay up late every night like this. But don't worry, we can look at the photo albums more again tomorrow. But now it is time for bed, so I will wish you sweet dreams."

Harold kissed the Audrey doll on the forehead, closed its eyes, laid down on the cot next to her, turned out the lights and went to sleep.

Harold woke up early the next morning and the first thing he did was check on the Audrey doll. He looked her over carefully. She really did look so lifelike that he couldn't tell the difference when she was in the bed like that. He went over to her, gently began stroking her hair and whispering to her. "Wake up Princess, we have a busy day today." He slowly opened the doll's eyes. "I hope you slept well. It's time for breakfast. We are having cereal today, but I picked out all the marshmallows to save just for you, because I know that they are your favorite."

Harold prepared the breakfast, and set aside a bowl full of marshmallows in front of the doll. As he poured the milk on his cereal and began to eat it, he spent the entire meal staring across from him into the eyes of the doll. When he had completely finished with his cereal, he turned to the doll and said, "Aren't you going to eat your marshmallows? I picked them out especially for you."

The doll continued to sit there with a vacant stare.

Harold shook his head. "Well, if you're not going to eat them, I guess I will." And he began to eat the marshmallows, looking every couple of seconds at the doll.

Once he had cleared the table, he sat down across from the doll and began chatting. "Today daddy is going to go out on an important mission. Today I am going to go outside. It might be very dangerous out there and I don't know what time I will be back. So I want you to stay here and keep careful watch over the shelter while I'm gone. Can I count on you to do that?"

The doll continued to sit there, motionless.

"Good, I'm glad that we understand each other. I will try to be back by dinner time, but if you want to have a snack in the meantime, that would be perfectly fine with me. But just one, we have to conserve food and watch our figures."

Harold patted the doll on the head and left the shelter.

He decided that he would try walking into town to see if there were any supplies that could still be used. Tomorrow was Audrey's birthday, and dammit she was going to have a memorable birthday. You only turn 13 once.

The walk into town was a long and difficult one. Luckily Harold had bundled up with a scarf, gloves, aviator goggles, his hunters cap, thick black boots and several layers of clothing. At his side, as always, was his pistol. He sincerely hoped that he would not have to use it.

He arrived in town after about an hour of walking. He saw no signs of life and a large number of abandoned cars with their windows blown out. Everywhere he looked the windows were blown out of every place, although any pieces of broken glass were covered in a thick layer of snow.

After looking around for a while, he managed to find the party supplies place. Nothing inside appeared to be looted, although if anyone had survived the blast he supposed that party supplies might not be the biggest priority. Come to think of it, it probably shouldn't be his current priority either, but he wasn't going to let his daughter's birthday be ruined.

Most of the stuff in the store was at least somewhat damp and there was frost all over the place, but he managed to find a couple of bags full of balloons, various noisemakers and the crown jewels of the entire collection – a full-blown clown outfit! This was going to be Audrey's best birthday party ever. He wished that he could find some type of cake mix or candy that was still edible, but nothing that survived would be safe for human consumption, so he went with the next best option and found an inflatable birthday cake. It was better than nothing and he hoped that Audrey would understand.

Once he had gathered up as many party supplies as he could carry, he went in search of a shopping cart in order to bring all of this stuff home. It was a long walk back to the shelter and he didn't think that he could easily carry all of this stuff.

As he went down the block to look for a shopping cart, he couldn't help but notice an adult video store nearby. He shook his head, anything electronic would probably have been destroyed by the EMP damage. But sometimes these stores had more than just videos. If this was the one that he remembered, they definitely sold more than simply videos. They also sold various sex toys and pornographic magazines.

That was when he started to feel guilty to be thinking about these type of things when he was shopping for his daughter's 13th birthday. But a man has other needs as well, and he didn't want to have to make two trips. He decided that he would check it out while he was here.

The video store was much darker than the party supplies place. Even with the feeble light from the outside, he could see what he was doing in the party supplies place. The video store had a narrow entrance that didn't let in any light. Luckily Harold had remembered to bring his flashlight with him.

He managed to feel his way around and made his way into the back room. He found himself lucky enough to find a small cache of DVDs that appeared to be undamaged, although he wouldn't know until he got home. Aside from that he just gathered up a couple of porno magazines and a plastic sex doll.

Once he had loaded up a shopping cart with as much stuff as he could fit, he began the slow journey home in the biting cold.

He managed to make it home before nightfall, which he was grateful for, because as cold as it was during the day time, he was sure that it would be even worse at night.

"Audrey, I'm home," he said as he pushed open the shelter door before stopping in his place. "I have surprises for you, but you will have to wait for tomorrow. So close your eyes now." He ran over to the doll, gently closed its eyelids and then quickly unloaded the shopping cart in the back room, after first taking a couple of minutes to warm himself up, as the cold had left him numb.

He was quite pleased with what he managed to gather on this journey. Although he didn't find much that was of any practical use for survival, he was beginning to realize that there is more to life than simply surviving.

He decided to put "Audrey" to bed early, right after they had their dinner. He then spent the rest of the night going through the things that he had brought home and seeing what worked.

The DVDs that he had gathered, unfortunately, were completely useless. The EMP had done its damage. But at least he had the magazines and his new doll, quite different than the Audrey doll, and not quite as lifelike. But it would have to do.

Although he realized that the plastic doll he had brought home wasn't really alive, he still decided that he needed to fix himself up to make himself more presentable to it. He went to the bathroom, shaved for the first time since he had been down here, washed his face and made a crude attempt to cut his hair and straighten it.

Once he had gotten himself all fixed up, he crawled into bed with the plastic sex doll. It didn't look anything like his wife, and was cold and rubbery, but he decided that he would call it Barbara. "So baby," he said as he put his arm around the doll, "it's been a long time since I have gotten any. You feel like warming me up?"

The doll sat there motionless.

"Maybe I just need to get you in the mood first," he said as he got up and began to undress. He stood in front of the doll, stark naked. "Like what you see, Barbara?"

He got back into bed and began gently caressing the doll's rubbery breasts. "You know I really miss this. We haven't spent this much time together in I can't remember how long. But I guess now we've got all the time in the world."

The doll rested in his arms as he drew it closer and wrapped his arms around it as he began to kiss it lightly on the cheek. "So, this is getting you all hot and bothered?"

The doll continued to sit there, and although he knew it was a doll, he was getting rather frustrated at the lack of response. He looked over to the copy of 50 Shades of Gray sitting on the floor. "I know what you like, you dirty girl," he whispered in the doll's ear. "You like it rough, don't you?"

He climbed on top of the doll and began rubbing himself against it very rapidly. He then squeezed its breasts very hard until he thought they might burst. "How's that feel baby?"

Next he turned the doll over and began doing it from behind as he slapped the doll on the ass. "You like that, don't you, you filthy whore!" He turned the doll over onto its back and began slapping it in the face. "Take that bitch! You love it rough, don't you? Don't you!"

Leaping up and off the doll in a moment of frustration, he stood up and pushed the doll off of his cot. "Why don't you say something to me!" he shouted as he began to kick the doll. "Talk to me dammit! Why won't you talk to me?"

Gaining control over himself, he looked at what he had done to the doll and then fell to his knees, put his hands over his face and began crying. He started pounding his fists on the floor in frustration. "Why, why, why Barbara. Why didn't you listen to me? Why?!" He then said softly one last time, "Why?"

Harold woke up the next morning still sitting naked on the floor next to the doll. He had cried himself to sleep. He got up and looked at himself in the mirror. He couldn't help but laugh when he noticed that he was standing there naked staring at himself and what a wreck of a human being he had become.

"Audrey's birthday!" he shouted, suddenly remembering. "This is no time for self-pity. I have a lot of work to do."

He looked over at the clown costume and quickly got dressed. He then blew up the plastic birthday cake and set it down on the TV tray. He started blowing up the balloons, but they just fell to the floor. That was when he remembered that they weren't going to float without any helium. That made him angry, but regular balloons are better than no balloons at all.

Once he had gotten everything all set up for Audrey's birthday party, he realized that he neglected one thing. He went over to the Barbara doll, sitting there completely naked on the floor, and realized that that wouldn't do. He opened the shelter door, ran upstairs into the freezing cold and into his wife's bedroom. He looked through her closet until he found her best outfit that she only wore on special occasions – a green sunflower dress. It had been her favorite while she was alive and today was definitely a special occasion.

Being overcome with cold, he quickly ran downstairs and dressed the Barbara doll in the sunflower dress and sat her up at the table.

Looking over the scene everything seemed perfect. He may not have had everything exactly the way he wanted it, but this was still the best birthday party he could set up under the circumstances, and that made it perfect to him.

"Time to wake up, Audrey, "he said as he went to the cot and raised the doll up. He sat her across from the Barbara doll at the table with the birthday cake between them and then sat down next to "Barbara", with him in his clown suit. Slowly he reached over and pushed open the Audrey doll's eyes. "Surprise! Happy birthday darling."

The Audrey doll sat there staring blankly at her father dressed as a clown sitting next to a sex doll dressed up as her mother.

"You're 13 today! You're entering into those awkward teenage years. You're a woman now."

The doll continued to sit there staring blankly.

"Well go ahead, make a wish and blow out the candles. But don't tell us what you wished for, or it won't come true."

The doll sat there motionless.

"Did you make a wish? Good." Harold stood up and began dancing with "Barbara." He spun her all around the room making sure to stay right in line with the Audrey doll's line of sight.

Harold began laughing hysterically. "Isn't this fun dear? Here we are all together once again. Just one big happy family."

He put Barbara down on the couch and continued to stare ahead vacantly at Audrey. "Well dear, do you like your party?"

Audrey sat there motionless.

"You know your mother and I went through a lot of trouble to set all this up. Don't you want to say something?"

Audrey continued sitting there motionless.

"How about you?" Harold turned to Barbara. "Do you have anything to say on this special occasion?" He paused and waited for a response, but did not get one. "Don't any of you have something to say?" He looked at Audrey, then looked back at Barbara. He stood up and shouted, "Why won't any of you say anything!"

Suddenly he found himself infuriated. He kicked over the table and popped the birthday cake, then started stomping on balloons. He started flipping over the cots and knocking the books and DVDs off of the shelves.

"Well this is a fine mess we have here," he said as he looked over at all the damage he had done. "Is anyone going to help me clean it up?" He looked at the two dolls sitting there on the floor. "No, just going to sit there staring at me and laughing, laughing at the clown." He picked up the TV tray and smashed it into the computer screen, shattering it. "This is pretty funny isn't it? I spent all that time and money building the shelter so that we can all survive, and now here I am, destroying it all."

He couldn't stop himself from laughing hysterically as he began to completely trash everything in the shelter. He tore apart the couch, ripped open the easy chair, tore apart the mattresses on the cots, ripped up the books and went into the bathroom and smashed the mirror with his bare fists, cutting his hands in the process. As he looked at his reflection in the broken pieces of glass on the floor, he began to come to his senses. "What's wrong with me," he said to himself.

Exiting the bathroom, he looked at the mess that he had made. Lying on the floor in this mess were Audrey and Barbara. He walked over to them and propped them up against the wall and then sat across from them. "I'm sorry," he said to them. "Here this was Audrey's special day and I ruined it. I was a real jerk and I hope that I could somehow make it up to you, both of you. You girls are the most important thing in the world to me, and it took the end of the world for me to fully appreciate that." He stood up and dusted himself off. "I know how I can make it up to you. I know that you don't like spending all your time cooped up here in this musty old shelter. No one should spend their birthday locked inside. Let's go for a walk. I am sure that it's a lovely day."

Without even bothering to change his outfit, he threw Barbara onto his back, and picked up Audrey in his arms, went upstairs and they walked outside into the cold. The sky was just as dark as ever and the area just as silent.   He sat down in the snow on his front lawn and put his arms around Barbara and Audrey. It was so cold that he could see his breath in front of him and could feel his body going numb. He drew Barbara and Audrey closer to him in an effort to keep them warm. As he could slowly feel all feeling leaving his body and his eyes beginning to freeze shut, he laid them all down with him in the middle and they all looked up at the sky together. As things began to go black, Harold clutched his girls tightly with his numbed hands and thought to himself that this really was a very special day and he was glad that he was able to spend it with his family.

He went to sleep with a smile on his face for the first time in a good long while.

The Fifth Horseman

He arrived in the Arizona desert at around noon, and the sun was bright in the cloudless sky. It was a nice, warm, sunny day, perfect summer weather. As he looked across the desert he found the quiet desolation to be very peaceful. Maybe it won't be so bad when the entire world looks this way.

Except that when the world ends, it will not be this peaceful.

He walked for several hours without encountering barely a soul. Every so often a car or a truck would pass by, but no one offered him a ride until well into the afternoon. He wasn't expecting much and wasn't very bothered by the heat, so much as he was by the indifference.

The first person who did stop to acknowledge his existence was a truck driver named Morty Engleman, who pulled over to the side of the road. "Do you need a lift stranger?" Morty asked as he opened the door.

The man nodded and got in next to Morty. "Thank you," he said as he buckled his seatbelt.

"How long were you wandering out there in the desert?"

"I would estimate a good couple of hours now. You're the first person to stop for me all day. It is amazing how you could be driving on an almost empty stretch of road for several hours without seeing another soul, and then when you do to completely pass by them without acknowledging their existence."

"A lot of people are quite indifferent to their fellow man."

"It's not indifference that worries me the most."

"I'm sorry," said Morty as he looked over the man to see that he was dressed in nothing but a white T-shirt and jeans and appeared to be covered in sweat. "But would you like something to drink?" Morty handed him a water bottle.

The man took the water bottle, chugged down a couple of gulps and said, "Thank you. That is mighty kind of you."

"Don't mention it. Say, I never even asked your name. I'm Morty."

The man shook Morty's hand but said nothing.

"You don't have to be shy, but I understand if you don't want to tell me your name."

"I guess you could say that I really don't have a name, so call me whatever you would like."

"Don't have a name? What you mean by that?"

"Just what I said. I really don't have a name."

"I've never met a man who doesn't have a name before. Do you mind if I ask you where you were from or where you were heading? That's kind of important if you want me to help you."

"Let's just say that I'm not from around here." The man laughed after that statement.

"Did your car break down?"

The man shook his head and laughed again.

"What's so funny about that?"

"I don't have a car."

"You were walking in the middle of nowhere. I just naturally assumed that your car must've broken down. It's not very often that you find people just walking along a road in the desert miles from civilization. If I didn't know better I would almost say it seems like you just dropped out of the sky or something."

With that the man erupted with the loudest burst of laughter so far. "You know you're a very perceptive individual. You don't find that very much these days."

"Well I try my best. But I can understand that you seem to be a person who doesn't much like talking about themselves. But it is important to know where it is you are heading if you want me to help you."

"I'm not heading anywhere in particular."

"Just going for a walk and got lost?" Morty laughed.

The man smiled. "Something like that. But to make it simple and to answer your question I will go as far as you'll take me. Where is it you are heading?"

"I was heading back to Phoenix. I thought that I would stop by the bar on the way home."

"That sounds perfect. I could sure go for a drink after walking in the desert all day. Preferably something really powerful."

"You like your whiskey strong, huh?"

"In my line of work you develop a strong tolerance."

"What line of work are you in?"

The man laughed again.

"Another one of your secrets I take it?"

The man nodded gently. "You might say something like that. Let's just leave it at I'm in a very stressful line of work that few would understand."

"Fair enough. I won't pester you any more about it. We should be in Phoenix shortly."

Within a short time they arrived in Phoenix and stopped at the first bar they came to.

"Get whatever you want," said Morty, "it's on me."

"That's very kind of you," said the man, "but I couldn't impose after all you'll already done for me. Let me buy you a drink."

"You don't need to feel obligated."

"Please, it's the least I can do. Besides, money isn't a problem for me. In fact," he said as he began to raise his voice, "drinks are on me for everyone tonight!"

The bar erupted with cheers and hollering.

"Well that's a very generous offer," said the bartender, "but I have to see the money before I start serving any drinks. Last guy who came in here saying that drinks were on him ended up stiffing me on the bill."

"Not much trust around here, is there?" asked the man.

"I'm afraid not, not when it concerns money."

"Well that's a damn shame, but no worries." The man pulled out a wad of bills from his pocket and laid it down in front of the bartender whose eyes lit up.

"Well folks it looks like drinks are on this man tonight," shouted the bartender to more cheers and hollering. "Say what's your name, stranger?"

"Let's just say that I'm a friend, and I'll have a whiskey sour."

The bartender quickly prepared his drink and slid it down to him.

"You really are a very generous man," said Morty. Morty had began to wonder where some wandering hitchhiker in the middle of nowhere managed to have so much money on him and started to worry that maybe he had acquired it through dubious means, although he didn't want to voice that opinion aloud for fear of offending the man. He always tried to believe the best of people and give them the benefit of the doubt until given sufficient and just cause to think otherwise.

The man drank down his whiskey sour very quickly and then started to walk over to go to where the televisions were. Aside from sports, one of the televisions was turned to a evangelical preacher.

"And the Lord's judgment will soon come upon the world and all of the Satanists, abortionists, sodomites, adulterers, fornicators and harlots will all face the wrath of the Lord," said the preacher. "The day of judgment is soon near. Will you be saved or will you be among the damned?"

The man sneered.

"Not a fan of televangelists?" asked one of the men near the television wearing a cowboy hat. "Don't think that judgment is upon us?"

"Actually, I do," said the man with a bit of a laugh, "I just don't agree with his criteria for who will be judged and why."

"Oh, and what criteria do you believe that people be judged by?"

"I believe that they will be judged by the content of the heart and the quality of their character."

"So do I. I just don't agree that Satanists, adulterers and homosexuals have good hearts. And the abortionists, they're just common murderers. They are all perverted against the will of God."

The man gave a disapproving look. "And you know what is in a man's heart?"

"Only the Lord knows that, but the Bible serves as a guide to who you shouldn't be trusting. Today we live in a country that not only tolerates but celebrates sexual deviants, atheists, Muslims and other preachers of falsehood. People who spend their life defying the will of God cannot hope to be spared his righteous and holy judgment."

"I really doubt that God gives a damn what people believe about him and what they do in their bedrooms, so long as they treat everyone with dignity and humanity."

"But the Bible says –"

"The Bible says a lot of things, and not all of it is accurate."

"You better watch what you say around here. If you doubt the Bible you will not be spared when the day of judgment comes."

The man scoffed. "I think I know a lot about who will be spared, and it is not a burden to be borne lightly."

"Nobody knows better than God himself. Who do you think you are to question his holy word?"

"You have no idea who I am and I don't think that you are ever going to know."

The man started to walk away with his back turned towards the man in the cowboy hat.

"Hey, don't you be walking away from me when I'm talking to you. I asked you who do you think you are?"

"Calm down Earl," said the bartender, "I don't want you starting anything again."

"I said I asked you a God damn question," said Earl as he grabbed the man's shoulder. The man pushed away Earl's hand and Earl responded by punching the man hard across the face. He then dived on top of the man and began pounding on him.

"Hey get off of him," said Morty as he pulled Earl off of the man, knocking off his cowboy hat in the process.

"That's it Earl, get out of this bar and don't come back until you've sobered up," said the bartender. "I should call the cops on you, but I know that you already have two assault charges against you and if you get one more you're going to find yourself in prison for quite some time."

Earl dusted off his hat and put it back on. "You're all sinners! You'll see. The day of judgment is upon us and most of you will not be amongst the saved. Look to the signs – wars and rumors of wars, earthquakes, fires, floods and famine, rampant immorality in the streets. Repent!"

"Okay, that's enough now Earl," said the bartender. "Take it elsewhere before I call the police."

Earl walked off in a huff and Morty helped the man to his feet. "Thank you," said the man as he dusted himself off.

"Don't mention it. But it looks like he gave you quite a shiner. We should get some ice for your eye. My apartment isn't very far from here."

"I don't want to be of any more trouble to you that I already have been."

"Nonsense, it just wouldn't be right of me."

The man looked at Morty for a moment and could see in his eyes that he wasn't going to take no for an answer, so he simply nodded. "Okay, let's go."

They got back in Morty's truck and began to drive home.

"Don't mind Earl, he's a bit hotheaded when he drinks. He's a bit of a fire and brimstone fundamentalist type. Pretty much hates everyone who disagrees with him."

"Unfortunately I know the type all too well."

"That's why you should never mention politics or religion, especially when you are drunk." Morty laughed, the man did not. "So are you religious or something?"

"Not in the conventional sense, no, but you might say that spirituality is sort of a big deal to me."

"Oh, is that so? In what way?"

The man laughed again as he rubbed his eye. "Let's just say it's my calling in life."

"Sort of a man on a mission type of thing?"

"You might say something like that."

"I've never been particularly religious myself. I've just always tried to live by the Golden rule of do onto others as you would have them do onto you."

"It is best when people stick to the basics. It is when you stray too far from that that the trouble starts."

"Amen to that, brother."

The rest of the ride proceeded without much conversation and they soon arrived at Morty's apartment. The elevator was broken and they had to walk up several flights of stairs until they came to a door at the end of a long hallway. He turned his key in the door and shouted, "Honey, I'm home. And I've brought a guest."

"Oh, I wasn't expecting a guest," said a blonde haired woman who was wearing a leg brace and walking with a limp towards the door. "Not that I mind. Everyone is welcome here. I'm Allison."

She held out her hand and the man shook it. "Pleased to meet you. Your husband was kind enough to give me a ride into town."

The woman blushed. "We aren't married, not yet anyway. We can't quite afford a decent wedding on a single income."

"I'm sorry to hear that," said the man as he took a look around the house to realize that it was fairly rundown and sparsely furnished. Most of the furniture looked like it was a decade or two old and ripped. The room itself was dark and only had a single window with a half dead fern in it. The walls were yellowing and were desperately in need of a paint job.

"Oh, don't be sorry for us," said Allison as she waved her hand dismissively. "We have a lot more than a lot of people have. I'm sure things will improve soon."

The man knew that that was not true, but he didn't want to say anything that would sound unkind to his gracious hosts.

"Do we have any ice?" Morty asked.

" Ice?" Allison asked.

"Yes, we had a bit of a run in with Earl at the bar and he gave my friend here quite a shiner."

"Not that Earl again. Let me guess, it was about religion again wasn't it?"

Morty nodded and Allison shook her head as she went into the kitchen to get the ice mumbling to herself, "Damn Bible thumping fundamentalist." Within a minute she came back with an ice pack and handed it to the man.

"Thank you," the man said as he placed the ice pack against his eye.

"Are you sure you shouldn't see a doctor?" Allison questioned. "You might have a concussion."

"Oh I'm sure it's nothing serious," said the man. "It's just a black eye."

"Someone should call the police on that stupid Earl." Allison shook her head again. "He's so hotheaded about every little thing and is always picking fights. He thinks he is so holy and righteous, but he would never turn the other cheek. He's convinced that the four horsemen of the apocalypse are about to descend upon the world."

The man laughed.

"What's so funny?" Allison asked.

"Nothing," said the man. "It's just that that Earl fellow wouldn't know the four horsemen of the apocalypse if they were standing right in front of him."

"That Earl doesn't know anything about anything," said Allison. "But try to take your mind off of him. You're welcome to stay for dinner if you're hungry. I wasn't expecting guests, but I always have extra spaghetti and meatballs."

"I would love that," said the man, "but I feel guilty imposing anymore upon you than I already have."

"Nonsense," said Allison. "We might not have much, but we always have enough to spare. So won't you please stay for dinner."

The man smiled. "Well I am awfully hungry."

A few minutes later Allison came limping out of the kitchen carrying a plate full of pasta. "Let me get that," said the man as he helped her to bring the food to the table.

"I'm sorry I'm so slow," said Allison. "I actually used to be a waitress, if you can believe it, until I injured my leg."

"I'm sorry to hear that," said the man. "Do you mind if I ask how it happened?"

"It was a car accident," said Morty. "A hit and run. The bastard banged into her leg and worried that she would sue and drove off before she could even get his license plate number. That's the kind of people in the world these days. Allison lost her job as a result of that and we didn't have any medical insurance. Luckily we have been able to get by me running extra shifts on my trucking run. The worst thing is that now we don't get to spend nearly as much time together since I am always on the road, and it will be a good long while before we can afford to have a decent wedding."

"I'm sorry," said Allison, "I didn't mean to burden you with our problems. I think that Morty is more angry about it than I am."

"You're damn right I'm angry about it," said Morty. "That bastard should pay for what he's done. But I don't mean to sound bitter. I believe in forgiveness, but it just makes me so damn angry that people can get away with stuff like that."

"Mercy and forgiveness are increasingly rare qualities these days," said the man. "They are some of the most neglected virtues in the modern world. But I believe that justice will prevail in the end. But I don't believe in judgment in the same way that that Earl fellow does."

"Earl," said Allison contemptuously, "I wouldn't take anything he says seriously. But now here I am rambling on and dinner is getting cold. So please, dig in."

The meal proceeded quietly with very little being said. Allison seemed to pick up on the fact that the man wasn't the most sociable individual.

"Thank you for the wonderful meal," said the man after he had finished. "It is the best I have had in I can't remember how long."

"Well you're welcome Mr.," Allison paused, "I'm sorry, how rude of me, I never even asked your name."

"Let's just say that I'm a friend and leave it at that," said the man.

Allison nodded, not wanting to push the issue.

"Well it is getting late," said the man, "I should be looking for a place to spend the night."

"Nonsense," said Allison, "you can just stay here for the night."

"No, no," said the man, "I have already imposed on you far more than any stranger could be reasonably expected to do."

"Please," said Morty, "we'd be honored if you would spend the night. The couch pulls out into a bed."

"That's a very generous offer of you," said the man. "It is rare these days to find people who are so hospitable and trusting to a person that they barely know."

"Well I've always depended on the kindness of strangers," said Allison in an imitation of a thick southern accent. They all had a good laugh at that.

"Well," said Morty, "like we said, you're welcome to stay the night. But I have to be getting to sleep because I have to get up early tomorrow for work. So I will have to say good night for now and I hope that you are feeling better in the morning. That Earl can really throw a punch."

"Thank you," said the man as he began to prepare for sleep.

The man waited for Morty and Allison to fall asleep before gently walking into their room as quietly as possible. Their bed was hardly more than a cot that barely fit the both of them, with Allison's injured leg jutting out prominently. He slowly approached their bed and gently grabbed Allison's injured leg and a mysterious red glowing energy was emitted by his hands. Allison moved a little bit in her sleep, but she did not wake up.

The man then went into the kitchen and saw some stationary sitting out on the kitchen counter. He turned on the light, took out a pen and began writing a note, then took $10,000 in cash out of his pockets and placed it under under the note. He then turned out the light and quietly let himself out the door.

The next morning Morty got up at 5 AM to eat breakfast before going to his trucking job. As he was looking through the refrigerator he noticed that the man had left. He also noticed the note the man had left on the countertop. He began reading:

Dear Morty and Allison,

I hope it is not rude of me to be leaving in the middle of the night like this, but I felt it would be easier to leave you this way, as I had not meant to stay as long as I have. I can't fully explain who exactly I am or what exactly I was doing in the middle of nowhere where you found me. But you'll remember I said that I had a calling in life and that I was something of a man with a mission. My mission is simply to repay human kindness in those rare instances where I encountered it. The two of you were the only genuinely good people I met on my current outing and I thought it only fitting that I repay you in kind. With this note you will find the sum of $10,000 in cash. You can do with it whatever you prefer and I will not come looking for any type of payback. The money is yours and I assure you it is not counterfeit and was not acquired by dubious means. I can't tell you how I acquired it, but needless to say money has never been a problem for me. I don't know if you'll ever see me again, but I do hope that you will have a happy life together. I will not lie, the times ahead are going to be difficult, and not just for you, but for all mankind. Once again, I cannot explain to you fully what I mean or how I know what I know. I will just end by saying that in addition to the money I also took the liberty of taking care of Allison's leg. I wish that I could do more, but at least I was able to do this much. Once again I would like to thank you for your kindness and wish you a long and happy life.

Signed,

a friend

Morty put down the letter and saw the $10,000, all of it in $500 bills. He counted it up three times just to be sure and looked at it under a light. He didn't know exactly what counterfeit money looked like, but as far as he knew this money looked as though it were real. That was when he remembered the other things mentioned in the letter.

"Allison," he shouted as he ran into their room.

"What is it Morty?" she said as she rubbed her eyes. "Is something the matter? Why are you shouting?"

"The man, he's gone and he –"

"Oh my God," she said as she put her hand over her mouth and sat up straight in bed, "he didn't rob us did he?"

Morty shook his head. "No, in fact he did the exact opposite."

"What do you mean?"

"Look." Morty threw the bills into her lap.

"Is this for real?" Allison said as she began counting the bills. "There must be thousands of dollars here."

"It's $10,000, I counted it three times."

Allison shot him a puzzled glance and scratched her head. "Are you telling me that the man left this money here and then vanished?"

"Well he also left a note. That's right, he mentioned another thing."

"What?!" she shouted.

"Let me take a look at your leg."

"My leg, why do you want to take a look at my leg?"

"Just let me see it!"

"Okay, okay," she said as she lifted her injured leg.

Morty examined her leg very closely. "Let me take off the leg brace."

"Why?"

"Just do it!"

"All right, hold your horses," she said as she slowly removed the leg brace. To her great surprise her leg was feeling perfectly normal and perhaps even better than it ever had before. She slowly began to get up and put pressure on it.

"Careful," Morty said as he helped her up. "Just go very slowly."

Slowly and carefully Morty helped Allison to stand up straight. "Oh my God," she said as she began to slowly walk around the room, "it's completely healed! It's a miracle! What's going on here?"

Morty handed her the note and told her to read it. After she finished reading it she looked up at Morty with a stunned look. "Is this for real?"

"I wouldn't believe it if I didn't see it with my own two eyes, but your leg is obviously completely healed and the mysterious man left us $10,000 in cash."

"Do you think he was some type of a guardian angel?"

"I don't know what exactly he is. But I do know that your leg is healed and this money appears to be real. I also don't have any idea where he came from, who he was or where to find him. I don't even know what his name was to send him a thank you note."

"So what are we going to do now?"

"I'll tell you what we do," said Morty as he grabbed Allison's hand and spun her around, "we celebrate!"

Morty and Allison danced around for several minutes with an ease which they never thought would be possible again. Then they made love for the first time since Allison's injury.

Morty decided to take a sick day and investigate whether or not the money was counterfeit. After determining that it was legitimate he quickly deposited it in the bank.

Allison went to the doctor to confirm that her leg was indeed healed. The doctor had no explanation for how she could spontaneously heal like that and declared it a genuine miracle. She didn't tell him about the mysterious man, she only said that she woke up and found that her leg was suddenly better. The doctor continued to express disbelief, but even he couldn't deny what he saw with his own eyes.

The two of them met up for dinner at a fancy restaurant that they hadn't been able to afford in years and then returned home for another night of passion. It was the best time that they had had in a long time.

After they had got over their initial shock at the miraculous events, things slowly returned to normal. Morty and Allison got married in a small ceremony. Although they now had a little bit of money, they were still far from rich and couldn't afford any major extravagance. But they were happy just to be together.

After taking a week off for their honeymoon, Morty resumed his work as a trucker and Allison managed to get her job back as a waitress. Times were difficult, but with the extra money they were able to live decently and spend more time together. They even managed to buy some new furniture as well.

Every night they would thank God or good fortune or whoever it was that sent the mysterious man to them. Allison strongly believed that he must have been an angel, although Morty held out hope that maybe he could somehow find the man and thank him for his kindness. $10,000 and a miraculous healing were far too generous for a ride into town, a spaghetti dinner and a couch to sleep on.

But despite searching online and giving out descriptions all over the city in a desperate attempt to find the man, they never were able to find him again.

As the years went on, things gradually got more difficult, not just for Morty and Allison, but for the entire world, just as the man had said it would. Always skeptical of apocalyptic claims and prophecies, even Morty had to admit that things were getting rather bad. The big war that everyone had long awaited finally broke out in the Middle East. Attacks with both chemical and nuclear weapons killed millions. Following those destructive exchanges on the other side of the world, the fallout led to outbreaks of pandemic diseases that killed many more millions. It also rendered the region completely inaccessible to the United States. This led to the biggest gasoline shortage in recorded history and a complete worldwide economic collapse. Many governments fell into anarchy and the state of worldwide war led to mass famine. As the headlines put it – the four horsemen of the apocalypse were riding across every inch of the Earth.

Morty and Allison tried to ignore the news as much as possible, but they were just barely getting by. Crime had reached epidemic proportions and Morty had to admit, with some degree of shame, that if he had met that same man today he probably would not have been so trusting. They had been robbed several times, and Allison narrowly avoided being raped on several occasions. It was no longer safe to leave the house at night, and it was barely safe to leave the house during the daylight hours, despite the implementation of martial law in most major cities in the United States.

In addition to everything else the climate had taken a turn for the worst. Even the most zealous climate change deniers were admitting that something was not right. Millions were forced to evacuate entire regions. Whole cities vanished from the Earth and some regions of the planet looked like giant refugee camps. With rationing of everything from fuel, to food, and even water and electricity, no one had enough of anything and people would frequently resort to violence to get whatever they needed.

There was one type of person who was doing just fine, and unfortunately that type of person were people like Earl. In the midst of all this chaos he had managed to amass quite a following of believers. While the majority weren't sure where their next meal would come from, Earl was head of a mega-church, drove around in limousines and had numerous mansions. This time of trouble was a time of plenty for the exploiters of human misery and the voices of ignorance and hatred.

"And the wrath of the Lord is upon the world," came Earl's voice over the radio, "and soon his judgment will be upon the world. Are there seriously people in the world who believe it is coincidence that in just a few short years of the legalization and legitimization of gay marriage that the entire world has rapidly gone to hell in a handbasket? Is it any coincidence that our nation first started to decline after the passing of Roe V Wade? But the times are changing fast. Soon the atheist socialist government of the sodomites, the whores and the adulterers will be no more. They thought they could defy God's will so brazenly and now they are on the brink of collapse. Soon will come the final blow and the day of judgment will be upon us. Will you be saved or will you be amongst the damned?"

"You turn that garbage off," said Allison.

"Gladly," said Morty as he turned off the radio. "I just wanted to hear the news but it seems like Earl is on pretty much every local station now."

"Well that's the way it goes. When the world goes to shit you know there have to be a lot of assholes around to benefit."

"You know my feelings on all of this apocalypse stuff, but even I have to admit –"

"That things have never been this bad so quickly."

Morty nodded. "And I also can't dismiss what the man said. He knew things were getting pretty bad and that they would get worse. And the fact that he managed to heal your leg still has no explanation, so he obviously knows something that mere mortals do not."

"I still think that he is some type of an angel."

"The question that I keep asking myself is that if he was an angel, then where is he now when we need him the most?"

"I don't know, but I really wish he were here."

"So do I. But there is nothing we can do about that."

"I had checked the Internet posting that we made seeking information about the man and if anyone had seen him."

"And?"

"I heard a couple of unconfirmed reports of a man fitting his description on the East Coast who was performing alleged miracles only to then disappear. But I was never able to confirm them before we lost complete contact with the Eastern half of the country."

"Does anyone know if Washington is still functioning?"

"No one has heard any news from the government in over a week, although I have heard various rumors that Washington was blown up in a terrorist attack and a series of EMP attacks are what wiped out the entire eastern seaboard. All the other news that I have heard has just been local, and Earl's broadcasts are hardly to be trusted."

Morty began to put on his jacket.

"Where are you going?"

"I am going to go down to the bar to see if anyone has any new information."

"I'm not sure if you should. It's very dangerous out there. I don't feel fully safe here by myself."

"I promise I will be back before nightfall; I'm not stupid. Just make sure that you don't answer the door for anyone and keep the gun by your side."

Allison nodded reluctantly, but the look on her face betrayed her true feelings.

Morty started walking to the bar. It was only about a mile away and it was too expensive to buy gasoline anymore. What little came in had to be rationed down to the last drop. He also didn't want to spend any more time near the gas station and risk getting caught in a gas riot like he did the last time and he barely made it out of there with his life.

As he walked to the bar he kept constantly looking over his shoulder to make sure he wasn't being followed. He had a weapon concealed under his pant leg that he hoped he wouldn't have to use. Even with armed guards posted every couple of meters he never felt fully safe leaving the house without a weapon of his own. Besides, he wasn't quite sure whose side the soldiers were really on. And with no news from Washington there was a no effective leadership beyond the local level.

He made it to the bar just in time as another one of those horrendous sandstorms was whipping up. Now he would be stuck at the bar until it had let up a bit.

The bar was extremely dark, since no one could afford to keep the lights on during the day anymore. There was a single television on but the only thing playing was a message from Earl, who was unfortunately made by circumstance into the most influential individual in the city. There was surprisingly little resentment against a man who had amassed a fortune in a time where most people had limited electricity and went to bed hungry every night.

"Has anyone heard any news from Washington?" Morty asked as he sat down at a table with a couple of the regulars.

"Washington," said one of the men contemptuously as he spit at the floor. "What good are they in a crisis? They were the ones who started all of this. They are aligned directly with the forces of Satan."

"Where did you hear that?"

"According to Earl –"

"I wouldn't put much stock in anything that bastard said."

"You better watch what you say," said one of the other men. "Around here Earl's word is law."

"I think that the mayor –"

"The mayor has fled the town and we haven't heard anything from him since the blackouts on the East Coast. Now Earl has filled the void of leadership. In the absence of any government Earl's word really is the law. And Earl's orders come directly from God."

"Says who? Earl? You know as well as I do that Earl was a legendary bullshitter."

"Then why is Earl doing so well. God has allowed his own to prosper."

"No, you have allowed Earl to prosper. It isn't God that is giving him all of his wealth and power, it's you guys! He's taking advantage of you, playing on your fears and insecurities and, worst of all, your hatreds."

"I think maybe you had better shut your mouth before you say something that you regret," said the first man as he drew a knife.

"Okay," said Morty as he put up the palms of his hands defensively and slowly started getting up. "I don't want any trouble. I was just looking for information."

"Well, we ain't got any, so now you can leave."

Morty slowly backed up and walked out of the bar. Unfortunately the sandstorm was still raging so he had to walk with his arm shielding his eyes. After a few minutes he remembered that he brought a protective face mask with him that he put on.

The whole time that he was walking he got the distinct feeling that he was being followed, although he couldn't see more than a few feet in front of him or behind him, and he had to assume that if there was anyone behind him they would be similarly impaired.

Once he had reached his apartment he felt a tap on his shoulder. He turned around quickly and drew his pistol. He put it down as soon as he saw who it was – it was the man, the man who had healed his wife's leg and given them the money that they needed to get married. He was standing right in front of him with his eyes wide open, apparently not bothered by the sand and the dust. And he was wearing the same outfit that he had worn all those years ago.

"It's you," said Morty as he put his gun back under his pant leg.

"I can see you are not as trusting as you once were, but I do hope that you will invite me in." The man smiled, still apparently not bothered by the sand.

He led the man upstairs and slowly opened his apartment door. Allison jumped up ready to reach for her gun, but she put her hands over her mouth in stunned silence as soon as she saw who was with Morty. "Oh my God, it's you!"

"Nice to see you again," said the man with a forced smile. "I think we have lots of things to talk about."

Morty and Allison began to prepare dinner for their old and mysterious friend and they all sat down for a spaghetti and meatball dinner.

"I remembered that you enjoyed this meal last time," said Allison. "I apologize that we don't have as much food as we did last time, but you're welcome to whatever we do have. I wish we could give you more, considering all that you gave to us."

"Thank you," said the man as he slowly ate a little bit of spaghetti. "I remembered your hospitality too. I suppose you have lots of questions, but I only have a limited time to answer them, so I'll cut right to the chase."

"Who, or rather what, are you?" Morty asked, not quite sure if he wanted to know the answer, however curious he might be.

The man wiped some sauce from his face with a napkin, drank a glass of soda and placed his silverware down on the table. "I guess I should start at the beginning. You will probably find what I have to say to be difficult to believe."

"I am walking because of you," said Allison, "so you might find me more open-minded than you think."

The man nodded and smiled briefly. "To put it in the simplest terms I am the fifth horseman of the apocalypse."

Morty and Allison shot each other disbelieving glances before looking back at the man.

"I can see you are still skeptical."

"It's not so much that," said Morty, "but aren't there only four horsemen of the apocalypse? I'm no biblical scholar, but I have heard enough preaching about the Apocalypse to know these details."

The man smiled and began to laugh. "I don't appear in the Bible, and that is by design. People aren't supposed to know that I exist at all. That is why I was purposely kept out of the Bible. And besides, so much of the Bible has been lost and mistranslated over the years that you should never take it too literally."

"I agree," said Morty, "but on the other hand even I have to admit –"

"That there is something to all of those prophecies after all," said the man as he leaned back in his chair with a somewhat smug look on his face. Morty nodded in acknowledgment.

"So which horsemen is the fifth horseman?" Allison asked with some nervousness. "All of the other horsemen were about famine, war and plague and death. But you don't really seem like the sinister sort."

The man laughed some more, before frowning slightly. "I am the horsemen who has the most difficult task of all. My name is Mercy and I am the horsemen of forgiveness. I was sent to this world to search for those who were worthy of being shown mercy."

"So that day I saw you in the desert, you literally appeared –"

The man nodded. "I pretty much dropped out of the sky."

"And why did you choose to show mercy to us."

"Mercy is shown to those that show it to others."

"But surely there must be others more deserving than we are," said Allison.

"Don't underestimate yourself. Your husband was the first person to stop all day and you were both some of the only people I have met who would take a stranger into their house, feed him when they could barely feed themselves, and trust me enough to spend the night in your house without robbing you."

"Well our trust certainly wasn't misplaced," said Morty. "Maybe not many people would invite you into their home to spend the night, but it is also true that it is even more rare to allow a stranger into your home and instead of them robbing you they leave you $10,000."

"You've got me there," laughed the man. "But now I have come back to you to offer you something even better."

Allison and Morty looked at each other, not quite sure what the man was talking about. "What exactly is that?" Allison finally asked.

"I am here to spare you from any further suffering. For the last couple of years I have been traveling around the country, talking to people, observing them and blending in as best as I could. The majority of people will simply ignore someone like me. Most take complete disinterest in their fellow man. But that isn't the worst thing that I have observed. The main thing that I have observed is that for every person like the two of you, I can name probably dozens who aren't just indifferent but actively hostile."

"Like that day in the bar," said Morty.

"Exactly. But you should know that I was never any real danger. If I had really wanted to I could have killed every single person in that bar simply with a wave of my wrist."

"Why didn't you?" Morty asked, immediately regretting that he asked such a thing.

"That wouldn't be very merciful of me, would it?" The man laughed, but then quickly frowned again. "For all my travels in this world I have seen that as things get worse and worse people have grown less and less merciful towards one another. So many people look forward to what is to come. So many self-righteous individuals, so assured that they are in God's good graces actively look forward to seeing those not like themselves suffer. They view the apocalypse as the great day of vengeance."

"Isn't it?" Morty asked.

The man shook his head. "It is the day of justice. It is a day that need not happen and that you have brought upon yourself. You have desired this as a way of seeing your enemies and your neighbors suffer. War, religious hatred, terrorism, it's all just a symptom of a merciless and self-righteous cruelty. People take delight in the idea that those not like themselves will suffer a horrendous death followed by further torture in a terrible afterlife."

"Sounds like Earl," said Allison.

The man nodded. "Exactly."

"And I am guessing that there isn't any truth to what Earl says," said Allison.

The man shook his head. "What do you think? No, there is no truth to what Earl says. This day is not divinely ordained. The Apocalypse and all the prophecies were simply warnings, a cautionary tale if you will. But you have desired it in your hearts and made it reality. There is no suffering beyond this world, not for anyone. But that was a part of the Bible that was lost in all the centuries of dogma."

"So what is going to happen?" Morty asked.

"I have been sent here to save those worthy of being spared any further suffering. I was not allowed to come here until it was clear that you were going to destroy yourselves. And I wasn't allowed to begin taking people away until after you had already begun the process. Already a fourth of the world has died and the rest will perish in the next couple of years. I was sent before the worst of it. And now I am offering to take you with me."

"Take us with you?" Allison questioned as she scratched her head.

"Yes, exactly as I said. I have come to take you away from this place. I know that you don't have anyone except each other and that your leaving this world wouldn't inconvenience anyone. No one will suffer as a result. That is an important part of the equation as well."

Just as Morty was about to say something, the power suddenly went off and everything went dark.

"Oh no, the power just went out," said Allison.

"I think that I heard something outside," said Morty.

They all went to the window and saw people gathering outside. It looked like most of them were carrying weapons of some kind.

"Morty Engleman," shouted the leader through a loudspeaker, "we have your apartment surrounded. Come out quietly and we promise that no one in your building will come to harm."

He recognized the voice immediately. It was Earl, and he had come with his followers.

"What are we going to do?" Allison said. "You're not going to go down there are you?"

"I don't have a choice," said Morty. "If I don't go down there they might burn down this entire complex or slaughter everyone inside."

"You don't have to do this," said the man.

"A wise man once told me that mercy is shown to those that show it to others," said Morty as he began to open his apartment door and walk down the hall.

"Morty, come back!" shouted Allison as she ran after him.

"I have to do this, otherwise people could get hurt," said Morty as he grabbed Allison. "Just stay here."

Allison began to cry and Morty hugged her. "I promise I will be right back," he whispered in her ear as he went to open the door.

"What is this about?" said Morty as he approached the crowd.

"This is a purging," said Earl.

"A purging? A purging of what?"

"I have heard from my informants that you have been saying stuff about me, spreading rumors and doubt."

"So now you have informants? Who put you in charge?"

"I speak directly to God. And God will not tolerate unbelievers in his presence."

"Do you think you can just get away with this? You don't think that the police –"

"The police are with me," said Earl as he pointed to several police officers at the head of his crowd. "In case you haven't noticed, things have changed around here. People will no longer listen to the godless government, who have fled like cowards in the face of God's wrath. Now I am the one in charge. God has chosen me to do his holy work."

"No good ever follows people who use those words."

"Blasphemer!"

"Go to hell Earl," said Morty as he turned his back to the crowd and began to walk away. But before he could walk more than a few paces he heard the sound of gunfire and soon fell to the floor covered in blood.

"Morty!" shouted Allison as she ran to his side. She looked up at Earl. "You killed him!

You bastard!"

"Well why don't you join him," said Earl as he fired a single shot into Allison's chest with his pistol. She fell down dead at Morty's side.

The man walked over and stood in front of the bodies of Morty and Allison.

"And who the hell are you?" Earl asked as he raised his gun towards the man.

"I am mercy, the fifth horseman."

Earl laughed. "The fifth horseman. There are only four."

The man smiled.

"What are you smiling about?"

The man started laughing hysterically and holding his belly.

"What's so damn funny?"

The man continued laughing and pointing at Earl.

"The hell with this," said Earl as he fired his pistol at the man. But the man did not fall down. Earl fired again and again, but the bullets did nothing. Then the man began to emit a blinding glow that caused everyone to cover their eyes. When the light diminished enough that people could look at it without being blinded they saw that Morty and Allison were standing next to the man with no signs of injury and big smiles on their faces.

"What the –" Earl began.

"Mercy shall be shown to those that show mercy," said the man as he began to point at Earl accusingly. "This man is not merciful. He is a false prophet."

Morty, Allison and the man all began to glow even brighter until they will once again blinding and then the light was gone and so were they.

Earl dropped his pistol at his feet, as a wind came by and blew his cowboy hat off. He turned to his crowd of followers who were all looking at him with different eyes. He began to slowly walk backwards away from them. "You don't believe that crazy man, do you?"

"That man just performed a miracle," said the chief of police. "He said you were a false prophet."

"And you're going to take his word over mine?"

"What miracles have you performed lately?" A woman in the crowd asked him. A bunch of others in the crowd began shouting with her in agreement.

Earl backed slowly away.

"That guy took all of our money," shouted another person in the crowd.

Earl looked the crowd in the eye, slowly turned around and began running. The last thing he heard was the sound of gunfire.

The man continued to wander. He would continue to wander the Earth for what little time it had left. He would continue to seek out the merciful in order that they may be shown mercy. But that was why his was the most difficult task of all. He had to pick out the few.

And only the few.

Front Row Seat

"Will you turn that stupid game off," shouted Kimberly.

"But this is the greatest game in the world," shouted Erik as he pressed his controller rapidly. "The game is based around the idea that the world is ending and you have to battle alien zombies. It's like having a front row seat to the end of the world."

"Alien zombies?" Kim asked. "That doesn't even make sense."

"It makes perfect sense," shouted Erik's best friend Jim as he stuffed a handful of popcorn into his mouth. "A bunch of aliens come down and start turning people into zombies to take over the world."

"Why would they even bother with such an idiotic strategy," said Kim. "If they were really that advanced they could just take us over without the need for zombies."

"Well that would be boring," said Erik as he continued to click away at his controller.

"I will never understand guys and their obsession with these idiotic video games," said Kim as she shook her head.

"Then grow a penis," said Jim as he turned to laugh at Kim. "Oh shit, now look what you made me do. I got distracted and zombies ate my brains!"

"Well that wouldn't be much of a meal," snorted Kim. "I'm going to go see if there is anything on the news."

"Well that's pretty damn boring," said Jim. "Aw fuck, now I got killed." Jim turned to Erik. "You know, your girlfriend is a real buzz kill around here."

"Yeah, but she's hot," said Erik with a perverted look in his eye.

"That she is," said Jim as he slapped Erik five.

In the kitchen Kimberly flipped on the news and there was an urgent report.

"And as crazy as it sounds," said the newscaster, "we are now seeing confirmed reports that seemingly extraterrestrial spacecraft have entered Earth's atmosphere."

"This must be some type of stupid movie," said Kim as she change the channel. "Let's see what the other news stations have to say."

"Alien invasion!" shouted the newscaster on the next channel. "This is not a test people. This is mother[bleep]ing aliens."

"You can't say that on the air," said the female newscaster next to him.

"It's the mother[bleep]ing Apocalypse, I'll say whatever the [bleep] I want you stupid [bleep, bleep]."

"Hey guys," shouted Kim into the living room. "You might want to come and see this."

"Yeah, later," shouted Erik. "Right after this level."

"No, seriously, you guys really want to see this, right now!"

"Are you naked back there?" Jim shouted.

"No!" Kimberly shouted.

"Then it can wait," Jim shouted back before the power suddenly went out.

"Ah, shit," yelled Erik. "And we didn't even get to save the damn game. Well Kim, you might as well tell us, what was so important?"

"On the news on several different channels they were talking about alien spacecraft being spotted entering Earth's atmosphere."

"Are you mocking us?" Jim asked.

"No, that is really what they said on the news."

"If alien spacecraft are entering Earth's atmosphere I think we would notice," said Erik.

"Well there's only one way to settle this argument," said Kim. "Let's go outside."

Erik and Jim shrugged, not that Kimberly could see them with the lights out. "I guess we've got nothing better to do," said Jim.

The three of them went outside in the pitch dark wielding flashlights.

"I don't see nothing," said Jim as he was suddenly enveloped in a bright blinding light along with the others. He looked up to see a gigantic circular alien spacecraft. "Well, I suppose I owe you an apology," said Jim before they all disappeared.

They emerged to find themselves standing together naked in a bright white circular room with Kimberly between Jim and Erik. They all looked back and forth at each other.

"Holy shit," said Jim as he looked over Kim, "I can see your boobs. What are you, like a C cup?"

"Hey, stop looking at me you pervert," said Kimberly as she covered her breasts with her hands.

Before any of them could say anything else, they all turned to face forward where they saw a giant pink octopus like creature with multiple tentacles and a face full of eyes.

"Our first words spoken to alien life, and it was I can see your boobs," said Erik as he put his finger on his chin and began tapping it. "Awesome!" He slapped Jim five once again.

"Silence," said the octopus creature as it raised one tentacle in their direction.

"Dude, it speaks English," Jim said as he turned to Erik.

"Do you understand silence!" shouted the tentacle monster (although from where they couldn't be sure, since it didn't appear to have a mouth) as it pointed at Jim. "I can also speak in Spanish."

"No no," said Jim as he held his hands up. "This is America, so speak English. Wait, are we still in America?"

"Actually, you are in an alien spacecraft several hundreds of miles above your planet. Behold!" said the tentacle monster as it pointed to the window to reveal the Earth floating in space.

"Cool," said Eric, "but why did you bring us here?"

"We have been studying your planet for a long time and decided that you are planet of complete and utter imbeciles who, if they somehow managed to survive on their own, would probably pose a threat to all other life in the universe, so we decided to invade your planet and wipe out all life."

"Dude, that is so not cool," said Erik. "But why did you save us? You're not going to probe us, are you?"

"No-no," said the tentacle monster as he waved a dismissive tentacle at Erik. "We just thought that we should save a couple of human beings to put in our alien zoos."

"That doesn't sound like a lot of fun," said Jim.

"We are going to take you to our pleasure planet where you will be bred like animals," said the tentacle monster.

"Oh...so does that, like, mean we are going to get to have a lot of sex and stuff?" asked Jim as he scratched his head.

"That is pretty much all you will be doing!" shouted the tentacle monster as it raised its tentacles to the ceiling. "I even took the liberty of getting rid of all of your clothing in preparation."

"Awesome," said Erik and Jim as they slapped each other five. "Dude, I can see your junk," Jim added.

"Good grief," sighed Kimberly as she pressed it her fist against her forehead.

"Don't worry," said the tentacle monster as it wrapped its tentacle around Kimberly's shoulder, "you will have a selection of the most attractive men and they will be your complete and willing slaves."

"Well," said Kim with a smile, "I guess it can't all be bad then."

"That's the spirit," said the tentacle monster as it slapped her on the back. He then turned to Erik and Jim. "In the meantime please enjoy a front row seat to the end of your planet."

"I'm not sure if I can take the destruction of my home planet so lightly," said Erik.

"What if I told you you could help us to blow it up," said the tentacle monster as he handed Erik and Jim what looked like game controllers. "Just zoom in on any location on the planet and fire. And it's as simple as that. You can wipe out an entire country with the press of a button."

"Well," said Jim as he turned to Eric, "I suppose that planet really was just full of assholes anyway."

"Yeah," said Erik, "screw those losers. We survived the Apocalypse and are going to be the fathers of a new and superior race of mankind. And we are going to get to have a lot of sex."

Jim and Erik slapped each other five once again and began annihilating what was once their home planet.

"Hey Kim," said Erik, "why don't you join us?"

The tentacle monster held out a third controller and placed it in Kimberly's hands. She grabbed it and shrugged her shoulders. "Sure, what the hell, why not?" she said as she began to help in the destruction of her home planet.

The tentacled monster then left the three of them and went to confer with several of his other tentacled friends.

"Why did you lie to them?" asked one of the other tentacled monsters.

"Let them enjoy themselves," said the tentacle monster as he waved his tentacle dismissively. "Why ruin their day by telling them that we are just going to breed them so that we can eat them later?"

And so our three intrepid space travelers had fun helping to destroy their own home planet. They later traveled to the aliens' home world where they enjoyed large amounts of sex and had many children, all of whom were then dismembered and eaten as entrées.

The looks on all of their faces were truly priceless.

I Dream of Armageddon

I remember the day that the world ended. It was a Tuesday in September. I had woken up early because I had been late to class several times and if I was late today I would end up getting detention again.

But I woke up late that day. I slept very soundly, only to wake up and find that the power had gone out in the middle of the night, meaning that my alarm did not wake me up.

I looked out the window to try and get a sense of what time of day it was. That was when I realized it was still pitch black out. And not just nighttime black, but I mean a total black gaping void. There were no clouds, no stars and no moon. I thought that was particularly bizarre, but I shrugged it off because I did not want to be late for class.

I went downstairs to eat breakfast only to find that my parents and sister were missing. "Mom, dad, Lucy!" I shouted, but I received no answer.

I shrugged that off as well and decided I would start making my own breakfast. I opened the refrigerator to find that it was completely empty even though it had been completely full the night before. "Dammit," I cursed under my breath as I slammed the refrigerator door shut.

Disappointed that there was nothing to eat in the house I figured I would just get something to eat at school. I quickly got dressed and went out to wait for the bus. But it was still pitch dark out even though my wristwatch had said it was 7:30 AM. This wasn't right, I thought to myself.

I didn't have long to dwell on that thought because that was when I noticed that shambling towards me was an awkward looking woman who seem to be disturbed. "Hello," I shouted, but she made no response. That was when she started moving towards me more quickly until I realize that she was running right at me. Not only was she running right at me but she seemed to be drooling blood all over her coat!

I began to bolt but the woman followed me in quick pursuit, blood dripping from her mouth as she snarled loudly.

I ran down several streets until I thought that I had lost her. I started to lean against a tree to catch my breath and that was when she got me. The woman dived on top of me and I could see her face more clearly now, just inches away from my own. Her eyes were glowing yellow, her face was a pale gray and she was drooling blood right into my mouth. I grabbed her by the neck and tried to push her off of me. The stench of decomposing fresh was overpowering and I began to throw up.

Just as the woman was about to bite into my neck I was saved at the last moment as I saw her face split down the middle and then falling into two pieces into my lap.

I pushed the woman's body off of me and spit up the blood that she had spat into my mouth. Then I vomited some more. I was so preoccupied with getting the disgusting taste out of my mouth that I did not even notice the other woman standing in front of me.

She was stunningly beautiful. She appeared to be oriental, dressed in metallic battle armor and a blue skirt and carrying a bloodsoaked samurai sword. She had long pink hair full of lots of multicolored hair clips that appeared to be filled with jewels.

She reached out and offered me her hand, but I just stood there staring at her.

"Well do you want me to help you up or not," she finally said. "Or do you just want to sit there staring at my breasts."

"Thanks," I said as I took her hand and she helped me up. Now that I got a better look it was true that she had pretty nice breasts. I tried to wipe the blood off of me, but unfortunately it had completely stained my shirt.

She looked me over carefully. She then looked me right in the face. "You got blood on you," she said. "You've been infected."

"What you mean infected!" I shouted as I drew back. "Did that woman have AIDS or something?"

"No you moron, she was a zombie!"

"A zombie?!"

"Yes, a zombie. Haven't you ever watched TV or movies?"

"Of course I have. But zombies are fiction."

She looked at me like I was a deranged mental patient. "Where the hell have you been?"

"I just woke up and was going to go to school when this crazy bitch attacked me," I said as I kicked the decapitated zombie woman's body.

"How did you not know about the zombies?"

"There were no zombies yesterday, at least not that I remembered."

She gave me another look of disbelief. "Are you feeling okay?"

"Not really. I mean I was just attacked by a zombie, which isn't exactly the kind of thing that happens every day."

"It does here. But seriously, how could you not know about the zombies?"

"Look I didn't ever see a zombie before today. But actually, now that I think about it, I suppose it doesn't make much sense that there is a completely black sky at 7:30 AM with no stars, moon or clouds. I haven't seen that before either."

"You really need to get out more. But look, it's not safe out here on the streets. I was just out looking for supplies but I need to be getting back. Do you have any place safe to go?"

"Well I was on my way to school and –"

"Are you dense or something? Haven't you taken a look? There is no school. This is the freaking apocalypse!"

"The Apocalypse?"

She slapped her forehead in exasperation. "Look, we can't just stand around here. Do you want to come with me or not?"

I nodded and began to follow her but then I remembered my family. "Stop," I said as I came to a halt.

"What is it?"

"I can't leave my family behind."

"Where is your family?"

"I don't know. I woke up this morning and they were missing."

"Well, we can't stop to look for them."

"I can't just leave them."

"It's up to you," she said as she shrugged her shoulders. "But I can't go back to look for them with you."

I paused and stopped to think for a minute. If my family had left why had they left me behind? That didn't make any sense.

"So are you going to come with me or not?" She started tapping her foot impatiently.

"But my family?"

"You can look for your family later, but right now we got to get out of here before they wake up."

"Before who wakes up!" I shouted as I jumped up in frustration.

"Sssshhhh," she said as she held her finger up over her lips and covered my mouth. But that was when I heard it. It was a loud shriek unlike anything I had ever heard in my entire life.

"Now you've done it," she said as she pushed me away from her. "You've woken them up."

"Woke who up?"

"The bats," she said as she pointed to the sky. And surely enough there was a huge group of giant flying bats coming right at us.

"Holy shit!" I said as I began to shake in fear. "What do we do?"

"Run you moron!"

We started running as the bats flew overhead and started swooping down at us. She took her sword and managed to decapitate the bats, splattering bat guts all over both of us. "Ewww," I said as I tried to wipe the bat guts off of me.

"It's just a little bat guts," she said as she wiped the bat guts off herself. "Besides, you've already been infected with zombie blood. So you're pretty much doomed anyway. I don't even know why I am bothering with you. Don't think that I won't use this on you,"-she raised her sword at me-"once you begin turning."

"You mean I am going to become a zombie?" I began to grow pale with fear and started swallowing deeply.

"You probably already are. Look!" She pulled back my sleeve to reveal that my flesh was already beginning to decompose.

I began to vomit some more as I slowly looked over my rotting arm. "What the hell? Is there anything I can do?"

"I could cut your arm off," she said as she raised her sword towards me. I closed my eyes and started to shake violently in fear. When I opened my eyes she had put her sword down.

"Well," I demanded.

"Well what?"

"Are you going to cut my arm off?"

"Do you want me to?"

"Not really. Isn't there some other way?"

"Well maybe if we can get you a vaccine. But you have to take it within 24 hours of infection or you're pretty much doomed."

"Why didn't you say that in the first place!"

She shrugged her shoulders and put her sword back in its sheath. "I thought that it was common knowledge. But if you want the cure we will have to get back to the laboratory quickly."

"And how far away is that?"

"Three blocks from here."

"Finally, some good luck for a change." I wiped the sweat from my forehead.

"It's not as easy as it looks," she said as she shook her head.

"Why's that?"

"The laboratory is surrounded by giant three headed dogs, Cerberuses."

"Giant three headed dogs! That's the most ridiculous thing I have heard all day. Then again I was attacked by a zombie and giant flying bats, so I suppose I should be a little bit more open-minded about these things. So how do we get past the dogs? Are you just going to cut their heads off?"

"I could, but it might be easier to use these," she said as she pulled two giant machine guns off of her back and handed me one of them.

"Wait, you had these the entire time? Why didn't you use them when we were being chased by the bats and when I was attacked by the zombie woman?"

"Because I believe in conserving ammunition."

"Well then why are you willing to use it against the dogs?"

"Well, if you must know, I am allergic to dogs and I cannot get close enough to them to cut off their heads without risking a sneezing fit that would leave me vulnerable."

"That is the stupidest thing I have heard all day!"

"Do you want my help or don't you?"

I sighed. "Fine, let's just get this over with."

We walked a few blocks to where the dogs were. There were about four of them, each with three heads apiece, circling around Winston laboratories, which was where she said the cure was.

"Are you ready?" she asked. I nodded in acknowledgment.

"Then let's go," she said as she began to charge.

She wasted no time opening a hail of gunfire upon the first two dogs, managing to shoot five of their heads, but that was enough to completely disable them. I managed to take out the other two and surprisingly was able to shoot all six of their heads, which gave me a feeling of intense satisfaction.

"Come on," she said as she motioned me towards the entrance.

We went inside the laboratory. She turned on the light and fortunately the power still worked, probably because the laboratory had generators. We looked through several rooms before she finally found what she was looking for. "Here we are," she said as she held up a very large needle. "Give me your arm."

"I really hate needles."

"Do you hate them more than becoming a zombie?"

"No," I said as I shook my head.

"Then give me your arm."

I did as she said and she injected me with what I presume was the antidote. "Ouch," I said as I withdrew my arm.

"Don't be such a baby."

"So is that all? Simple as that?"

She smiled and nodded. "Simple as that."

"Well I guess I should thank you for all that you have done for me. So thank you."

"Don't mention it," she said as she patted me on the back.

"It looks like everything is going to turn out okay after all."

"Wait, I hear something."

I put my hand around my ear to hear better and that was when I heard loud grunting and the flapping of wings. "What's that noise," I asked her.

"Winged monkeys."

"Winged monkeys!"

"Quiet you moron, they'll hear you."

But it was too late. Flying towards us was an entire pack of monkeys with fangs dripping with blood. She quickly started shooting at the monkeys until she was out of bullets. Then I started shooting at the monkeys until I also ran out of bullets.

But the monkeys kept on coming.

"Now what will we do?" I shouted as I grabbed her arm.

"We'll have to do this the old-fashioned way," she said as she drew her sword. She quickly went to work slicing the monkeys to pieces until they were nothing more than a pile of bloody chunks.

"Take that you damn dirty apes," I said and then we both started laughing.

"I guess we make a pretty good team after all," she said. She smiled at me, and I smiled at her, and just as we went to hug, out of nowhere a giant pair of fangs came down and devoured her.

I started screaming as I backed up and away. Standing in front of me with blood dripping from its mouth, just like all the other horrible creatures I've encountered today, was a giant dragon. It roared loudly and started coming towards me. As its mouth came down around me I closed my eyes as I felt it begin to devour me.

"Ahhhhhhhhhh!" I screamed as I bolted up in bed.

"What's the matter darling," said my mom as she ran over to me and began stroking my hair.

"Mom," I said as I hugged her. "It's so good to see that you are okay. I thought that the zombies or the bats or the giant dogs had gotten you."

"The what?" She looked deeply into my eyes and began stroking my hair even more. "I think that you had a bad dream."

"I sure did. That was why nothing made sense. I dreamed it was the apocalypse. But I'm so glad that it was just a dream and that the world isn't going to end after all."

That was when my mom backed away, looked me in the eyes and gave me a sad look as she began to frown.

"What's wrong?" I asked her.

She began to cry and hug me tight. "You poor child. Of course the world is going to end. We've known about that for several months. But there's still a possibility that the rockets will manage to deflect the asteroid in time. There's still hope."

That was when I remembered and my heart sunk. The world was indeed going to end. I had been worrying about it and worrying about it and that probably was what caused the dream.

"Are you okay?" My mom looked at me with her sad eyes

"No," I said and I began to lie back down in bed in resignation.

I think I had better odds against the dragon.

It's the Apocalypse and I'm All out of Prozac!

He awoke with a headache, and not just any headache, but probably the worst headache that he had ever had in his life.

He attempted to get up but found that the throbbing in his head was too intense and his eyes burned. "What the hell," he muttered as he rubbed his eyes and forehead, which did little to improve his condition.

His entire body ached and he didn't feel fully up to getting up just yet so he laid back down, having not opened his eyes once, and fell swiftly back to sleep.

He awoke several hours later, this time with a noticeable metallic taste in his mouth. He slowly lifted himself up, his head still pounding, and very slowly opened his eyes.

What he saw was not reassuring.

He appeared to be buried under some type of rubble, and could feel blood trickling down his cheek. "What the hell," he said again as he wiped away the blood.

He attempted to lift the rubble off of him, but it was too heavy. Now what was he going to do, he thought to himself.

A quick glance of the room revealed that there was broken glass all over, lots of general debris, the ceiling was caved in on top of him, and the entire building seemed like it could collapse at any moment.

The most disturbing part of the whole ordeal was that he had no idea how this had happened. At least it was the most disturbing part until he realized that there appeared to be a dead body not far away from him. He couldn't get a good look at it, but on the other side of the rubble he could vaguely make out what looked like the body of a woman with her skull split open.

He turned to the side and vomited. He noticed that his vomit contained a fairly large amount of blood.

Looking over his situation more carefully, he noticed that the rubble mostly covered his legs up to his chest area. His arms were free but that was about all. He tried once more to push the rubble off of him but soon felt a shooting pain in his chest and he began to cough up blood all over himself.

This was when he noticed for the first time that he was very thirsty. When was the last time he had something to drink? He had no idea, but he felt like he was dehydrated.

Looking around the room once again he didn't see any signs of anything to drink. But he did look up where the ceiling should be and realized that it was an especially cloudy day. With any luck maybe it would rain and he would be able to drink the rainwater, not to mention wash all of the blood and vomit off of himself.

The next several hours passed by very slowly. He had nothing to occupy his mind except for the scene of carnage around him. He mostly passed the time trying to figure out what had occurred to have caused all this. But it disturbed him that he could not remember anything. He couldn't even remember his own name or who the woman was on the other side of him, the one with the cracked open skull whose brains were spilled all out on the floor. For all that he knew that woman could be his wife or lover. Thinking of that caused him to vomit up a little more, so he turned his head and tried his best not to look.

If that woman was anyone important to him, it kind of made him even more sick at the thought that her brains were splattered all over no more than a few feet away.

After several hours of boredom and pain, he eventually passed out from exhaustion once again.

He came to later on to the sound of someone hacking away. He looked up to see a disheveled looking bearded man in dirty ripped up clothing with a pickax breaking away the rubble on top of him.

"Hello," he said, but the man did not respond. "Hello, I say," he said again. "Thank you for helping to chip away all of this rubble on top of me. What's your name?"

The man continued to say nothing as he hacked away more furiously at the rubble.

"I'm grateful for your help, but it would be nice if you could tell me something," he shouted at the man. But the man kept on digging away until he suddenly stopped, looked him closely in the eye, and threw down his pickax and ran away.

"Hey, where are you going!" he shouted at the man, but as soon and as mysteriously as he arrived he had left.

He looked to his side to see that at least the man left the pickax within his reach. He slowly pulled it towards him and with all his strength used it to chip away at the rubble until his legs were freed.

Once he had freed his legs, he put the pickax down and slowly pulled himself out from under the rubble and began to examine his legs. They did not appear to be broken, but they were heavily bruised and cut, and most of his pants had been torn away.

He sat there for several minutes, trying to get the feeling back in his legs. He attempted to stand but fell backwards right onto his ass. He eventually managed to drag himself to the wall and using it for leverage managed to pull himself up.

As soon as he managed to pull himself up he screamed in pain. He felt excruciating pain in his chest that caused him to vomit up yet more blood. Fortunately he managed to anchor himself and lean against the wall so he did not fall down.

Slowly and carefully he felt his chest. He was no doctor, at least as far as he knew, but it appeared that he broke a rib.

Once he had rested for a little while, he slowly approached the dead body of the woman on the other side of the rubble. He fought back the urge to vomit as he saw her splattered brains once more near his feet. Seeing the woman up close didn't stir any recognition in him.

That was when he noticed her purse lying just a few feet away from her. He felt guilty rummaging through a dead woman's purse, but maybe it would be able to tell him something. He looked at her wallet and found that her name was Evelyn Proctor, age 36.

He could've hit himself in the head if it didn't hurt so much already. Why didn't he check himself for something similar? He reached into his pocket and found that he had a wallet as well. He checked the ID which had the name Richard Morgan on it, age 39. At least now he knew who he was, even if he didn't remember anything else about his life. But he did not appear to be related to Evelyn, whoever she was.

He put his wallet back in his pocket and continued rummaging through the woman's purse. He found just what he was looking for – a cell phone. He turned it on and tried dialing 9-1-1 but received no signal. Whatever caused this disaster, it wiped out all cell phone service.

He shrugged his shoulders. There is nothing else to do now but try to find some other people, he thought to himself as he slowly limped out of the building, pausing every few moments to clutch his chest in pain.

Surveying the landscape, he saw that the sky was very dark and thick with clouds. Off in the distance a city appeared to be burning. In fact, the burning rubble around him provided the only light in an otherwise darkened landscape.

What time of day was it, he wondered. He checked his digital watch to realize that it was completely smashed. Why he had not thought to look at it sooner he had no idea. But it was useless to him now, so he took it off and threw it to the floor.

"Hello," he shouted, only to then feel a surge of pain in his chest that almost caused him to fall over.

No one answered his cry for help.

He continued to walk around the devastated landscape looking for signs of life, but he didn't even see or hear any birds singing. He had not seen another single living soul, although every so often he would come across a dead body.

"I couldn't be the only survivor," he said to himself as he continued to rub his head. His headache had not gone away, and truthfully had gotten worse, far worse than a normal migraine, and every so often he would have to sit down to give himself a rest.

As he sat down and assessed his situation it did not look very positive. Something had happened on a devastating scale, perhaps some type of nuclear attack. That was what he felt was the most likely scenario. The dark sky, the burning buildings, the extreme cold. No sign of life anywhere.

"I guess I should consider myself lucky," he muttered to himself. "Given that I haven't seen any other survivors, I must be one of the few who made it through this catastrophe alive, although just barely."

He was probably being generous with himself. He may not be dead yet, but he was pretty close. He was in a situation where he had severe cuts and bruises on his legs that made walking difficult; at least one broken rib, if not more; a severe migraine; probable dehydration; and complete and total amnesia. If he didn't find other survivors soon he wouldn't last very long.

I've got to stay awake, he thought to himself. He needed to keep going as long as he possibly could. He felt that if he fell asleep again he might not wake up. He might have a concussion.

But maybe that would be better. Even if he did find other survivors, he can't imagine that this would turn out to be a world that is worth living in. But he also didn't believe in suicide. He knew nothing else about himself, but he felt like he was a survivor. And for all he knows he could have family out there who are looking for him. Then again, he could be a completely miserable and lonely bachelor with no family and friends in the entire world. And even if he did have friends and family, there was a high probability that they were all dead. But he tried not to dwell on the negative.

Looking at things more positively, the fact that someone came out of nowhere and gave him the means to free himself from under all that rubble could be a sign that someone up there wanted him to survive. He didn't know if he believed in God or any type of organized religion, but you still have to be thankful for small miracles, wherever they come from. So he would try to stay positive, even in the midst of this catastrophe.

His positivity was rewarded when several hours later, just as he was beginning to lose all hope, he saw his first sign of life since the crazy old man who had helped him, only to run off without telling him anything.

It was a dog. The first living creature he had seen in hours. It didn't look like it was in very good shape, seemingly wandering around in a dazed state. It also looked like it had burns all over its body. But it was alive! It might be dying, it might be in a terrible state, but maybe it would lead him to someone that could help him.

"Here boy," he said as he gestured with his fingers and made whistling noises at the dog. The dog looked up briefly, barked, but then went about stumbling blindly around. "Well," he muttered as she shrugged his shoulders, "it may not be much, but it could be a sign."

For the next hour or so he followed the dog, seemingly around in circles. The dog didn't seem to have any idea where it was going or what it was doing, but if it was alive it must have a source of food or water.

Every so often it would start to gently rain. At first he was going to drink the rainwater, but then he realized it was filled with ash. "Fallout," he said to himself as he sought shelter in a nearby car.

The car had its windows completely blown out and he had to clear away a lot of broken glass before he could sit down and rest inside the car, but it was better than being completely out in the open. At least this car seemed to still have a roof that would protect him, even if it wouldn't be adequate to shield him from the cold.

From the front seat of the car he continued to watch the dog run around in circles. He considered trying to beep the car's horn, but then he might scare away the dog. It probably wouldn't work, at any rate.

Eventually the dog ran off and he was tempted to run after him, but he didn't really want to expose himself directly to what he felt was radioactive fallout. He didn't know how he knew it was fallout, but somehow he knew. But he still did not know anything about himself beyond his name.

As he grew more and more comfortable sitting in the front seat of the car, he decided to put the seat back so that he could lie down in a way that wouldn't be putting as much pressure on his chest as it would leaning forward. His headache had still not gone away, his legs ached to the point where he could barely feel them and now he was becoming numb with cold. It was so cold that he could see his breath.

You have to keep going, he thought to himself. If you fall asleep now you're done for. But try as he might he did not have the strength to get up. As he stared out into the desolate landscape, watching the ash gently fall down all around him, he felt his eyes grow heavier and heavier and he could keep them open no longer. Just a few seconds, he thought as he closed his eyes. But that was all it took for him to be out like a light.

When he woke up he was surprised to find himself in a bed in a dark room lit only by candlelight. He tried to open his mouth to speak, but he realized that he had a tube in his nose going down his throat. He also noticed that his arms and legs were covered in bandages, as were his chest and head. He still felt rather sick, and his head still pounded severely, but wherever he was he felt warm and appeared to be getting nourishment because he had an IV pole next to him.

He looked more carefully around the room and saw that there were several other beds all packed closely together near his.

A nurse saw him motion towards her and she came running towards him. "This one is waking up," she shouted into the hallway and he heard the sound of feet pitter pattering on the floor. Within moments an entire team of doctors and nurses were crowded around his bed.

"Mr. Morgan," said an African-American woman wearing a white doctors uniform.

"As far as I know," he replied hoarsely, choking a little bit on the tube down his throat.

"Do you know where you are?" the doctor asked.

He shook his head.

"You are at Ravenswood hospital – a joint medical facility and psychiatric hospital. We found you unconscious in a car parked not very far from here."

"How did you find me," he said in barely a whisper.

"Oddly enough, a dog lead us to you. The dog kept barking until we decided to follow him thinking that he might have an owner that was in trouble."

"Well how about that," he said coughing slightly. "I guess that dog was like my guardian angel." He laughed before coughing again.

"Does the dog belong to you?"

"Not as far as I know," he said. "Unfortunately I don't remember anything about my life before yesterday."

The doctor shook her head. "You have been out for over three days. And I'm sorry to tell you that the dog passed away shortly after leading us to you. But you owe your life to that dog. If we had found you any later you probably would have died."

"What happened?"

"The dog was suffering from radiation burns and radiation sickness. I'm afraid there was nothing we could do for him."

He coughed some more, struggling to speak. "I mean what happened to the city. What happened to the world?"

The doctor gave a worried glance to her colleagues. Another man, who looked Indian, answered. "Nuclear attacks."

"I guess I was right. What brought that about?"

The Indian doctor gave him a look of shock. "You really must not remember anything."

He shook his head at the doctor.

"Well Mr. Morgan, there was a crisis over the Chinese invasion of Taiwan. We had been in a state of crisis for two weeks. We launched a small-scale tactical nuclear strike against the Chinese Navy, and they responded by attacking several of our bases in Asia. The exchanges continued for nearly 3 days until we lost contact. That was over a week ago. It's anyone's guess what is going on. But it seems like the entire world is affected. Nuclear winter."

He started to cough up more. It looks like he was correct after all, which certainly didn't put his mind at ease.

"Sorry to be the bearer of bad news. Do you remember anything, anything at all?"

He shook his head.

The doctor looked at his colleagues and frowned.

"You suffered a minor concussion," said the African-American doctor as she pointed to her head. "It is not uncommon to suffer memory loss when you have suffered a head injury. You also broke three ribs, have a punctured lung, badly injured legs, and when we found you were suffering from dehydration and hypothermia. We had to pump a lot of blood out of your stomach. It really is a miracle that you are alive at all."

"What am I doing in a psychiatric hospital," he managed.

"It is a psychiatric and medical hospital," said the Indian doctor. "It is the only hospital left standing in the area. All the survivors in the city and the surrounding areas have managed to find their way here or have moved on in search of relatives. We send out search parties in the local area to try and find survivors. But mostly we figure anyone who is still out there is most likely dead or dying. We have limited resources and you are welcome to stay here for as long as those last. But we don't know when, or if, we will be getting any new supplies anytime soon. This is the last surviving mental health facility that we know of. We are nearly out of medication but we can give you food, shelter and counselling, at least while that lasts."

"Will my memory return?"

"It is too soon to tell. Sometimes the memory will return when the concussion heals, but sometimes the memory loss is permanent. Many people have suffered similar traumas, and the Apocalypse is definitely a traumatic event for anyone. Your mind could also be repressing the memory in order to help you cope. If you can't remember anything about the event that caused all this then you're luckier than most. You're probably one of the few survivors with no memory of what you've lost. You should consider yourself fortunate."

"More fortunate!!" he shouted as he sat up, before gagging himself on his nose tube. "I'm not fortunate, I'm much less fortunate. I've lost everything I ever had. Memories of better times are all anyone has left, it's the only thing that gives human beings the will to go on living. What good is surviving if you can't recall anyone or anything, if you have no connections to the past which is now lost forever. I would rather remember losing everything than to live without the memory of having had things I cared about in the first place. Without that I might as well be dead."

The doctor motioned for him to lie back down. "I am sorry. I realize that might sound insensitive. I did not mean it like that. What I meant is that many of the people here have been traumatized by the memories of what they have experienced in the past week, some driven completely psychotic. I was just trying to look at it from that perspective. For all that you have been through you are in better shape than many and are very lucky to have survived at all."

He was going to say something but all he could produce was severe coughing and gagging.

"Please," said the African-American doctor as she produced a pan for him to gag in, "you must rest if you're going to get better. You have been through a lot and right now the best thing for you is to stay in bed and try and get some sleep. If you need anything we will have a nurse posted by the door making her rounds every couple of minutes. We don't have any electricity, but we will try to keep everyone informed of what is going on and check in on everyone as much as we possibly can. If you would like to talk to a psychiatrist, there are plenty available. I am Dr. Woodland, and the other man you were talking to is Dr. Singh. If you need anything we're here to help you."

He continued coughing and gagging into his pan and waved them away as he laid back in bed. The doctors left and he soon fell back asleep.

While he was sleeping he felt like he was having vivid dreams, although upon waking he could not remember what their content was.

"I see you are awake," said Dr. Woodland as she came over to him. "Are you feeling any better?"

"How long was I out for?"

"A couple of hours."

"What time of day is it?"

"The one working clock said it was around 3 PM when I last checked a while ago, although you couldn't tell because it looks as dark as night out pretty much 24/7. Can you remember any more about what had happened to you?"

"When I first woke up I was buried under rubble, but some crazy old guy with a beard had dug me out with a pickax and then run off without saying anything. That sounds crazy doesn't it?"

She shook her head. "Everyone responds to tragedy differently. Most people have lost someone or their entire families."

"I can't even remember if I even had one." He coughed some more.

"Well there was a picture of you with a blonde haired woman and a young boy at a beach of some kind in your wallet. I assume that they are your wife and child."

He slapped himself in the head. "Ouch," he said as he began to rub his head. "What an idiot I have been. When I checked my wallet the other day to see if I had any identification, all I did was look at my drivers license. I didn't even think to look at the pictures in my wallet."

"We often don't think of the most obvious things when we are in disorientating situations. And I think that would you have been through definitely counts as disorienting."

"Bring me my wallet."

She reached into the bag at the side of his bed where she kept all of his personal possessions, however meager. He took the wallet from her hand and flipped through it and started staring at the picture of the woman and the little boy and began to cry.

"Are you okay?" she asked as she put her hand on his. "Is it stirring any recall?"

He began to sob hysterically. "They are beautiful, but they are strangers to me." He threw the wallet back into the bag and fell back into his pillow.

Dr. Woodland started rubbing his hand gently. "You have to give it time. Your memory could come back gradually or all at once."

He shook his head. "Maybe Dr. Singh was right. Maybe it is better that I don't remember anything. For all I know the woman and the child in the photograph are dead. It will hurt less if I have no memories."

"Don't say that. You were the one who was correct. Memories are all that we have. All of these people here are suffering because they have lost loved ones, but those loved ones are still alive in their minds."

"But they are still dead physically." He pounded his fists into the mattress.

"You don't know that for a fact. You might wake up tomorrow, remember where you lived, find your way home and find that your family is alive and missing you just as much as you are missing them. You can't give up hope so easily. Do you believe in God?"

He shrugged his shoulders. "All I know about myself is that my name is Richard Morgan and that I am age 39. Beyond that I'm pretty much a blank slate. A name and an age mean pretty much nothing if you remember nothing about yourself."

She grasped both of his hands in hers and looked deep into his eyes. "I know that you are a survivor. And whoever Richard Morgan was, whoever you are, you have a family who could be looking for you right now. A name can help to identify you."

"That would be a miracle."

"Well even if you don't believe in God, I would say that you should still believe in miracles. It is a miracle you are alive and managed to find your way here. If anyone is prone to miracles it is you. So don't give up quite so easily. Where there is one miracle, there may very well be others."

He smiled slightly, then coughed some more.

"Is there anything I can get you?"

"Yeah," he said with a laugh, "get me some Prozac! The Apocalypse is depressing as hell."

She laughed and patted his hands. "You just get some rest. And if you would like to see a counselor, that's what we're here for."

He nodded, put his hands under his pillow and laid back in his bed.

After Dr. Woodland left he reached back into the bag at his side and flipped through his wallet. He appeared to have several credit cards and an ATM card, all of which would now be worthless, so he might as well just throw them away. He also had about $78 cash, a gift certificate to Red Lobster and a couple of coupons, also pretty much worthless. It seems he was a member of a fitness center, which is probably no longer standing and certainly not doing any business right now. So it was all basically worthless.

He then decided to look more closely at the photographs. Aside from the one of the woman and child, he also had a picture of himself in front of a red car. That really didn't do much good in helping to identify him as he couldn't even see the license plate number. At any rate, that nice looking car was probably a flaming heap of rubble somewhere. He hadn't even thought to check the area for his car. He didn't even look to see what the name of the building was where he found himself covered in the rubble. So he didn't even know where he worked, except that it seemed to be an office of some kind. So he was an office worker. So were millions of others, so not much help there.

This was useless, he thought. When a man's identity is reduced to the contents of his wallet he doesn't have much of a life left. Nothing in his wallet gave any useful identifying information beyond his name and birth date. After staring at the picture of the woman and child with him and struggling to try and remember, he gave up and threw the wallet back into the bag and decided to go back to sleep. There really wasn't anything else to do and his headache still hadn't completely vanished, even after three days.

The next day he woke up and was actually feeling better, until he remembered what his situation was. They finally removed the tube from his nose and allowed him to start drinking liquids in small amounts. They didn't want to give him food just yet, because with such limited supplies they didn't want to waste anything on anyone who might not get any benefit from it.

He got up and went to the window and looked out. It was bright and early in the morning but it might as well just have been midnight. You couldn't tell by looking outside. Off in the distance he could see flickers of light from the burning of the city.

He didn't stay at the window very long. The view was less than inspiring.

The nurse suggested that he try walking, so he went for a walk in the hallway, using crutches to help him, since he still hadn't regained his strength and his legs were still badly injured, though fortunately still functional.

The hallways were also lit with candlelight, which made getting around difficult. He saw others stumbling through the hallways that were in worse shape than him. He saw people that were almost completely covered in bandages because they had been completely burned all over their body; people walking around using a cane because they had been blinded; and others who were stumbling around in what seemed to be a state of complete confusion.

As he was walking past the nurses' station he accidentally brushed up against a woman. "Sorry," he muttered as he passed by.

No sooner did he turn around did the woman start to grab him screaming loudly. "It's the end! This is judgment day, revelations!"

"That's very nice," he said politely as he pushed her away, but she grabbed him tightly and looked him in the eye. "You have been bewitched," she said. "The spirit of the devil has come upon you. Devil! Devil!"

"Get off of me you crazy bitch," he shouted as he pushed her away.

Soon the nurses got up from their desks and began restraining the woman who was still pointing at him as they dragged away and continuing to shout various obscenities before falling to the floor, shaking and seemingly speaking in tongues.

"I hope she didn't hurt you," said one of the nurses putting her hand on his shoulder. "Some people just can't handle what has happened."

"I can't blame them," he said as he turned away from the shaking woman. "I think I'll return to my room."

He didn't leave his room for the rest of the day after that. He spent that time trying to get to know his various roommates, all of whom had tales of woe about missing families, dead friends and various sights of horror that they had witnessed in the past couple of days. He was beginning to feel that maybe he was lucky not to remember after all. But all of these men still had one thing that he didn't – something to live for. Many of them knew for certain that they had family members out there looking for them, although he didn't have the heart to tell them that they couldn't know that for sure. Having a memory tends to make one more hopeful.

Then some of his roommates had more exotic theories about what was going on.

"It was aliens," said Carl, a 45-year-old blond haired man.

"Aliens?" Richard said with his eyes raised.

"The aliens have been preparing us for this for decades. Then just when we need them the most, they're going to come down and promise to save our world for a price?"

"What price is that?"

Carl drew closely and whispered into his ear. "They are here for our souls."

"Our souls?"

Carl continued to whisper. "I'm not supposed to tell anyone this, but I had visions of this for years. God spoke to me directly and said that the aliens would come promising to bring salvation to the world, but that they aren't actually aliens, they are demons! They are the servants of Satan here to breed with us and create a new race of devils to wage war against God."

"Is that so?" Richard asked, trying not to show his disbelief.

Carl put finger up to his lips as he whispered again to Richard. "But don't tell anyone, it's a secret. God would be really mad if word got around."

Richard made a zipping motion across his lips. "My lips are sealed. You can count on me."

"And one more thing," said Carl as he whispered really closely into Richard's ear, "when the aliens come down to rescue us, don't breed with their women. If any of them try to seduce you just hum really loud, as demons can't stand the sound of humming. God told me that directly, so you can trust me, and he said that I can trust you."

"That is good to know," said Richard as he patted Carl on the back. "You can count on me to keep your secret, and I'll keep in mind what you told me. You don't have to worry, I'm not going to be seduced by any alien demons, I've got a wife out there somewhere."

That was when a nurse came in and interrupted them. Carl returned to his bed but winked at Richard and he winked back.

He tried not to judge Carl. Under the stress of what has happened you really can't blame anyone for clinging to whatever will give them hope, and people in a psychiatric hospital probably aren't going to be very stable under the circumstances. But he was beginning to lose hope.

Later that day a psychiatrist named Dr. Moody came to see him and ask him how he is doing.

"I haven't made any progress with recovering my memory," he said as Dr. Moody wrote stuff down on the clipboard.

"How are you finding our hospital accommodations," asked Dr. Moody as he adjusted his glasses.

"As well as can be expected under the circumstances, but I am a bit concerned about my roommate Carl."

"Carl is one of our regular patients. He has been talking about the Apocalypse and various conspiracies relating to it for the better part of a decade. As you can imagine the last couple of days have been especially stressful for him."

"I think that they have been stressful on everyone. At least Carl has something to give him hope."

"I certainly won't dispute that anyone would be stressed out by the circumstances. I wish there was more I could do for you, but unfortunately all I could do is give you some antidepressants, and we are already running extremely low on them."

Richard waved his hand at Dr. Moody. "Drugs aren't going to help anything, unless you have a drug that can restore my memory?"

"I'm afraid not. You just have to give it time and hope for the best."

He nodded at Dr. Moody, who then went to talk to Carl.

Richard spent the rest of the day staring at the pictures in his wallet. Why couldn't he remember anything? Just give it time, he laughed as he thought of Dr. Moody's advice as he closed his wallet and put it back into his bag.

He had given it enough time. That was when he decided that tonight he was going to end it all. As a person with no memory, no family and friends and no one to talk to but the injured and the insane, he didn't figure that many would miss him. Besides, he was draining hospital resources that could better be used on those who had something to live for.

He grabbed a pad of paper and a pencil at his side and composed a short suicide note. He really didn't know what to say and figured that no one would care, so he decided to keep it as brief as possible. A man with no memory doesn't have much to say about himself. Under the circumstances suicide was fully understandable and he was sure that he wasn't the only person who would be ending their own life today.

He waited until dark and decided he would just go and slip out discreetly and hope that nobody noticed. Then he would go off into the cold and just let himself go to sleep. Maybe unconsciously that is what he had chosen back when he went to sleep in the car. It probably would've been better had nobody found him.

He began walking down the hallway and was approaching the exit. The nurses didn't notice and thought that he was just going for a walk around the hallway so did not question him.

"Richard," he heard a woman's voice say as he reached for the exit door. He turned around and standing there was the blonde haired woman and the young boy standing right behind him in the hallway.

"Oh Richard," she said as she hugged him.

"Daddy I missed you," said the boy as he hugged Richard's leg.

He stared at them both in shock as he walked back.

"What's wrong honey?" the woman asked. "It's me, Amanda, your wife."

"You're the woman from the picture," he responded. Then he looked at the boy. "And you're the boy."

"It's me, Rick," said the boy. "Don't you remember daddy?"

"We need to talk," Richard said as he put his hands on both of their shoulders.

They went back to his room where he explained everything to them. His wife managed to explain how she had gone from hospital to hospital looking for him. The place where he had worked was an office building and they lived about an hour outside of the city. They made their way there on foot to find him.

"So you don't remember anything," said Amanda as she put her arm around his shoulder and began to cry.

Richard shook his head. "No, but this feels right, familiar."

"When did the doctors say you will get your memory back?"

"It could be today, tomorrow or never." He sighed and drew her closer.

They weren't sure what to do, but Amanda decided that they should all sleep together tonight in the same bed. The hospital said that they were welcome to stay there for as long as is necessary, even if their supplies were limited.

So Richard went to sleep with his wife on one side, and his son on the other. He fell asleep rapidly and began to dream. He dreamed of warm beaches, family drives in his red car and a nice little house in the suburbs. He dreamed of weddings, birthdays and Christmases.

He awoke early the next morning with his wife and son at his side.

"How are you feeling?" Amanda asked as she rubbed her eyes.

He drew her and Rick close. "I don't remember everything, but I remember the most important things. I don't know how long it will take my memory to fully return, but you have given me something."

"What's that?" she asked as she grabbed his arm.

"You have given me something to live for. You know, I think I am perhaps one of the luckiest people here."

"Why is that?"

"Because all of these people have lost everything and everyone that they have cared about. And here I am with a loving family who managed to find me in spite of all the odds. And now I have something to look forward to. I get to look forward to getting to know you all over again."

She kissed him on the cheek and they laid back in bed.

As he lay there with his wife and child by his side he couldn't help but think he wished he had a camera. This would have made one hell of a picture for his wallet.

Cleanup in Aisle 7

Chad woke up with one raging headache, turned to the side of his bed and began vomiting. When he was finished puking his guts out he realized that he was extremely hungry. His first assumption was that he probably just had the munchies, as his last memory was of himself smoking pot. But that usually didn't make him feel as sick as this. He generally had a pretty positive relationship with marijuana.

He walked into his kitchen and shouted to his parents, "Mom, dad, I'm awake! Is breakfast ready yet?" But he got no answer, so he yelled again. "Mom, dad, pretty hungry here!"

He shrugged his shoulders, reached into the refrigerator and found that the power appeared to be out as the light in the refrigerator didn't go on. It looks like most of the food had spoiled. "Just great," he said as he slammed the refrigerator door shut. "Mom, dad, the power seems to be off. Where the hell are they? What time is it?"

He was starting to feel dizzy again and caught himself before falling over. He then decided he would try and find where his parents had gone. He ran into their bedroom to find them both still in bed. "Mom, dad, wake up! The God damned power is off."

They didn't respond.

"Yo," he said as he began to shake them in bed, "power outage here."

Still not getting any response he pulled the covers off of them and then lurched back in horror. His parents were lying in bed completely pale with blood oozing out of every orifice in their body. The entire bed and all the sheets were soaked with blood and human excrement. Flies circled around the maggot covered bodies and a putrid smell assaulted his nostrils.

He ran over to the garbage pail and began to vomit.

"What the hell," he said as he slowly raised his head out of the garbage after several minutes of puking. He felt his face had several days of beard growth when he remembered going to bed clean shaven. Slowly he backed out of his parents bedroom and closed the door behind him.

"Okay, get a hold of yourself," he said to himself as he sat down at the kitchen table, still feeling quite nauseous. "I know!" He ran to the phone only to find it dead. He then reached into his pocket to take out his cell phone only to find that it didn't get any reception.

Now what was he going to do?

"The neighbors!" he shouted as he ran out into the streets. What he saw was not encouraging. He saw several cars crashed with their owners' blood drenched bodies flung several feet from them and numerous telephone poles down. The bodies looked like his parents bodies. They were decomposing and were already in a pretty advanced stage of decomposition. He was no doctor, but he knew that something must be seriously wrong if no one has come to take care of all this chaos. He noticed that there were also several dead birds and the neighbor's dog was sitting out in their backyard completely stiff as a board. In the distance he saw smoke rising from what seemed to be numerous fires.

It didn't take long for him to decide to run back inside his house after seeing this. Once more he vomited, this time all over the kitchen floor. He then ran to the bathroom as vomit continued to dribble out of him and puked up a tremendous amount in the toilet.

This was when he noticed that he was feeling rather feverish. Reaching into the medicine cabinet he took a Tylenol and then took his temperature. His temperature was 100.6°. So he seemed to be at least mildly ill. But did he have whatever it was that killed his parents? Was he going to die as well?

He started to panic. The phones were down, everyone was dead except for him and he was feeling as sick as hell. This was not good and he didn't know what to do. He got undressed and began to take a cold shower in hopes that it would bring his fever down. He was sweating bullets and even the shower didn't help him to feel very refreshed.

Next he managed to stumble back into his room and collapsed onto his bed. His nausea was becoming uncontrollable, so he did what he always does in this type of situation. He reached into his drawer, moved aside the porno magazines and took out his little baggie full of marijuana. Pot always helps with nausea.

With shaking hands he managed to light up and start smoking his pot. He soon began to feel very relaxed, and even the nausea seem to subside for a while. Once he had finished smoking one joint he decided to roll over and go back to sleep. If he was going to die he might as well do it while baked so that it wouldn't hurt.

2

He woke up as the sun came through his window on what he assumed was the next day. He still wasn't feeling very well, but the nausea had gone away, and his temperature had apparently gone back to normal. The power was still out and the food in the refrigerator had gone bad. He reluctantly looked in his parents' bedroom hoping that it had all been a nightmare, but as soon as he opened the door the smell caused him to start gagging and he slammed it shut.

"I have to try and find some help," he muttered to himself as forced himself to go back into his parents room one last time to search for their car keys, which he found on their dresser.

Going to the garage he found that the car was still intact, but with so many cars crashed outside there was no way he could navigate the roads with the car. He threw the keys down in frustration and went back inside to his room. He sat down on his bed and thought for a while. "I guess I'll just have to walk," he said to himself.

After loading a few supplies into his backpack, including what remained of his marijuana, he started to hike through the town. Everywhere he looked was a scene of devastation. There were fires burning all over the place, bodies lying on the streets, of both people and animals, and cars crashed in every direction. Whatever caused this happened rather quickly, if not instantaneously.

After walking around for an hour he did not see another living soul and decided to sit down on a park bench and assess his situation. There was only one explanation for what he was seeing – alien invasion. Sure he hadn't seen any aliens yet, but this could just be the first stage.

As he contemplated all of this he began to feel really paranoid. There could be aliens lurking around any corner just waiting to eat him. But maybe he was jumping to conclusions too fast. After all he still was pretty baked, and he had a major case of the munchies.

"The supermarket," he shouted to himself. "They'll have at least some food that I can eat."

With only occasional pauses to catch his breath, he rapidly made his way to the local supermarket. The entire parking lot was littered with rotting corpses and the smell was almost too much for him to take. But he had to get something to eat. He wasn't sure how many days had passed, but he hadn't eaten in a while and all he had was some warm beverages in that meantime, and most of that he had thrown up. He was probably at least mildly dehydrated he figured.

The doors to the supermarket were automatic and they would not open without the power on. Looking around he didn't see anything he could use to break the glass with. He tried kicking the glass in but was unable to manage. Stupid Plexiglas. He decided to go around the back to see if the doors were open there. With much luck he saw that someone had gotten the door open.

Once he entered the back door he found himself in the storage room. There was a dead body rotting on the floor that he stepped over while holding his nose, due to the stench of rotting flesh.

Looking at the supermarket, he saw that dead bodies littered the floor and that most of the shelves had been knocked over. This was going to be messy.

"Cleanup in aisle 7!" he shouted as he laughed for the first time since this began. What happened next he never expected in a million years.

"Who's there?" came a feminine sounding voice.

He turned around and standing there before him was a tall, skinny blonde woman wearing designer sunglasses, a fancy looking pink outfit with a miniskirt and a lot of expensive looking jewelry.

"Well, are you just going to stand there staring at me or are you going to say something," the woman snapped at him.

"I'm Chad," he said as he extended his hand.

"I'm Patrice," she said as she shook his hand.

They stood there staring at each other in a state of shock before he broke the silence. "Hey, I know who you are!"

"You do," said Patrice with a look of shock.

"Yeah, you're Patrice Hensley. I asked you out once."

"I don't remember that."

"I guess I didn't make that much of an impression on you then."

She stood there with her hand on her cheek as though she were deep in thought. "Who are you again?"

"I'm Chad, Chad Phillips. I'm in a rock band."

She stood there for another minute processing this before snapping her fingers and pointing at him. "I think I remember you!"

"You do?"

"You're that lowlife punk rocker, the one who is always smoking pot behind the bleachers. If I recall correctly when you went to ask me out you asked me if I would like to go get high and watch you play the drums."

"You do remember!"

"I also recall telling you that I wouldn't go out with you if you were the last man on earth."

Chad looked from side to side and then stretched out his arms wide and slapped the palms of his hands against his jeans. "Well?"

"Well what?" Patrice lowered her sunglasses and looked at him in a patronizing manner.

"Well I don't see any other men left around. Now I probably am the last man on earth. Does that change your decision now?"

"Look Chet –" she began.

"Chad."

"Right... Chad. The thing is you just not my type of guy."

"I still have my pot if that would influence your decision." Chad gave her a big goofy stoner smile.

"See the thing is, you're kind of poor, and I'm kind of really rich. I just don't think that it would work out."

Chad frowned. "Well you're a rather stuck up bitch. You would think that given the circumstances you wouldn't be quite so picky. Fine, if you're going to be like that, I don't need you." Chad began to walk away.

"Wait," said Patrice as she extended her arm towards him. "I suppose I was a bit rude."

"So have you changed your mind about me?"

"Well, no."

"Then screw you," Chad said as he pushed her hand away.

"Wait!" she shouted as she grabbed him and took off her sunglasses revealing that her eyes were filled with tears. "I'm scared alright. What's going on here?"

Chad shook his head. "I don't know. But I do know that if we don't eat something we are going to starve to death. And I also know that we might be the only two people left alive in the entire town. I think it would be a good idea for us to stick together."

Patrice gave a feeble nod.

"So," said Chad, "would you like to help me gather up some supplies?"

Patrice nodded again and then they went up and down the aisles with shopping carts, filling them with as much food and beverages as they could possibly contain. The task was made more difficult by all the rotting bodies, which made the smell in the store almost unbearable. They were both glad to get out of there.

"So do you have any place to go," Patrice asked as they wheeled their supplies into the parking lot.

"Well I have a house not far from here, but it's nothing impressive, and it stinks up something bad."

"Why don't you come stay with me? I have plenty of room." She smiled sweetly at him and any hostility he might have felt towards her earlier quickly melted away.

Chad nodded and they slowly started to make their way back to Patrice's mansion.

3

Patrice's mansion was bigger than anything Chad had ever seen. Fortunately she had a generator so they were able to cook up some of the food that they brought home.

"I don't know how long this will last," Patrice said. "The generator only has so much fuel. But for now we should eat pretty well."

"So what happened to your parents?" But Chad regretted asking as soon as he said that. "Sorry, I didn't mean to be impolite."

"No, it's okay. I was never really close to my parents. They were emotionally distant and I was largely raised by nannies. My parents were on vacation when all of this happened and I have no way of reaching them. I guess they were lucky to not be here when all of this happened. But we still have no idea just how far this thing extends. Phones, Internet, television – all of it seems to be down."

Chad nodded. "I was never very close to my parents either. They were always on me to get better grades and start thinking about college and a career and all that stuff."

"What did you want to be?"

"I wanted to be a famous rock 'n roll star. But the best I could do was become a Walmart greeter. I don't really have any money and my grades weren't good enough to get me into any really decent college. So I spent most of my days just hanging out, killing time and getting high."

"How ambitious," she said with a laugh.

"Hey, not all of us can be born with a silver spoon in our mouth." Chad hung his head. "Sorry, I didn't mean for it to come out that way."

"No, you are right to be mad. I was kind of rude too. I suppose none of that matters now and we are both kind of useless under the present circumstances. A spoiled rich socialite with no real skills and a pot smoking, punk rocker, Walmart greeter are hardly the ideal for rebuilding civilization."

They both laughed at this.

"So, do you still have that pot?" Patrice asked with a flirtatious smile.

Chad smiled and they both lit up joints.

The next several hours passed rather quickly as they spent their time sitting around giggling like idiots as they rapidly got baked. By the time that they started to come off their high it was already fairly late.

"I guess it's getting pretty late," said Patrice as she began to get undressed.

"Yeah," said Chad as he scratched his head and politely looked away.

"So do you want to come to bed with me," said Patrice.

"What's that?"

"Do you wanna fuck," she said as she stood there naked in front of him.

Chad smiled his big stoner grin and nodded. It seems like the end of the world might not be that bad after all, he thought to himself. This really was some good weed.

4

They were awoken the next morning by the sound of breaking glass. "What was that," Patrice asked as she woke up rubbing her eyes.

"What was what?" Chad asked as he stood up naked and scratched his ass.

"I thought I heard someone downstairs. It sounds like someone was breaking the glass."

"Oh, well, shit."

"Well."

"Well what?" Chad stared at her as he continued scratching his ass.

"Well what are you going to do about it!"

"What do you want me to do?"

"You're the guy, shouldn't you be the one to go check it out."

"I see you're not one of those ass kicking liberated female types."

"And I can see that you're kind of a pussy!"

"Why don't you yell louder so whoever's down there can hear us!"

"There's a gun in my parents room in the safe."

"What's the combination?"

"I forget."

"Well a lot of good that does us!"

"Sorry, my memory is a little fuzzy because I spent last night baked out of my mind screwing some pussy ass Walmart greeter!"

That was when they heard footsteps coming up the stairs.

"Shit," Chad said as he started looking around in panic.

"Freeze," came a male voice from the doorway of the bedroom.

The first thing Chad noticed was a gun pointed at them, so he put his hands up. "Please don't shoot us," he said with his junk hanging out as he started to tremble at the knees. He closed his eyes and prepared for the worst.

"Bang," said the voice in the doorway. That was when Chad noticed that he recognized the voice.

He slowly opened his eyes and saw standing in front of him in the doorway was an African-American man dressed in a suede outfit wearing lots of flashy jewelry. "Jamaal," he said as he slowly put his hands down.

"Hey, it's my man Chad," said the man as he put his gun away and came to embrace Chad, before remembering that he was naked and backing away. "Why the hell are you naked?"

Jamaal then looked to the side and saw Patrice using her bed sheets to cover up and shaking in fear. "Oh," said Jamaal with a smile that revealed he had one gold tooth, "I see what's going on here. You fucking this bitch?"

"Kind of," Chad laughed.

"She's a pretty fine bitch," laughed Jamaal.

"I'm sitting right here," Patrice yelled. "I'll thank you not to refer to me as some fine bitch. And I only slept with him because I was baked out of my mind. And what the hell do you think you're doing in my house uninvited anyway? "

"What the hell do you think I am doing? Everybody's dead, so I figured that property rights no longer apply, and this house looked like it might have some neat bling. Rich people always have nice shit."

"Chad who the hell is this guy?!" Patrice yelled.

"This is Jamaal."

"He looks like some lowlife street criminal. You know how those people are."

"Those people? What you mean by 'those people'?" Jamaal said pointing at Patrice. "You think I'm some sort of lowlife criminal just because I'm black. Well you are one racist bitch."

"I think you're lowlife criminal because you broke into my house and pointed a gun at me!" Patrice said as she threw the blanket off of her, before covering herself up again once she remembered that she was naked and started blushing.

"I'll have you know that I am no lowlife."

"Chad," Patrice whined, "who is he?"

"He's Jamaal, my dealer."

"Your dealer? You mean drugs. So I was right, he's a lowlife."

"Hey," shouted Jamaal, "not all of us are born rich. Some of us have to work for a living."

"By selling drugs to people?" Patrice scoffed.

"Hey Missy," said Jamaal as he pointed at her, "I bet those drugs that you got baked on last night were from Chad, and he got that from me. So you're welcome."

"You broke into my house!" Patrice shouted as she shook her bed sheets in frustration. "And don't call me Missy."

"Hey, it's the fucking Apocalypse sweetie. The rules have changed."

"So it's okay for you just to break into people's houses and steal stuff?"

"Hey," Chad interrupted, "he's right. These aren't normal circumstances. For all we know we could be the last three people on earth. So can't we all just tried to get along?"

"Fine, whatever," said Jamaal.

"Patrice," Chad said as he looked in her direction lacing his fingers together as though begging.

"Fine," she said as she turned her head scornfully.

"Glad that's settled," said Jamal. "No put on some fucking pants boy. I don't need to see your junk hanging out like that."

After everyone got dressed they went downstairs to eat lunch together and discuss the situation.

"So what do you think happened," Patrice asked.

"I don't know, it seems like some type of a plague based on what I've seen," said Jamaal. "I've just been going from place to place looking for supplies for the last couple of days."

"But everyone seems to have dropped dead pretty much where they stood," said Patrice, "so whatever killed them looks like it killed them pretty much instantaneously. But why did it kill them and not us?"

"I don't know," said Jamaal she shrugged his shoulders and took a bite of his sandwich, "but I know that when I woke up I was feeling sick as a dog."

"So did I," said Chad.

Patrice nodded. "Me too."

"So whatever it was," Jamaal said taking a sip of his milk, "it was enough to knock everyone out. But maybe it was like some type of deadly gas, like you always hear about Middle Eastern dictators using to kill their people with, usually with our help."

"So you think this is a terrorist attack?" Patrice asked.

"I don't know," said Jamaal shaking his head. "But whatever it is it seems to have a pretty high mortality rate, and it seems like even those of us it didn't kill were still pretty badly fucked up by it."

"I think it's some type of alien invasion," said Chad.

"Boy are you trippin," said Jamaal as he started to laugh.

"Well I was pretty baked last night," said Chad, "as well as the day day before that."

"So in other words you are doing things pretty normally for yourself," said Jamaal with more derisive laughter.

"That's not funny," said Patrice.

"Hey, I'm glad he's alive," said Jamaal, "he's one of my biggest customers. My job in life is to see people like him stay completely baked all the time. You've been a good friend and a good customer Chad, but I think all those drugs have fried your brains. Alien invasion, seriously?"

"It's as good as explanation as anything," said Patrice. "I mean it does sound pretty crazy, but who else has weapons like this?"

"I don't know," said Jamaal, "the government has all sorts of crazy shit they probably aren't telling us about. So who really knows. Could've been those crazy Muslim fuckers or North Korea. Your guess is as good as mine."

"So what do we do from here," asked Patrice. "Our supplies are only going to last so long."

"What the hell you talking about," said Chad. "We have entire supermarkets here for the taking. There is probably enough food to last us several lifetimes."

"Food goes bad," said Jamaal. "Eventually we're going to have to find some type of long-term food source, especially for someone like you who has the munchies all the time."

"True," laughed Chad, "I have to admit that I'm still pretty hungry even though I have been stuffing my face. It's good to know that even in the apocalypse we won't be short on food for a while."

"How far have you traveled?" Patrice asked turning to Jamaal.

"Just around the local area. You were the first people I have come across. What are the odds? I'm a drug dealer and I found that one of the few survivors in a town of over 30,000 people is my best customer."

"I guess it's a sign from God," said Chad. "I must be like the chosen one or something."

"Somehow I feel like a failed rock 'n roll star Walmart greeter stoner isn't what God would have in mind as the savior of humanity," said Patrice, "no offense intended."

"All right," said Chad, "that's fair enough. Maybe I am not the savior of mankind. But I do think that we need to form some type of leadership in this crisis. So I vote to make me the new president."

"I don't think the line of succession works that way," said Patrice.

"Like Jamaal said earlier, the rules have changed. So I elect myself super president of the United States of kick ass!"

"I call VP," said Jamaal as he laughed.

"What does that leave for me?" said Patrice as she stood up and put her hands on her hips.

"You can be my first lady," said Chad.

"What makes you think I want to be first lady?"

"Well, you might be the only woman left in the world, and I think that last night the president rocked your world, even though I can barely remember it because I was so out of my mind on drugs."

Patrice rolled her eyes and shook her head. "So this is the new leadership of the world. A Walmart greeter president, vice president drug dealer and myself. Somehow I think maybe I should be president."

"What qualifies you to be president?" Jamaal asked.

"Well, I am rich. Usually the richest person wins the elections. I think I am more qualified than a drug dealer and a stoner."

"Or buys the election," said Jamaal.

"But if you're the president," said Chad, "then that makes me the first lady. I'm not your bitch, you're my bitch!"

"I ain't nobody's bitch!" Patrice said as she slammed her hands down on the table.

"Let's put it to a vote," said Jamaal. "Who thinks that Chad should be president?" Jamaal and Chad both raised their hands.

"Now who thinks I should be president," said Patrice as she raised her hand. Nobody else raised their hand.

"Well it looks like it's 2 to 1," said Chad, "I win by a landslide. And as my vice president I will take Jamaal, and you can be first lady."

"Looks like we beat your privileged ass," said Jamaal.

"Why do I even bother," said Patrice as she put her face on her hand and shook her head. "I guess you couldn't be worse than a majority of our presidents."

"Let's celebrate our inauguration by getting wasted and then, after that, getting baked," said Chad.

"I've also got some ecstasy," said Jamaal.

"To the future of America," said Chad as the three of them clinked glasses and downed their alcohol.

5

The three of them woke up the next morning with one hell of a hangover.

"I knew I should've stuck to pot, guess it really is a gateway drug," said Chad. "This isn't the best way to start the first day of my administration. As my first act I am going to legalize everything."

Chad then tumbled onto the floor and began to puke.

After they had recovered from their hangover they decided to have breakfast and discuss what they should do next.

"I call this first cabinet meeting to order," said Chad as he banged his beer mug on the table. "Our first order of business is ensuring that we have an adequate food supply. We should also send out an expedition to see if there are any more survivors."

"Agreed," said Patrice. "But how are we going to travel with all the roads blocked off?"

"Ever heard of walking," said Jamaal.

"I guess that will have to do," said Chad. "We should go exploring. Maybe we could use some bicycles or something to gather supplies. We can all take some backpacks with us and see how much we can carry back to the house. I think that we should all stick together, that's probably the safest."

Jamaal and Patrice nodded and they prepared for their journey.

The first place that they decided to go was back to the supermarket to try and bring back as much food as they could carry. It took them several trips back and forth pushing shopping carts to stock up on all food that wouldn't go bad. They also tried to get as much food that they could eat before the expiration dates to eat right away. They then went back one final time to procure three bicycles from the bike rack for further exploration.

"I think that this is as much food as we can fit in the refrigerator and cabinets," said Patrice." I don't know how long the generators are going to last. They run on gasoline and I think we are already running out. I know that there are gas stations around, and hopefully they haven't caught fire yet. Luckily the fires don't seem to be close to this house, yet, but it is something we might have to worry about in the future."

"If that happens I guess we'll just have to move," said Chad.

"I don't want to move," said Patrice. "This house has been in my family for two generations and is worth $10 million."

"I'm no economist, but I think the collapse of civilization might have devalued all currency down to basically worthless," said Jamaal. "Money doesn't mean anything anymore. Money only has value if there is some functioning society to back it up. Now it's just take whatever you can get. Too bad too, as I got thousands of dollars worth of drugs that I could've sold if society hadn't collapsed."

"What a tragedy," said Patrice. "Although I guess you are right. But still, I'd rather not abandon my home if at all possible. This place is now the unofficial presidential palace, or the new White House."

"You're house isn't white though," said Jamaal.

"I meant that figuratively," said Patrice.

"Well the house is okay for now though," said Chad. "So for now I think this is a pretty good base of operations."

"Yeah," said Jamaal, "this place is pretty swanky. Better than the shithole I lived in."

"So," said Chad, "anyone want to get baked again?"

"Don't you think about anything else?" asked Patrice.

"Well, I think about sex a lot."

"Maybe we should conserve our drugs," said Jamaal. "I have a lot, but my supply wasn't meant to last forever. As far as I know the Mexican cartels that I get them from are probably dead or avoiding this area. But if I could get the proper ingredients I could probably make a meth lab."

"No," said Patrice. "I have nothing against drugs, but we are not going to turn the presidential palace into a meth lab! I think that we should try to stay clearheaded while we are looking for survivors. We want to get our new civilization off to a good start. This is our chance to rebuild society as we desire it. We can rebuild it as a better society, a more enlightened one, one that doesn't treat women like sex objects."

"Whatever bitch," said Jamaal. "If you ask me the old society wasn't all that impressive to begin with, so it's a pretty low bar."

Patrice threw up her hands. "This is all giving me a headache. I give up. Pass me a joint."

6

The next day they decided it might be more practical to put aside doing drugs for a day and go ahead with their plan to explore the area in more extensive detail, in hopes of finding survivors. They got on their bicycles and headed up and down the street not far from the supermarket to see if they saw any signs of the survivors. They shouted in hopes that people would hear them, but they got no responses.

Eventually they came across the town library and decided to check it out. The library was a place where survivors might come to seek out information on the rebuilding of society.

"Do we really have to waste our time here?" Chad asked. "I feel intimidated by all these books. It is like I am back in school or something."

"We are going to need books if we are going to rebuild society," said Patrice. "There could be lots of useful information to be gained by the books here. There could have been other people who had the same idea."

"I think maybe we should just burn the whole fucking place down," said Chad.

"Place might burn down on its own if those fires don't stop burning," said Jamaal. "Soon the entire town might burn down. So we should investigate while we can."

"I'd rather knock stuff over," said Chad as he pushed over a bookcase which had a domino effect on the bookcases behind it.

"Hey, what do you think you're doing!" came the shout of an unfamiliar voice.

They all looked up at the top floor of the library to see where the voice had come from, and saw that it came from an African-American man with graying hair and who appeared to be going bald. He was wearing a gray suit and really thick glasses.

"Who are you?" Chad shouted to the man.

"Stop knocking stuff over and I will come down and talk to you," said the man who quickly ran off to the staircase.

They met him at the bottom of the stairs.

"My name is Prof. Washington, professor of political science at the community college," said the man. "And I don't appreciate the desecration of this library. I cleared all the dead bodies out of this library specifically to make sure that it would be safe from any type of outbreak of disease. This library represents what might be the last refuge of civilization and human knowledge. So I would ask you to try and show more respect in the future. And who are you people?"

"I'm Chad," Chad said as he pointed to himself, "and these are my friends Jamaal and Patrice. I am new president of these United States."

"I don't recall getting a vote," said Prof. Washington.

"Well you weren't there when we took the vote, otherwise we would've included you," said Chad. "So it seems there are other survivors."

"I'm not the only one," said Prof. Washington. "There are a few others with me."

"How many others?" asked Patrice.

"I will show you, if you follow me."

Prof. Washington led them down to the library's basement where he had set up a couple of cots. There appeared to be a disheveled bearded man looking like he hasn't had a bath in a long time, a senile old man sitting in a wheelchair babbling to himself, and a young girl holding a baby. She looked far too young to possibly be the baby's mother.

"I'm Rusty," said the bearded man with a hiccup.

"The man in the wheelchair is Adam," said Prof. Washington. "I found him at the nursing home and he seems to not to be aware of what is going on. I'm guessing he is probably somewhere in his late 70s to early 80s."

"I'm Jasmine," said the little girl. "And this is my baby brother Justin." She held up the baby boy.

"How long have you all been here for?" Chad asked.

"A couple of days," said Prof. Washington. "I found the girl wandering the street with her baby brother. I found Rusty sitting outside on a park bench passed out drunk, and I found Adam when I was raiding the nursing home for medical supplies."

"I woke up to find my parents were dead and that I was confused," said Chad. "I then decided to raid the local supermarket for supplies where I met up with Patrice and we went to her mansion. Jamaal then broke into the house while scavenging for supplies, and then for the last couple of days we've been mostly just eating what we can find and doing drugs."

"Oh," said Prof. Washington, with a clear tone of apprehension and disapproval. "I am sorry to hear about your parents. In the last couple of days we must all have lost lots of people who were near and dear to us."

"You're more than welcome to stay with us," said Patrice. "We decided to come to the library in hopes of finding books on how to rebuild civilization and see if there were any other survivors. I guess it was just dumb luck that we found you."

"Or maybe God told us to come here," said Chad. "I have a theory that I might be his chosen savior."

"Did you come to that conclusion before or after you did all those drugs," asked Prof. Washington, looking at Chad with an understandable level of skepticism and scorn.

"Fair enough," said Chad. "But I still think it's not coincidence that we all managed to find each other. I think that we all stand a better chance of surviving if we all stick together."

"That's all well and good," said Prof. Washington, "but I don't think it is wise to do drugs under the circumstances. Doing drugs will just just lead to accidents and increasing danger to ourselves and others."

"I've got a lot of drugs," said Jamaal, "just in case you change your mind. The

Apocalypse can be rather depressing you know."

"Yes," said Prof. Washington, "it certainly can be. How are you holding up for supplies?"

"I think that we are doing pretty good," said Patrice, "but we really aren't sure what to do for the long term. We kind of figured that maybe the library would have some useful books."

"That was what I was figuring as well," said Prof. Washington. "I still think it might be better to stay here in the library where we will be near the books and can protect them, and also to make sure that nobody steals them or knocks them over." He looked at Chad when he said that last part.

"What?" Chad asked, clearly not picking up on Prof. Washington's implication.

"Nothing," said Jamaal as he patted Chad on the back, "nothing at all Mr. President."

"I still think I want to talk to you about that whole President thing," said Prof. Washington.

"You don't have to call me Mr. President, Chad is fine by me," said Chad with a laugh.

"But what about the others?" asked Prof. Washington. "Do you have enough room for them at your mansion?"

"I have numerous bedrooms and guest bedrooms," said Patrice, "so I don't think that that will be a problem. There is more than enough room for everyone. And if our population begins to increase too much there are a couple of other really big houses next door that, as far as I know, seem to be abandoned."

"That sounds pretty good," said Prof. Washington, "so I think I will accept your generous offer and hopefully we can all be of help each other. Jasmine and Rusty can walk, but I might need some help with Adam, as I don't think he likes to be moved."

"What's wrong with him?" Chad asked.

"He appears to have some type of senile dementia," said Prof. Washington shaking his head. "Poor guy. He doesn't seem to have the slightest idea what is going on. But I am more worried about his health. I really couldn't find any information about him on the hospital computers since all the power was down. If I hadn't found him he no doubt would've starved to death. I think that he might have some type of medical condition. And his constant shaking makes me think he might have Parkinson's disease. I just wish that we could find some type of a doctor. None of you happen to be a doctor by any chance, do you?"

"I was a Walmart greeter," said Chad with a laugh, "and now I am president of the United States of America. We are going to rebuild this country on sex, drugs and rock 'n roll!"

Prof. Washington frowned, then laughed hesitantly and insincerely and turned to Patrice.

Patrice pointed to herself. "Me? I was kind of independently wealthy."

"Did you go to college or anything?"

"Not really. I have to admit I don't really have many useful skills."

"Well that's okay," said Prof. Washington. "When I was your age I didn't know very much either and wasn't sure what I wanted to do with my life. But you have managed to hold up pretty well. What about you?" He turned and looked at Jamaal.

"Well you could say that I am involved in the pharmaceutical industry," said Jamaal.

"Really," said Prof. Washington with the first sign of real enthusiasm.

"Oh for Christ's sake," said Patrice with annoyance, "you're a freaking drug dealer. Pharmaceutical industry my ass."

Prof. Washington put his hand to his head and shook his head back and forth muttering to himself. "Okay, I think that maybe I should take charge here."

"Who decided to put you in charge," said Chad. "I'm still the president here."

"Young man, with all due respect, you are too young to be the president of the United States. The president of the United States has to be at least 35 years old and you barely look like you are 20."

"Well it's the Apocalypse," said Chad, "that kind of changes the rules."

"We don't even know that the President of the United States is dead or if any members of his cabinet survived. We don't know how extensive this thing is. All we know is that it extends at least throughout this entire region. Now I'm not going to claim I should be any type of president or anything, but I am 58 years old and I have a degree in political science. I think if anyone is qualified to be a leader here it is me."

"Political science is pretty useless in this type of world old man. This is survival of the fittest, and I could kick yer ass any day of the week."

"Look," said Patrice as she interrupted, "this type of fighting isn't going to get us anywhere. And to be honest I think he has a point Chad. I don't think that you know anything about leadership. And if we have to put it to a vote again I would vote to make him our leader."

"So you want to screw this old man as his First Lady?" Chad asked.

"I never said anything about that! Why does your mind automatically go to sex all the time!"

"I kind of got to agree with Patrice," said Jamaal. "Besides, brothas gotta stick together." Jamaal stood next to Prof. Washington and held him close to him, which clearly seemed to make him uncomfortable.

"This is treason," shouted Chad.

"Well it's my house and I say that everyone is welcome," said Patrice. "Maybe we can make this a truly democratic society and we will all decide on everything by consensus. We don't need a president in a society with only eight citizens. So I think it's a little premature to be worrying about those issues. Now let's get back home and try to make this whole thing work. Is everyone okay with that?"

Everyone nodded in agreement, although Chad waved his hand as he did so to show his annoyance.

"Good, so it's settled," said Patrice. "Let's try to get as many books as we can each carry and bring them back home."

They all packed their backpacks with as much as they could fit. They mostly carried back books about how to build things, how to fix things and how to survive in extreme circumstances. They managed to push Adam's wheelchair all the way back to the house, although he put up some resistance because he wasn't accustomed to being moved around. When they got home they managed to set everyone up in their own room, had a dinner together and then went to bed early for the night hoping to get a fresh start tomorrow.

7

After breakfast the next morning they decided to sit down and have a Council meeting, except of course for Adam, who had no idea what was going on. But they made sure to keep him in the room because they didn't want to leave him by himself in case he ended up hurting himself. Jasmine was too young to understand what was going on, so she just spent her time attending to her baby brother Justin.

"So do any of those books have any useful information about the rebuilding of society?" Jamaal asked as he looked at Prof. Washington. "As a political science teacher you must have some idea about how society works. I mostly have StreetSmarts, which might not be such a bad thing under the circumstances."

"Well usually in a crisis like this people look to a strong leader to restore order, although that often results in even greater chaos or some type of authoritarian political structure, much like happened in Nazi Germany."

"Are you comparing me to Hitler?" Chad asked as he stood up.

"No," said Prof. Washington, "I just was illustrating the point that in times of great crisis people often look for a Savior of some kind to restore things to the way they were. And a lot of time it results in persecution and destruction. But I don't think we need to worry about that here. A society of eight people is usually pretty limited in the damage it can do. I am hoping that we can avoid the mistakes of the past if this really is the end of civilization."

"What do you mean if!" Chad shouted. "Have you looked out there? I think we can be pretty certain that this is the end of the world."

"I think Mr.Washington has a point," said Patrice.

"Sure, take his side," said Chad as he folded his arms and looked away.

"You are being really immature about all of this Chad," she said. "We don't know just how bad the damage is. This might be some type of local catastrophe, and maybe the government will come in and restore order."

"But we don't know that," said Chad. "What about my theory?"

"You ain't talking about the aliens again, are you?" Jamaal asked as he laughed.

"We can't rule it out," said Chad. "It's as good as explanation as any."

"I think there's more likely a terrestrial cause," said Prof. Washington. "If this was some type of alien invasion, then where are the aliens?"

"Well, I don't know." Chad paused to scratch his head. "But maybe the alien could be one of us, like in Invasion of the Body Snatchers or The Thing."

"Those are some good movies," said Rusty in the first thing that he had said all day. "I think that Chad might have a point."

"Thank you!" Chad said as he patted Rusty on the back. "Finally we have a sensible person who can see my point of view."

"I remember this one time when I was in the park I saw this man looking at me, and I could swear that he was like some kind of secret alien or something," said Rusty. "It was like he was stealing my thoughts or something. It was shortly after that that I started drinking."

"Well Chad, it looks like you've finally met someone who thinks the way you do," said Patrice with a laugh.

"What's so funny?" Rusty asked as he scratched his beard.

"Nothing," said Patrice.

"I could really use a drink about now," said Rusty.

"Didn't you just have a drink a little while ago?" Patrice asked with exasperation.

"I'm an alcoholic," said Rusty. "And I think under the circumstances it is perfectly understandable behavior. Besides, if you're completely drunk then the aliens can't control your thoughts. Everybody knows that."

"Really?" Chad asked. "Maybe I'd better have something to drink as well."

"Well this is really turning out to be a real Algonquin Roundtable we've got here," said Patrice. "I don't know why I even bother."

"Well what do we really have to discuss any way," said Chad. "This is the end of the world. The way I see it we have plenty of food, plenty of drugs and plenty of everything that we need. If some problem arises will deal with it when we come to it. I say that we take advantage of the situation and do all the stuff that we always wanted to do but couldn't do."

"Like what?" Patrice asked.

"Well I've always wanted to run stark naked through the streets without getting hassled from the man," said Chad.

"Ladies and gentlemen, the President of the United States," laughed Jamaal.

"You know I think I have a Nixon mask somewhere," said Chad. "Does anyone want to go streaking with me?"

"I think I'll pass," said Patrice. "I think I have a little more class than that."

"Don't be such a snob," said Chad. "Social status doesn't mean anything anymore. We are all equal now."

"Some animals will always be more equal than others," said Prof. Washington.

"What the hell is that supposed to mean?" Chad asked.

"Nothing, it's a reference that you wouldn't get," said Prof. Washington.

"Why, you think I'm stupid?" Chad crossed his arms. "You know you educated types and you rich types are always such snobs. You go around waving your education or your money in the face of people like me. You just can't accept that in this type of world it is people like me that will thrive."

"That's just what I worry about," said Prof. Washington. "There are some of us who have higher ambitions in life than streaking through the streets wearing a Nixon mask. Here we have the opportunity rebuild civilization, and all you want to do is run around drinking, doing drugs and goofing off."

"Higher ambitions, I'm the freaking president," said Chad as he opened a beer and began to chug it down. "I can do whatever the hell I want to do. What more can anyone ask for in life? Your problem is that you just can't accept that there is an upside to being the only people in the world. There are no rules, no one telling you what to do or how to behave or forcing you to wear pants."

"Whatever Chad," said Patrice. "If you want to go run off naked through the streets, then be my guest. We'll be here waiting for you when you get bored of your juvenile antics."

"Fine. Does anyone want to join me? How about you Rusty?"

"Yeah, why not?" Rusty shrugged. "I could use some fun."

Chad and Rusty decided to go into town to have some fun by themselves. They decided to go down to all the fancy stores and go on a spree of looting.

"Woooooooo whoooooooo!" Chad said as he threw a rock through a fancy jewelry store. He then ran inside with Rusty and started piling Rolex watches into a sack. They then put several more watches on their arms.

"You know these watches are probably worth more than I've made in my entire life," said Rusty. "And now they are almost completely worthless and just there for the taking."

"I know it's great, isn't it?"

"I've been thinking Chad. Maybe the other guys had a point."

"What do you mean?"

"I never made much of myself. I went from job to job never succeeding in anything. I was later diagnosed with paranoid schizophrenia. And then my wife eventually left me and I started drinking. Soon my drinking got worse and worse and exacerbated my mental illness. I spent the last three or four years living as a bum. And now here I am wearing a bunch of watches that could have made me wealthy, and it all means nothing."

"The Apocalypse is the great equalizer. But what's your point?"

"All of this. We may all be in the same position, but it isn't a happier world. Having everyone being in a terrible state doesn't make my situation any better. And now that I look at the world going to hell, I don't know, I just sort of regret my entire life. I wish I had made something of myself when it still mattered. Didn't you have any higher ambitions?"

"Not really," said Chad as he shook his head. "I mean I did want to be a rock 'n roll megastar and have sex with lots of beautiful women, but I was never able to achieve that. If the world hadn't ended I would still kind of be a loser. So really the world ending and me being one of the last people on earth is kind of the biggest achievement of my life. I know that sounds ridiculous, but this is almost like the greatest thing to ever happen to me. Surely you must feel a little bit better? You can't be a bum in a world where there is no society left. Just the fact that you survived makes you important in some way. At least that's how I've always seen it."

"You know I kind of always wanted to be some type of an artist. I know that sounds silly now, but it had always been my dream. I never really cared much about money, although perhaps I should have cared a little bit more, then maybe my wife wouldn't have left me for a more successful man. But then I started with my delusions and hallucinations and I just hit rock bottom. And once I became homeless I pretty much just gave up on life and was living day-to-day by whatever I could beg for."

"But everything is different now."

"But I'm not. Maybe money doesn't matter anymore, maybe social status doesn't matter anymore, but I'm still not an artist. I'm still mentally ill, I'm still an alcoholic and I'm still a bum. The fact that I might be one of the last people left on this planet doesn't change that. Of all the people to survive the end of the world, I couldn't think of a more unworthy person."

"Dude, don't be so hard on yourself. It's the end of the world, and yeah that's kind of a bummer, but none of that stuff matters anymore. The fact is you are one of the last people on the earth and that makes you more important. And now we can do whatever we want. So you want to loot some more stores?"

"Nah," said Rusty as he waved his hand. "You know, I think maybe I just want to go for a walk alone for a while."

"You sure you don't want to streak? I've still got my Nixon mask."

"Nah," Rusty shook his head. "You go ahead. I'll catch up with you and meet you back at the house."

"Are you sure?"

Rusty nodded.

"Okay, I guess I'll see you later. But you're missing out on some good naked fun!"

Rusty walked off on his own and Chad spent the rest of the day running naked through the town and looting places. He filled several sacks and shopping bags with all sorts of jewelry and valuable electronic equipment, which in retrospect he realized was kind of pointless, considering there was no way to use most of it. He arrived back home late at night.

"I'm home," shouted Chad as he walked in and threw his bags to the floor.

"Did you have fun looting and streaking?" Patrice asked.

"Plenty of fun," said Chad laughing. "It was some of the most fun that I have ever had in my entire life. I just can't believe that Rusty didn't want to join me."

"Where is Rusty?" Prof. Washington asked.

"You mean he never came home?" Chad scratched his head. "He said that he would meet me back at the house later. I assumed he would be home by now."

"I hope he's okay," said Patrice. "How could you let him go off on his own like that?"

"He's an adult, he can take care of himself."

"No, he can't," said Prof. Washington as he stood up from the table. "Rusty is a severe alcoholic and schizophrenic, and he has been growing ever worse ever since this catastrophe happened. I am worried about him."

"He said he was just going for a walk. I'm sure he'll be fine. Is dinner ready yet?"

"Is that all you can worry about," asked Patrice. "One of our group is out there, possibly lost and injured, and all you can think about is dinner."

"I don't see what the big deal is. The man was just going for a walk."

"I think maybe we should go look for him," said Patrice.

"I agree," said Prof. Washington. "I don't think Rusty is safe out there on his own."

"I'm sure he'll be back by the morning," said Chad.

"I think we should go and look for him," said Patrice. "But someone needs to stay here with Adam and the children."

"I think maybe I had better stay here," said Prof. Washington. "I'm no doctor, but I think Adam's medical condition, whatever it is, is getting worse. I know some basic CPR and first aid. But I am also worried about Rusty."

"I think that Chad, Jamaal and I can find Rusty," said Patrice turning to Prof. Washington. "You just stay here and take care of Adam and the children. They know you better."

"Can we eat dinner first?" Chad asked.

Patrice slammed her hands down on the table. "Dammit Chad, all you think about is yourself. It's your fault Rusty is missing in the first place."

"Okay, okay," said Chad as he put his hands up defensively. "Let's go."

"What's happening, I heard shouting," said Jamaal as he entered the kitchen.

"Rusty's gone missing," said Patrice, "we need to go looking for him."

Jamaal nodded in acknowledgment and after getting some flashlights prepared they were off.

They searched for Rusty until it had begun to get dark and cold.

"Maybe he is back by now," said Chad.

"But what if he isn't?" Patrice said, and could see her breath in front of her due to the cold.

"I'm worried about Rusty too," said Jamaal as he hugged his body, "but it's getting freezing out. If he isn't home by now he might already have froze to death. I don't think he took a jacket with him when you guys left, did he?"

Chad shook his head. "No, he didn't."

"As much as I hate to admit it, we might have to go back," said Patrice. "It's getting too dark to go on looking and I'm beginning to lose hope that –"

"What is it?" Chad asked as he saw Patrice suddenly freeze in her tracks.

Patrice put some binoculars up to her eyes. "Up there!"

Chad and Jamaal looked up to where she was pointing the binoculars, and on top of a tall building they saw a figure standing on the ledge.

"Give me those," said Chad as he took the binoculars away from her and pointed them up. "It's him, it's Rusty. It looks like his pants are at his ankles and he is holding his belt."

"I think he's going to jump," Patrice shouted. "We've got to get up there."

They quickly ran to the roof of the building and started running and shouting at Rusty.

"Stay back," said Rusty as he turned around to face them.

"Calm down Rusty," said Patrice as she slowly backed off. "We aren't here to hurt you. We just want to bring you home."

Rusty started laughing hysterically as he shook his head and outstretched his arms. The other three looked back and forth at each other and then looked forward again to Rusty.

"What's so funny, buddy," asked Chad as he laughed nervously.

"They're coming," said Rusty as he stared straight forward at them.

"Who's coming?" Chad asked.

"The aliens," said Rusty as he began to laugh hysterically. "They are coming and there's nothing we can do to stop them. You are right Chad. They could be all around us. It could be anyone. Trust no one."

"We're friends," said Patrice. "We're here to help you."

Chad and Jamaal nodded in agreement.

Rusty laughed even louder as he shook his head. "I have no friends. Any of you could be one of them. You're here to suck out my brains. But I'm not going to let you."

Rusty started to step backwards.

"Whoa buddy," shouted Chad, "don't move. It's all going to be okay."

"No," Rusty said as she shook his head. "It's never going to be all right. This is the invasion, the end of the world! There is only one way to escape."

Rusty stepped back to the edge of the ledge, outstretched his arms like Christ on the cross and then started to fall backwards.

"No!" shouted the three of them in unison. But it was too late, as Rusty went over the side of the building.

They took a moment to compose themselves and then quickly ran down the stairs and onto the street below. They slowly approached Rusty's body, but he did not move. Patrice checked for a pulse and only got a faint one.

Chad kneeled slowly forward to try and turn Rusty over onto his back. Rusty reached up, grabbed Chad by his jacket and whispered into his ear, "don't trust anyone." Then he laid back and stopped breathing.

8

The next few days following Rusty's death passed in almost total silence. Hardly anyone said more than minimal amount to anyone else. Even Adam seemed to be more agitated than usual, as though he could sense the tension in the air and knew that something wasn't right. And even though they tried not to, they all drank and did drugs more to try and numb the pain. Even Prof. Washington began to drink, despite the fact that he had sworn off alcohol years ago.

Chad grew more and more paranoid and started avoiding the others altogether, spending his days alone in his room, always carrying his gun at his side and muttering to himself inaudibly. Patrice began to become more and more worried about him, but she tried to keep her feelings to herself, although she was sure everyone else was just as worried.

Another week passed and another tragedy struck. One morning when they were waking up to feed Adam, they found that he had stopped breathing in the night and had died. They didn't know what had killed him. Prof. Washington ruled his death to be natural causes, although he admitted that he had no idea if that was true. Adam was an old man, but clearly he had something wrong with him.

They decided to bury Adam's body in the backyard and marked the spot with a simple headstone. They didn't know if he was a religious man, although he wore a Star of David, which they thought they should bury with him out of respect.

"Does anyone want to say anything," Patrice asked as they stood solemnly around the grave.

"I didn't know Adam very long," began Prof. Washington, "and I didn't know anything about him beyond his name. But I cared for him like he were my own child. In the short time we had together I grew incredibly fond of him, and it saddens me greatly to be burying him so soon after we have all witnessed so much death and destruction. The only consolation is that, unlike the rest of us, he probably did not realize the horror that he managed to survive the way the rest of us did. I only hope that wherever he is now he has found peace, and I would like to ask for a moment of silence to honor Adam, and Rusty and all the other people that we have lost."

The moment of silence was finally broken by Chad who said the first thing directly to anyone that he had said in several days. "They got him," Chad muttered, "and they are going to get the rest of us as well."

Patrice, Jamaal and Prof. Washington all gave each other worrying looks, while Jasmine just stood there holding her baby brother in total silence.

That night they all ate dinner in total silence. Nobody said a single word beyond pass the ketchup, although Chad was staring off into space muttering to himself increasingly. It was difficult for them to ignore. All he just kept saying under his breath was "they got him, they got him."

"We're getting low on food," Jamaal said finally breaking the silence. "I think we are going to have to go for another raid on the supermarket soon."

Everyone nodded in agreement, except for Chad who just kept muttering to himself.

"I think we should go tomorrow," said Patrice.

"They'll get you," Chad said in little more than a whisper, without even looking at anyone. They just ignored him.

"I think Jamaal and I can handle it by ourselves," said Patrice. "Do you think you can watch the place while we are gone Prof. Washington?"

"I think I can handle it," he said as he nodded.

They all finished their dinner without saying anything else.

9

The following day Patrice and Jamaal went to the supermarket and gathered more food, only to find that a lot of it was now expiring and going bad without refrigeration, so the pickings were getting slimmer. When they got home they opened the door and Patrice screamed. Lying on the floor was Prof. Washington in a pool of his own blood. They ran over to him and shook his body.

"Find Jasmine and her brother and get them out of here," choked Prof. Washington.

"Who did this to you?" Patrice asked.

"It was Chad, he's gone crazy."

That was when Patrice felt the nozzle of a gun against her back. "Freeze," came Chad's voice. "And get up slowly."

Patrice and Jamaal slowly turned around and found themselves facing Chad who had a gun pointed at them.

"Chad, why?" Patrice asked.

The gun started shaking in Chad's hand. "He was one of them."

"One of who?"

"The aliens! He was always undermining my authority as president. Rusty knew what he was. Prof. Washington is a shape shifting bodysnatcher."

"You are tripping bro," said Jamaal. "I've got to stop giving you so many drugs."

Chad pointed the gun at Jamaal and he suddenly shut up.

"What did you do with Jasmine and her brother," said Patrice as she began to cry.

"They're fine," said Chad as the gun continued to shake in his hand. "They are tied up in the basement. But now there's the question of what to do with you."

"You could let us go," said Jamaal with a bit of nervous laughter.

Chad laughed as he continued to shake. "And let you suck out my brains. I don't think so. How do I know you're not one of them?"

"I'm your friend," said Jamaal. "If I was going to suck out your brains I would've done it one of those times when you were high."

"But how do I know you're really my friend? An alien shape changer could've killed Jamaal and taken his form."

"I can prove that I'm the real Patrice," said Patrice. "Remember we slept together on that first night that we met."

"Indeed we did," said Chad as he laughed. "But if you sucked out Patrice's brains you would have her memory and would know that."

Chad continued to shake more and more and then turned to the side and began vomiting. Seeing his opportunity, Jamaal leapt forward and tackled Chad. Patrice ran to the stove and picked up a large pot. In the struggle she heard a gun go off and saw Jamaal fall to the floor clutching his stomach. As Chad was getting up Patrice took the pot and smashed it down hard on his head several times causing him to drop the gun. She quickly picked up the gun, pointing it at Chad's unconscious body as she knelt down by Jamaal.

"Jamaal," she shouted.

"I knew I should've voted for you," Jamaal said as he laughed and started spitting up blood.

"You're going to be okay Jamaal," she said.

"It's nice of you to lie like that," said Jamaal. "Let's face it, I'm fucked. I managed to survive the Apocalypse and now here I am dying of a gunshot wound. The universe sure has a funny sense of humor."

"Maybe we could get you a doctor," said Patrice. "Don't quit on me Jamaal. I can't be left alone like this."

"Go take care of Jasmine and make sure you tie Chad up," choked Jamaal as he began gagging up tons of blood.

"But what about you," said Patrice.

"Go!" coughed Jamaal as he started to convulse.

Patrice ran upstairs as quickly as she could, reached into her drawer and took out some novelty handcuffs. She quickly ran downstairs, turned Chad over onto his back and handcuffed his hands behind him. By then Jamaal was no longer moving and she could not deny that he was already dead. She started to sob hysterically, but then she remembered Jasmine and her brother. She quickly went down into the basement and untied Jasmine and Justin. Jasmine was really shook up, but otherwise seemed to be fine.

But now what was she to do about Chad?

Patrice wasted no time handcuffing Chad to a chair and tying up his feet. He seemed to still be breathing but might have had a concussion. He also looked extremely pale and sickly.

She cleared the bodies out of the house, dragging them into the backyard and did her best to try to soak up the blood with some towels. She really had no idea what to do in the circumstances. Once she had managed to compose herself she attended to Jasmine and Justin. She asked them if they wanted anything to eat later on, but Jasmine shook her head. But together they slowly spoon fed Justin's baby food to him.

"What's going on," Chad said interrupting their vigil. "Why am I tied up? I'm the president, untie me at once."

Patrice looked at him with disgust. "You murdered two innocent people."

"They were one of them."

"Dammit Chad, there are no aliens. You're just insane. I wish I had never met you. I should just let you die."

"Then why didn't you?"

"Because I'm not a murderer."

"You're going to have to untie me at some point." Chad turned to the side and vomited.

"You are ill Chad."

"No, you're just infected me. My body is being taken over. I knew that the aliens were coming when I saw their spaceship flyover earlier."

"What do you mean?"

"I saw a light in the sky."

Patrice suddenly started to feel hopeful. "Was it a helicopter or airplane?"

"That's just what they want you to think."

"No Chad, it means someone is coming to rescue us. And when they arrive I think you are going to be going to prison or the insane asylum."

Chad started laughing hysterically before vomiting more all over himself. "You're crazy. When they arrive they are just going to suck out your brains. There are no more prisons and mental asylums. We are just going to be food for aliens."

"I'm going to keep you tied up until they do arrive. Then at least maybe you'll get some help."

Chad just started laughing maniacally and Patrice decided it was best to take Jasmine and Justin upstairs into the bedroom with her.

"What's wrong with him," Jasmine finally asked.

Patrice started stroking Jasmine's hair to comfort her. "He's gone a little bit crazy. I think it will be safer up here. I think that help is going to arrive soon. We just have to keep him restrained until the authorities arrive."

"What about all that weird stuff that he was saying," Jasmine said as she began to cry. "Are people really coming to get us?"

"People are coming to rescue us Jasmine. We just have to hold out a little bit longer. For now we are just going to have to keep him tied up and hope that help arrives shortly."

"Can I sleep with you tonight?"

Patrice drew Jasmine and her brother closer to her. "Of course you can. It will be better if we all stay together. Don't worry, it'll all be better in the morning, I promise you."

10

Jasmine was the first one to wake up the next morning. She quickly nudged Patrice to wake her up, but she didn't wake. "Patrice, Patrice wake up," she said as she shook Patrice's body. But then Patrice's head fell forward and she started hacking up blood from her mouth all over her bed sheets. "Are you okay?!" Jasmine shouted.

Patrice jumped up out of bed and started vomiting up a bucket of blood into her wastebasket.

"What's wrong?" Jasmine asked with fear in her voice.

"I think it's food poisoning," Patrice said as she continued to gag, before falling over onto the floor.

Jasmine ran over to Patrice and began shaking her. "Wake up, wake up!!"

"Don't...eat...the food," Patrice coughed before closing her eyes.

"Wake up, wake up!" Jasmine cried as she shaked Patrice's body. But Patrice did not move and did not appear to be breathing.

Jasmine then ran downstairs to see what was happening with Chad. She ran over to the chair where he was tied up to find that he had fallen over onto his side and there was a big puddle of blood that appeared to have come out of his mouth.

This was when Jasmine suddenly noticed that her own stomach was hurting a lot and she turned to the side and began vomiting. She then fell on her knees and vomited a large amount. Once she had stopped vomiting, she went back upstairs to check on her brother. He was crying.

"I'm sorry little brother," she said as she shook Justin's fragile body and cried, "but I can't give you any food. The food is poison. We'll just have to wait until help arrives."

But as the hours went on Jasmine felt sicker and sicker and couldn't stop vomiting. She was beginning to feel delirious, but didn't want to leave her brother alone. She decided that she would write a note explaining what had happened and put it in her brother's crib. When she had finished her note she left it in the crib with Justin and decided to go to sleep on the couch.

11

"Check in here," said a man in a biohazard suit as he kicked in the door of Patrice's house where he saw the dead bodies on the floor. "We've got bodies here, and they look fresh. There could be survivors."

"There's some more bodies out back," came the voice on his intercom.

"There seems to be another body upstairs," came a third voice. "They look like they just died recently, so these people must have survived the attack."

"I can't imagine what they must have gone through," said the first man. "This is the worst biological weapons accident in the history of the world, and there were some people who were unfortunate enough to live through that. We'll have to do an autopsy on these bodies." That was when he noticed Jasmine's body and went over to her to find that she was not breathing. "I found another body, it's just a little girl."

That was when he was interrupted by the sound of a baby crying.

"I think we've got a survivor," he said as he ran over to Justin's crib. "It's a baby, and there appears to be a note with him."

He picked up the note and began to read to himself.

Deer riscoo peeple. My nam iz Jazmine, lik the pincess. I m olee 8 yeers old and I am dislexsik, hat meens I can't reed and rite so god. My mummy and daddee died of soom bed germs, but this kice man foond me and we went to the liberry. Thin anuther groop of peeple foond us end we wet 2 this manson. Bi thin evreone went krazee and got all sik and evrebudee died. My timmy herts beekoose I 8 sim bed food. Peelase riscoo my babee brather and fid him. But dan't fid him the bed food hat kiled all mi freends. He lices the abble flavired babee food. Tank u, Jazmine.

The man fell back onto the couch next to Jasmine's dead body, dropped the note on the floor, and took off his biohazard suit. Then he fell to the floor and began to cry.

Countdown to Doomsday

Andrew was excited when he heard the announcement. School was being canceled and all of the students sent home early because the nation was under attack. He didn't quite know what that meant, since he was only in first grade, but he realized it was something important enough to cancel school.

The teachers did not seem to be as excited as the students. All of the students were jumping up and down with excitement that they would be getting a day off from school.

"Do you think they will cancel school tomorrow too?" Andrew asked his best friend Mark.

"I hope so," Mark replied as he jumped up and down in his seat. "Maybe we could hang out or something and play video games."

"No talking children," the teacher said. "This is a serious matter. You are all to wait here quietly until your parents come to pick you up."

One of the girls raised her hands. It was Emily, the school smarty-pants. Andrew never liked her very much because she was the teacher's pet.

"What is it Emily?" the teacher asked.

"I'm scared," she said as she began to cry. "Are we all going to die?"

"No, just you!" shouted Dennis, the class clown.

"Dennis!" the teacher shouted as she waved her finger at him disapprovingly.

Emily began to sob hysterically and the teacher went over to comfort her.

"Look, Emily wet her pants," Dennis shouted as he began to laugh, soon joined in by most of the class.

"That is enough!" the teacher yelled. "There is not to be another word out of you until your parents arrive. Now everyone put their heads down on their desks."

Andrew thought that Dennis was really funny. It's not like the teacher could punish him either. If the school was going to be shut down due to some type of crisis they might have a really long vacation. He started fantasizing about all the things that he would do if that were the case. He could play the new military videogame without having to worry about his homework, and maybe he would be able to hang out with his friends until really late at night since he wouldn't have to get up early to go to school.

But before he had much time to think about that his mother had arrived and immediately hugged him.

"Mom, not in front of the guys," Andrew said as he pushed her away.

"I'm sorry honey," she said as she wiped away a tear, "mommy is just very worried."

"Why are you worried?" Andrew didn't understand as he had never seen his mom like this since grandma had died.

"I'll explain to you when we get home," she said as she patted him on the head.

"Do you think I can hang out with Mark later?"

"We'll see darling, we'll see."

The car ride home was eerily silent. Usually his mom was asking him all types of questions about his day. But then he thought that today was really short, so maybe she forgot.

"I got a B+ on my math test," he finally said, interrupting the silence.

"That is wonderful dear," she said as she kept her eyes straight forward on the road. There was a huge traffic jam and they were hardly moving.

"Why aren't we moving," Andrew said as he tugged on his mom's arm.

"Because everyone is crowding out of the town. Everyone is all panicked."

"Why is everyone afraid?"

"Because some very bad people on the other side of the world have started trouble."

"But if they ever come here I'll take out my gun and blast them away," he said as he took out his toy pistol from under the seat.

"Put that thing away," she scolded him with an unusual harshness. "You know I don't like you playing with toy guns."

"But what if the bad guys come?"

"You let mommy and daddy worry about that."

Finally the traffic started moving again, but as they passed by the accident site they saw lots of police cars and large numbers of people being arrested.

"Why those people being arrested?" Andrew asked.

"Some people can't handle a crisis. People are just very afraid. But don't worry, we'll be home soon."

Andrew's mother noticed what seemed to be a person on the floor with their brains blasted out and a gun at their feet. "Don't look out the window," she told Andrew.

"Why not?"

"I don't want you to see something."

"You mean like that time we saw the guy peeing on the side of the road?"

"Something like that."

"That was funny!"

"Well this is no laughing matter. Just keep your eyes staring at the floor until I tell you."

They passed by the site of the accident rather quickly and then she gave him the okay to look forward.

The rest of the trip home proceeded without incident, and as soon as they arrived Andrew's mom ran into the house to find her husband waiting at the door. She immediately hugged him.

"Dad," Andrew said, "you're home early from work. Did you get the day off like I did?"

He nodded as he drew Andrew closer. "Everyone is getting out early today."

"Because of the bad guys?"

"Yes son, that's exactly why."

"Do you think maybe later we can play baseball?"

"We'll see son, we'll see," is all he said as he led Andrew into into the house.

Andrew's parents immediately turned on the TV and Andrew saw an image of the president talking.

"I want to watch cartoons," Andrew said.

"I'm afraid cartoons aren't on right now," said his father. "Right now the president's talking to the country."

"But that's boring," said Andrew as he began to sigh. "Can I go hangout with Mark?"

"Not now son," said his mother. "Just go play quietly in your room. We have to call your brother."

Andrew went to his room but couldn't remember the last time he saw his parents act this nervous. He decided he would eavesdrop on them.

"Have you heard from Kevin yet?" his mother asked.

"No," said his father as he began to draw her closer to him.

That was when the phone rang. Andrew picked it up. "Hello," he said putting the phone to his ear.

"Hey little brother," came the voice on the other line.

"Kevin!" Andrew shouted. "Mom and dad have been waiting to hear from you. They sound like they are worried. Is that because of the bad guys that you're fighting over there?"

"Something like that," Kevin said.

"Andrew, is that your brother?" his mom asked.

Andrew nodded.

"Give me the phone," said his father, and he did as he was told.

Andrew's father went into the other room and motioned for him to stay there. Why didn't his father want him to listen. He decided to run into the other room and pick up the other phone so that he could listen secretly.

"Everyone on base is on full alert," Kevin said. "Everyone here is worried that the enemy would attack and we are all just waiting for information. I would've called sooner but you can understand why he wasn't able to."

"Of course I do," said his father.

"How is Andrew taking it?"

"He's too young to understand these matters. But we have been waiting to hear from you all day?"

"Are you safe?"

"Well we don't have a bomb shelter or anything. You are probably safer than we are at the base."

"Not if we take a direct hit."

That was when their conversation was interrupted by the sound of an alarm.

"What's that noise?" Andrew asked before catching himself and realizing that he just revealed that he was eavesdropping.

"Andrew, get off the phone," his father yelled.

But before he could put the phone down he heard a loud crackling and suddenly they got a dial tone telling them that the number they had tried reaching was no longer in service. He heard his father click the phone down.

"What happened dad?"

"You shouldn't have been listening in on our conversation," his dad yelled.

"I'm sorry, I just wanted to talk to Kevin."

"It's okay son," said his dad as he drew him close and hugged him tightly.

"Come quickly," came the voice of his mother from the living room.

Andrew and his father quickly ran into the living room to see that the president was making an announcement that our overseas bases had just been attacked.

"Oh my God, Kevin," his mom said putting her hand over her mouth.

"What's wrong mom?" Andrew began to look worried.

"It's nothing son," she said, although she sounded like she was lying. Andrew could always tell when his mom was lying.

As they stood there staring at the TV suddenly there was a flash on the screen and the president's image disappeared to be replaced by static.

"The TV just went out," his mother shouted as she began flipping through the channels to see that the other channels were either out or had the emergency broadcasting symbol on it.

"The president was in Washington," his father said. "That's only 35 miles away from here."

That was when they heard a loud booming sound and all the power suddenly went out and the window shattered. They all fell to the floor and started screaming.

"Is everyone okay?" his mother asked.

"Yes," said Andrew and his father in unison as they slowly stood up.

They then all went over to the window and saw a large cloud of light rising in the distance.

"What's that big cloud?" Andrew asked.

"It's nothing dear," said his mom, but he could hear she was gently sobbing.

Andrew wasn't sure what to say in this situation so he just said the first thing that came to mind. "Do think we will have school tomorrow?"

"No, school will be cancelled tommorrow," said his mother drawing closer to him and still sobbing.

"Can we go to the park tommorrow?"

"No dear."

His father began to hug him tight, as did his mother.

"What about the day after that?"

"We'll see dear, we'll see."

The Party at the End of the World

I awoke to find myself lying on a bed that I did not recognize in a room that was unfamiliar to me. I could hear music pounding loudly and that did not go well with the headache I was developing. This was not good. When you wake up with a headache and don't know where you are that is never a good sign.

My line of thought was interrupted when I heard a knocking on the door. What should I say? What should I do?

"Hey, is anybody in there," came a loud and angry male voice as they pounded more loudly on the door.

"Yeah, somebody is in here," I shouted back.

The knocking stopped and I decided to look out the window to see if anything looked familiar. I looked out the window and into the backyard below to see that it looked like there were hundreds of people gathered around dancing to a live band and a really amazing light show.

It looked like a pretty good party was going on, but where the hell was I? Well, I thought, only one way to find out.

I slowly opened the door and walked into the hallway which was packed with people holding drinks of various kinds. I pushed my way through the crowd until I managed to get downstairs. I didn't see anyone that I knew, but then somebody bumped into me, spilling their drink on me.

"Hey, watch where you're going," he said as he pushed past me.

I went over to the nearest table and got some napkins to wipe myself off. I looked at the napkin to realize it looked like a custom-made napkin for the occasion. It had a picture of the Earth blowing up and said "End of the World Baby" on it in be bold, golden lettering. Kind of a weird napkin I thought, but I didn't give it much thought beyond that and threw it right in the trash.

I made my way outside where the majority of the party guests seemed to be. It was a pretty big place, a mansion in fact. But it still didn't look very familiar to me.

"Excuse me," I said as I approached a man who looked reasonably friendly.

"Yeah," he said as he took a sip of his drink.

"I think I might've had a little too much to drink," I said as I rubbed my head a little bit. "So my memory is a little bit fuzzy here. I'm just wondering if you could tell me what exactly is it we are all celebrating?"

The man laughed loudly as he held his belly and spit up a little bit of his drink.

"What's so damn funny?" I honestly had no idea why he was so amused.

"You mean you really don't know?"

"No, that's why I'm asking."

"Is this some kind of a joke? Who put you up to this?"

"It's not a joke and nobody put me up to it. I just want to know what the big celebration is all about."

"You really must've had a lot to drink," he said as he slapped me hard on the back. "We're celebrating the Apocalypse."

"The what?!"

"You know, the end of the world, doomsday and all that jazz."

"It's the end of the world and you're celebrating?"

"Hey we all gotta go sometime, we might as well all go together with a real kickin sendoff."

"Wait, what exactly is gonna cause the world to end?"

"Who cares man, it's the end of the friggin world!"

"But why do you think the world is going to end?"

"I dunno, like I said, who cares? Let's just party!"

This guy obviously wasn't taking me seriously, and he was probably just as drunk as anyone. I slowly slipped away without saying anything and decided I would just watch the light show that was going on. They did have a live band after all.

I got up close to the stage so I could hear really well and listened carefully to the song. Within a few minutes I realized what the song was. It was "It's the End of the World As We Know It (and I Feel Fine)" by REM. Maybe it was just a coincidence.

"Great party isn't it?" said the guy standing next to me who was wearing a T-shirt that had the same design as the napkin. It was a picture of the Earth exploding with the words "End of the World Baby"on it in gold lettering.

"Yeah, it's a great party," I said, not sure how else I could possibly respond without sounding crazy. But I wanted to know more. "Say, mind if I ask you a question?"

"Sure, it's a free country, at least while it still exists it is. That won't be too much longer though."

"I'm just wondering why you are wearing that shirt that you're wearing."

The guy started laughing.

"What's so funny?"

"You're wearing the exact same shirt as I am." And wouldn't you know it, I was. Now I felt really stupid. Here I was wearing a shirt with the same emblem on it celebrating the end of the world and I hadn't even realized it.

"So they gave us all the shirts for free?" I certainly didn't remember buying it.

"Everything is free now. Money isn't worth anything. Why would money matter when the world is about to end?"

"Yeah, I suppose that wouldn't make much sense would it?"

"Hey why save your money when were all going to be dead in a couple of hours anyway, right?"

"Exactly." They were really taking this all pretty seriously. I was beginning to feel like someone who was the butt of a joke that they weren't in on and that everyone was in on it but me.

"So what did you spend all of your money on?"

"What do you mean?"

"I spent all my money buying explosives and fireworks. Then I burned down my whole fucking house. Ka-boom!" He started making explosion noises and moving his hands outward in imitation of an explosion.

"Why the hell did you blow up your house!" This guy was crazy!

"Why the hell not? It's not like it's going to be there tomorrow anyway."

"So you spent all your money just blowing up your house?"

"No, of course not. I had a lot more money to spend after that. I bought a new car and then I crashed the whole thing through the store where I worked."

"Why? Are you crazy?"

"No, I'm not crazy. It's not like he can fire me or sue me or anything. Did you ever just want to just completely go crazy and let out all your pent-up frustration in one big glorious orgy of destruction?"

"Well I guess everyone has thought about it." This conversation was getting awkward. "So you spent all your money blowing up your house and crashing a brand-new car into the store where you worked."

"I still had plenty of money left after that. I spent the rest of that on drugs and strippers. If the world weren't ending I would feel pretty dumb getting coked out of my mind and stuffing thousand dollar bills into a stripper's G string."

"So I guess now you are completely broke?"

"Not by a long shot. Speaking of which," he said as he took out a $100 bill, lighting it on fire and then putting it to his mouth to light a cigarette. He then threw the burning hundred dollar bill to the floor and stepped on it.

"You just burned $100!" I couldn't believe this guy.

"I know, it's great isn't it! Do you need a light?"

"No, I'm good. But what if the world doesn't end tomorrow? I mean tomorrow is when the world is supposed to end right?"

"It's supposed to end sometime tonight," he said as she shrugged his shoulders. "I don't remember exactly when. But I'm sure we'll notice it. Kinda hard to miss something like that."

"And you're not the least bit concerned about the fact that we are all going to die!"

"Hey man, don't be a buzzkill, you're totally making the apocalypse a downer."

"My humblest apologies."

"It's cool. You just need to relax and enjoy yourself. Would you like to snort some cocaine? I still think I have some left in my pocket."

"No, I think I'll pass on that as well."

"Whatever man. But if I were you I would enjoy this night. Party like there's no tomorrow, because there isn't."

"I'll keep that in mind. I think I'm going to go get a drink."

"Just make sure you drink a lot, nobody wants to be sober when the world ends."

It felt good to get away from that guy, he was starting to make me feel uncomfortable. Clearly he was completely off his rocker. Surely this is all just some sort of theme party with no reality behind. Probably everyone was just playing into some type of role-playing and didn't want to break character.

I went over to the drink table, poured myself a beer and chugged it down really fast. I still wasn't sure what was going on, but I think that that guy was talking to was right about one thing – this is not the time to be sober.

I sat down next to one guy who had his head down flat on the table. "Are you okay," I asked him as I tapped him on the shoulder to make sure he was still conscious.

"Okay. Okay! It's the end of the freaking world and you think I'm okay with that?!"

"But it's all just a theme party, isn't it? I mean it's not like the world is really going to end."

"What the hell you talking about? Of course the freaking world is going to end! Where the hell have you been?"

"I don't know, I woke up feeling like I was hung over and I just happened to be at this party."

"Well join the club," he said before belching loudly in my face, the smell of alcohol strong on his breath. "Excuse me, I'm a bit wasted. But can you blame me?"

"No, I guess not."

He started banging his head on the table and moaning loudly and I decided to get out of there.

I decided to go back over to the stage because I thought maybe listening to the music would help take my mind off of this. I was quite shocked when I suddenly noticed the significant portion of the audience was buck naked. Those who were dressed were wearing the same shirt that I was – the picture of the Earth exploding. If this really was the end of the world people were sure going about it rather casually.

"Hey this is a pretty great party isn't it," asked the guy standing next to me.

"Yeah, sure," I said, not sure what else to say.

"The end of the world really causes people to let go of their inhibitions. If only the world weren't ending it would be pretty great if it could've been like this all along."

"People are being pretty casual about the end of the world, don't you think?" Perhaps I shouldn't have said that, seeing as the other responses I have gotten tonight were less than encouraging and made me think that maybe I should just keep my mouth shut.

"Well who wants to get all weepy about the end of the world? I mean if the world is going to end anyway we might as well enjoy it, don't you think?"

"I guess so."

"I, for one, am enjoying the unprecedented amount of naked female flesh on display here. I could do without all the drunken guys waving their dicks around, but I guess you gotta take the good with the bad, you know what I mean? I'd get naked myself, but I'm self-conscious about the tattoo that I got yesterday while drunk. I know I shouldn't care, what with the world ending and everything, but I think I have to get a bit more drunk before I am ready to take my pants off. Know what I'm saying?"

"Umm, yeah, sure, whatever."

"You know what, screw it," he said as he began to pull down his pants. "I'm not going to let myself be all uptight at the end of the world. If I'm going to meet my maker I'm going to do it the way I was born – totally freaking naked!"

"You sure you want to do that? I mean a lot of people here have camera phones and once that stuff gets on the Internet it won't be going away anytime soon."

"Who cares," he said as he took off his shirt. "The world isn't even going to be here tomorrow. You know what someone told me once?"

"What?"

"Someone once told me life was a gift and that was why it was called the present, and I can safely say that right now I see a tasty little morsale I wanna unwrap right now." As he said that he pointed to a woman dancing on the stage in nothing but a bikini.

"It's kind of hard to get turned on when you know you're about to die in a couple of hours."

"Whatever dude, but if the world's going to end I'm going to get laid one final time if it kills me. And if it does, well the most I've lost is a couple of hours." And with that he pulled off his underpants and started running around swinging them wildly and cheering.

"Wow, this is all so crazy. The end of the world does some strange things to people."

I was always really uptight and concerned about the future. Now it's the end of the world and here I was at a bitchin party with lots of hot drunk, naked female flesh and all I can think about is the non-existent future. Well I guess there's not much more left to think about.

Well there was one thing. I realized that I had been drinking a lot of beer and my bladder was getting rather full. Time to make a trip to the bathroom.

As expected when I got there there was a long line of people, most of whom were holding alcoholic beverages as they waited in line. I got in place and stared straight ahead to notice that I was staring at a pretty hot redheaded girl.

"Hi, I'm Amy," said the girl when she noticed I came up behind her.

"Hi, I'm, you know I forget my name." I suddenly felt very awkward. I was so wasted I can't even remember my own god damn name. So much for first impressions.

"Well you look like a Jack," Amy said as she laughed. "I knew a guy named Jack who looks just like you."

"Okay then, I'm Jack." Maybe that really was my name. At this point I guess it really doesn't matter.

"This is a pretty long line," she said as she took another sip of her beer.

I started to look down at her cleavage and realized she was pretty stacked.

"Like what you see?" Amy asked as she smiled.

"I didn't mean to stare." I began to blush.

"I don't mind." That was when I noticed a wet spot begin to form on her jeans and trickle down her leg. "Oh damn, looks like I went and pissed myself. I must be pretty drunk."

"Maybe there is something you can change into around here."

Amy shrugged her shoulders and began taking her pants off.

"What are you doing?" She really was crazy, just like everyone else.

"What do I need pants for? The world's going to be ending in a few hours anyway. I can't waste time worrying about waiting in line for the bathroom or whether or not I'm wearing pants. Let's just have fun."

I stood there staring at her not sure what to say.

"So do you wanna go do it?" she suddenly asked me.

"What?"

"Do you want to go have sex?"

"Right now?"

"Sure, why not?"

"Right here?"

"Well we can go into a room if you want. So, do you want to?"

This girl was clearly drunk out of her mind and it would be wrong to take advantage of her in such an obviously inebriated state. Then again, what the hell? It's the end of the world, she obviously doesn't care and I don't even know what my name is, so I might as well enjoy myself.

"You know what Amy, sure, let's go."

I led her to the nearest room and I knocked on the door. Nobody appeared to be inside the room that I had left earlier, so we both went in.

As soon as we were in the door, Amy flung her shirt off, ripped her bra in half and flung her panties to the side of the room. She stood there in front of me stark naked when I realized that she had tattoos on her body. On both of her breasts was that same symbol I had seen on all of the T-shirts – her breasts were two small globes exploding.

"Like what you see?" she said as she stood there with her hands on her hips.

"I do," I said, and it was the honest truth. "I just have one question."

"Yeah?" She stood there tapping her foot impatiently.

I was going to ask her why she had that symbol tattooed on her breasts, but you know what, who cares? "Never mind, let's just do this."

I quickly threw my clothing to the side and stood before her completely naked.

"Hey, great tattoo," she said with a big smile on her face as she began to giggle.

"What tattoo?" I started to look down and realized that across my entire chest and stomach area was a tattoo of the world exploding. I then looked at her breasts again and started to laugh. "I guess we were meant for each other."

"What do you mean?" She obviously didn't get what I was talking about.

"Never mind," I said as I slowly crawled on top of her and started going to work on her.

The next hour or so went by in a blur. I had sex with her, she had sex with me in a variety of positions that I could hardly even remember. But when it was all over with I was feeling pretty damn pleased with myself. I turned to Amy and smiled. "It looks like for us the world is going to end with a bang!"

"What do you mean?" She obviously didn't get that either. She really was wasted. But I didn't even care.

"Never mind," I said as I looked up at the ceiling and put my hands behind my head with a strong feeling of satisfaction. Then I turned back to her. "So did you enjoy it is much as I did?"

She turned to me and smiled. "Normally I would regret sleeping with you, but I normally expect to be alive the next day, so I guess it's your lucky night!"

That wasn't the response that I was hoping for, but who cares? The world was going to end in a few hours and my last act in this world was to have sex with a hot woman at a random party and I didn't even know what my own name was. I think I was finally starting to lose my inhibitions and enjoy myself.

"So Amy, wanna go get high and run around naked?"

She sat up in bed, paused for a moment as though deep in thought, and then nodded. "Sure, why not? Besides, I can't even remember what I did with our clothing. I think I threw it out the window."

I started laughing and Amy joined in. We then ran out of the room completely naked, grabbed the nearest alcoholic beverages that we could find and chugged them down. Before I knew it we were both up on stage shaking our naked, and apparently also tattooed asses in front of a cheering crowd to the hundreth rendition of It's the End of the World As We Know It (and I Feel Fine). And the truth was I did feel fine. In fact I never felt better in my entire life. It may have been the end of everything, but it was probably the best night I have ever had and I owed it all to the Apocalypse.

Why was this happening? How was it happening? And who was responsible? Well I found the answer. Okay, so maybe I didn't find the answer, but then who cares, it's the end of the world after all. It only comes once so I might as well enjoy it. I lived more in this one night than I did in an entire life of careful planning, proper diet and regular exercise, well assuming I actually did those things.

As it turns out, the world ended not with a bang, not with a whimper, but with a full blown rock concert and I was center stage with a beautiful naked woman. Now that's an apocalypse! I almost wish these kind of things would happen more often, but unfortunately the Apocalypse is a one time only event.

Well I guess there's not much more left to think about. Here comes the Apocalypse and all I can say now is that at least I enjoyed it!

Party on.

The Deletion of the World as We Know It

My name is Jonathan Drake and I am the creator of this world. I find that the best way to unwind after a difficult day at the office is to spend my evenings living amongst my creations incognito. This is not without precedent. Greek mythology is full of tales of the gods coming to Earth in human form and living amongst their creations without them ever knowing the true nature of their reality.

I guess I am really not that much different from my own creations, as I don't know if I am the product of a greater reality beyond me. But I do know that I created this world all on my own. That doesn't make me unique by any means. Once the technology was perfected to create a perfect simulation of any world that you can imagine, it pretty much became the most popular form of recreation amongst those who can afford it, and to have the delusions of grandeur to want to. After all, who doesn't want to be a God?

Unlike God however, it only took me about four days to create the world, but I did it over the period of about four weeks on the weekends and evenings after work. By the time the world was up and running I figured I had put about four days work in total into it. I was a computer programmer by trade, so creating my own simulated universe was a lot easier for me than it was for some people. Some people will take weeks, months or years designing their own personal universe, but few have my level of motivation.

It is relatively simple to customize your own personal universe if you start from the original template. The program was created over a period of about 10 or 20 years before it went into mass-market production. Originally it was created by governments to create simulated worlds populated with real virtual people who think just like people in the real world, for the most part.

The way it works is that a sophisticated artificial intelligence would work with data from millions of uploaded brains from people all around the world. It would then populate these worlds with representative people that were composites of an average person from this world. There are of course plenty of different nations, religions and philosophies and lots of different personalities. All of the simulated people in these worlds, all the billions of them are fully self-aware and unique individuals created from all of the data from millions of people around the world and extrapolated into all the possible variations of human behavior.

Of course tailoring each world to your unique specific preferences is where most of the programming comes in. Everyone has their own ideal world. Some people create worlds populated only with one race, creed or color. Some populate entire world with one sex. Others like to mess with reality and create an entire planet of obedient slaves or change the laws of physics to make things more interesting.

I never went out for that. Sure our world is imperfect, but if you want to create a simulated world you need imperfection. So my template was pretty much the standard one that was supposed to be as much like the world as it actually is, but I would always inject new data to keep things interesting. But I didn't want to radically alter the laws of physics or anything dramatic like that. I felt I could create a more believable and realistic world by keeping it simple, although simple doesn't imply dullness.

The world that I created is more or less a perfect replica of the real world with a few minor alterations. I have decided that natural disasters wouldn't happen quite so often. And I decided to set the Earth's climate model to the way it was before the polar ice caps started melting, back when the world was a little bit more peaceful. But beyond that I didn't like to interfere with people's free will. That would make the entire thing quite boring. If the people of my world mess things up on their own at least it will have been their decision and I would be interested to see how they deal with the problem. That was, after all, the original intent behind creating the simulated worlds, before they went into mass-market for the entertainment of millions of bored people with a lot of time and money to spend on playing God.

But enough about all the technical details. The fun part about designing your own world is the fact that you can upload yourself into it. That's pretty much the whole idea. Some people just like to observe from a distance, probably because a lot of those people take delight in inflicting suffering on their peoples without wanting to be in the thick of it themselves. When most people play God it is more of an Old Testament type of God – the type that wants worship, blood sacrifice and blind allegiance.

When I play God I play the role of silent observer. I'm the type of God that doesn't interfere with people's lives or judge them. My pleasure comes from meeting random people and seeing how their lives have turned out in the world that I have created.

Today I decided I would observe my people in masculine form. That is what I usually do. I have of course tried out every race, sex and nationality in my world. That's a big part of the fun of it – getting to be a different person every time you visit.

But most of the time I visit as myself – a 45-year-old Caucasian male with a large waistline and receding hairline. Okay, maybe not entirely myself. I prefer to go as a more attractive younger version of myself when I am 30, buff and have a rich, thick head of hair.

So that is how I am going out on this particular evening. I decided to go to my favorite location of New York City, with a few minor alterations. In the world that I created the World Trade Center was never blown up and the sea levels had yet to rise to the point where the city was becoming a less attractive place to live. What can I say, I love New York, but I loved it more the way it was before all the catastrophes struck it. That was in New York that I grew up in, in a small apartment in Manhattan. Actually, I still live in a small apartment in Manhattan, except now a couple of hours each day I get to be God.

As soon as I put on my virtual reality headset and uploaded my brain I materialized in the men's room at Penn Station. It always scares the shit out of whoever sees me emerge. I could've easily had myself emerging invisibly and only become visible when it was appropriate, and sometimes I do that, but when the mood strikes me I love to see the expression on people's faces when they see a man materialize out of thin air. Every world needs its own mythology, and I have done this enough that there is now a legend that has developed in my world's version of Penn Station that every so often people see a mysterious man materialize out of thin air. Some people actually go there hoping to get a glimpse of it, and sometimes I like to fulfill their hopes. But like the alleged God that so many people around the world worship and believe in without proof, I never allow any evidence of my existence to remain. I always make it such that if anyone tries to videotape me or anything else like that that it just simply won't work. Yeah, I realize that can be kind of a jerky thing to do, but few people of faith complain that their God never appears on video.

Today when I emerged in an empty stall nobody saw me. One man commented that he didn't see anyone go into that stall, but I'm sure he'll never suspect anything. I know this because as God I am omnipotent of anything that happens in my world. All I need to do is look at a person and I will know everything I want to know about them. If I didn't like something about them I could easily change it, but I usually don't do that, because as I said earlier I don't like to mess with free will, well not too much anyway.

As I left the men's room I passed by a blind man with a violin case open to receive change. Sometimes when I see that man there I am tempted to perform a small miracle and restore his sight. But I realized that had he never gone blind he would never have appreciated music. But I am not a totally heartless God. Every time I pass by him he finds he gets a $100 bill in his violin case. What can I say, as a patron of music I don't want to see this man starved.

That's one of the moral dilemmas that you come across when you are God. How much do you intervene in human affairs? It always makes me sad when I see someone suffering in the world that I created, but I also wanted to keep things realistic. I have always taken a hands-off approach to controlling the universe. I am probably in the minority as far as that goes. I am the God of small miracles.

As I walk through the train station I get a strong feel for who the most interesting people are in the general area. Unlike the all-knowing all-powerful God of the Bible, I am not fully omniscient. I can change things and I can know everything about this world, but I can only observe one aspect of this world at a time. So unless I specifically choose to know what is happening with a given individual, I will remain ignorant. But sometimes I put out an alert so that I can mentally pick up on where interesting stuff is happening. I can probe the entire planet to know what type of things are going on that I might be interested in, but usually I can only handle so much data at a time. That is a limitation of this God.

After walking around for a while I came across a man harassing this woman. By looking at them I immediately knew that this man was abusive and that woman had been repeatedly harassed by him on numerous occasions. He was one of those rich jerks who never treated anyone with any respect. These are the situations that tend to get on my nerves. As a person who likes to follow a philosophy of noninterference, but who also has the power to change things, it creates a dilemma. What to do in such a situation?

What the hell I figured. I simply concentrated for a moment and the man harassing the woman suddenly found himself the proud new owner of two enormous breasts, a vagina and the most revealing outfit I could think of. So that will no doubt be a learning experience for him.

Okay, so I sort of violated my policy of noninterference. I find that I usually do at least once or twice a day. But in a world with billions of people few would notice. And since I can alter peoples' memories and perceptions of any changes I make I can make these changes without anyone noticing.

For example, that man I just gave an instant sex change to. Now you are probably assuming that that would have been done in front of a pretty large audience. But I also made sure to alter the memories and perceptions of anyone in the general vicinity. So nobody actually saw him turn from a man into a woman. To anyone who had been observing this event he had always been a woman. The only one who knows that anything has changed is him.

In addition I also changed life for the woman that he was harassing. Where she had been an underpaid secretary and he had been a rich playboy, now she is independently wealthy and he is a welfare recipient who will suddenly remember that he is married to an abusive 300 pound retired wrestler named Bubba. Never let it be said that God has no sense of humor. And "he" will be in for an even bigger surprise later on when he takes that pregnancy test to find it comes back positive!

But that is about the extent of my interventions. I will change things around here and there and will sometimes cause confusion, but if he says anything he will surely be considered insane. Maybe I will look in on "him" and change things back for him if he learns his lesson. Although from scanning his mind I can see that this change will probably not teach him anything.

Oh, what the hell. I concentrated really hard and this newly pregnant woman whose body he found himself in was soon going to find himself a bit on the chilly side when that highly revealing outfit disappears completely!

But something went wrong.

I had only meant to disrobe that one individual. But now I was looking around me to see everyone gasping in panic. I had just rendered the entirety of Penn Station completely butt naked! The only one still dressed was myself. Fortunately most people were too concerned with their own sudden and inexplicable nudity to take notice of me. They were busy trying to cover themselves up with whatever happened to be near them.

This certainly would not do. I would have to do a full-blown memory erasure and reverse this. I concentrated really hard, closed my eyes and opened them again. But when I opened them I was greeted by the same sight of hundreds of blushing, panicked nude men and women scrambling all about.

Why wasn't this working? I have never had this problem before. I figured my best bet was to simply vanish and hope that all memory of this event would vanish with me.

I immediately tore off the virtual reality helmet and was back in my tiny little apartment. I also noticed that I had a mild headache. That happened sometimes when I was in too deep, fully immersed in my own little world, but this one was very sudden and immediate.

"Maybe there is something wrong with the system," I said aloud as I scratched my head. But that was when I noticed it was already getting pretty late and I had to get up early for work tomorrow. Whatever the problem was it would have to wait until tomorrow. At least tomorrow was a Friday, so I would have all weekend to deal with this.

I had a restless night and woke up at least an hour early, unable to sleep. I made myself a quick breakfast and took some aspirin because my headache had not fully gone away. I just couldn't stop thinking about what had happened. I had never experienced anything like that before. I had been God of my own personal universe for nearly 3 years now and this was the first time I had ever noticed any type of glitch.

I continued to think about this on the subway and could barely concentrate at work that day. By lunchtime my coworkers could tell that something was perturbing me.

"What's wrong?" asked Paul, my close friend who had been working here with me for nearly 5 years. "You look like you've been hit by a truck."

"I'm having problems with my own personal universe," I said as I put my hands on my cheeks and sighed.

"Do you mean your personal life, who doesn't?"

"No, I mean literally my own personal universe."

"You mean the simulated reality universe?"

"Of course that's what I mean. Have you ever had problems with your own personal universe?"

"Nope. Every woman in that universe still thinks I'm the greatest thing in creation." He had a good laugh at that. Paul used his own personal reality stimulator primarily to create a universe where all women thought that he was a living God. He took the opposite stance to me. I always tried to be the God of the gaps so to speak. In his world everything is just like it is in this world, except that when he arrives there and materializes everyone immediately knows it's him, that he is God, and all the women want to have sex with him nonstop. So for him the personal universe was just a place where he went for a virtual booty call.

"So what seems to be the problem?"

So I explained the situation to him and what had happened. He had a good laugh about it.

"It's not funny," I shouted.

"What's not funny?" asked Jessica, another one of our friends and coworkers.

"John had a glitch in his universe. He made everyone in Penn Station completely naked and was unable to reverse it."

Jessica started to laugh. "Pervert."

"I'll have you know that originally I was just trying to teach this sexist jerk a lesson."

"Sure you were."

"I was! Besides, I've been to your personal universe, so don't play innocent with me."

Jessica was something of a radical feminist and she created a world where women held all the power and men were used solely for sex. Of course when she went into this world she was Empress of the world and all the men thought that she was the most beautiful person in the world. Truth be told, most people use their personal universe primarily to fulfill sexual fantasies. I won't pretend that I have never used it for that purpose, but for me it was never the primary purpose, and I would try not to use my godlike powers to make things too unrealistic.

Of course lots of people use their own personal universe purely as a way of self-aggrandizement or living out the fantasy of a world where everyone agreed with them or looked like them and thought like them. I know of several people who have created world where everyone had the same religion, the same race, sometimes even only the same-sex. Others had certain nations and nationalities nonexistent altogether, and many were sadists who use their godlike powers to smite entire peoples based on their own personal prejudices from this world. I once read that some of the biggest addicts of this new virtual world where religious fanatics and white supremacists.

So as far as God goes I was relatively sane.

"So what are you going to do about it?" Paul asked.

"I guess I will just have to reinsert myself into the universe and hope that I can correct the problem. Otherwise I guess I can always try calling tech support. But it's sort of a minor thing I guess."

"A minor thing!" Paul asked. "If hundreds of people in our world's Penn Station suddenly had their clothing magically dematerialize like that you can bet it would be big news!"

He was right. Since the memories of all the people of the world are constantly backed up I would have to find some way to change it or people in that reality would suspect something really weird is going on.

On the way home from work that evening I stopped by Penn station, the Penn station of this world of course. I have to admit I felt weird being there, almost like a criminal at the scene of his crime. I started trying to visualize the clothing of all the people around suddenly dissolving, but when I opened my eyes of course nothing had changed. Get a hold of yourself, I thought to myself. I didn't want to end up like a lot of the extreme addicts; people who spend so much time immersed in their own reality frequently find it hard to distinguish one reality from another.

When you start trying to influence the real world the way you would your virtual universe is when you might be slipping.

It was probably just the stress I told myself. Having seen the first glitch in my own personal universe has made me paranoid.

As soon as I got home I barely even took time to eat a TV dinner before I decided to get right back into my own personal universe to see how things were doing. Maybe that one little glitch would be no big deal.

I put on my virtual reality helmet and inserted myself into the men's room. As soon as I came out of the stall I found the bathroom to be empty. The bathroom was never completely empty. This was not a good sign.

I slowly walked out of the restroom to find myself in a completely empty plaza. Everything seemed to be cordoned off with police tape and there were all sorts of people in lab coats holding geiger counters.

"Hey you're not supposed to be here," shouted one of the security guards on duty as he began to run towards me.

I had to think quickly. I concentrated and immediately found myself on the subway. I hope that my mind wipe on that security guard worked.

Wait a minute, I hadn't intended to find myself on the subway. I had intended to place myself just outside of Penn station. Was this another glitch?

I decided to get on the subway and simply observe people's reactions. I sat down next to an attractive blonde woman who seemed to be reading the paper. The headline on the paper was about everyone being suddenly stripped naked in Penn station. So it seems like my mind wipe didn't work. I tried concentrating hard to undo the entire incident, but try as I might nothing seemed to change.

"So how about what happened at Penn station the other day?" I asked her, trying to make conversation.

"It was humiliating," she said as she suddenly began to blush.

"You mean you were there?"

"Yes, I was," she said with a degree of annoyance as she continued to grow redder. Maybe I should back off. But I wanted to find out more and I wanted to hear directly from people themselves, not just by reading their thoughts.

"So you mean you were one of the people whose clothing suddenly vanished?" I couldn't help but smile at that thought.

"I already told you I was there," she snapped. "And I will thank you not to smile about it."

"Sorry. It's kind of hard not to see the humor in the situation."

"Humor, you think it is funny that I was publicly humiliated?"

"Well, no, I guess that would be pretty embarrassing, not to mention terrifying."

"You're telling me."

"I didn't mean to pry into your personal life, I just find the whole thing extremely interesting because it is so bizarre. I am John by the way." I held out my hand to shake hers.

"Elizabeth," she said as she shook my hand.

"So what do you think caused it?"

She shook her head. "No one has any idea. It's the most inexplicable thing that has ever happened. There doesn't seem to be any rational explanation behind it. I mean how do hundreds of people suddenly just lose their clothing like that, like magic. How is that even possible?"

"Maybe there is a supernatural explanation."

"I'm not really a big believer in the supernatural."

"Okay then, what's the rational explanation behind it?"

"Well, I guess there isn't one. But just because we don't have a rational explanation for it doesn't mean that there is some supernatural reason for it? I mean what type of supernatural being would suddenly use their power to strip hundreds of people naked in a public area like that?"

I probed her mind just a little bit to discover that she was actually a strong skeptic of the supernatural and was a scientist. Here I felt like kind of a jerk. I kind of assumed that because she was attractive that she was sort of a dumb blonde, but according to the information I was downloading from her she had an IQ of 169 and had won a research grant. That was when the irony struck me – this woman was a product of my creation and had an IQ a good couple of dozen points higher than mine. So here I was, creator of the world ogling this young blonde woman who was more intelligent than me. How's that for a paradox?

That was when I realized I hadn't answered her question. "Well I don't know." I felt bad for lying, but what was I supposed to say? "What are other people saying?"

"Some people think it is terrorists."

"Why would they think it is terrorists, in this world the World Trade Center was never even bombed."

"What the hell are you talking about?"

I had completely forgotten, so my omniscience was not so great that I couldn't make a stupid remark here and there. I could know anything about this world, but I was still myself with all my shortcomings and memory lapses. "Nothing, forget I said anything. I was just saying why would terrorists want to strip people naked? And how would they do it?"

"That's the baffling thing. There is no rational explanation for this, but I'm sure there has to be one. I just hope that they find an answer to this soon."

Unfortunately I knew that they wouldn't, unless I can figure out how to erase everyone's memory and undo this. As much as this woman wanted there to be a rational explanation, I am sure that someone like her would never accept the answer I am God and I am the reason this happened, and I can't undo it because of some type of glitch. The people in this world are realistic, so most people would assume I am crazy, unless I specifically change their mind to make them accept the unacceptable, but like I've said, I don't like interfere with people's free will.

"Well hopefully it will just be a one time thing," I said trying to reassure her.

"Well I certainly hope so. It was the most humiliating experience of my life. If I were a religious person I would think that God was punishing me or something."

Way to guilt trip me. "I'm sure if there was a God that he would have better things to do with all of his power than simply stripping people of their clothing." The sad truth was, I really didn't. "But I'm sure it couldn't have been too bad, right?"

"Are you kidding me? Do you know how terrifying it is to have your clothing just disappear without any logical explanation with hundreds of others. I had to somehow get home like that. I didn't have any money because all of that was in my pocket book, which also disappeared. Luckily people nearby were understanding and managed to get us something to cover ourselves with, but you can't erase peoples memories and you can't erase the Internet. I saw plenty of people with camera phones snapping pictures of me. I just hope that no one I know recognizes me in the crowd of hundreds. I think I would just die. I was almost afraid to come into work today out of fear that it might happen again."

I began to probe her memory even more. I instantaneously learned that she was a very shy girl with lots of inhibitions and a tendency to blush excessively. I downloaded her memory of the event from the other day and could see everything she described. I could see her clothing magically disappear, feel the panic inside of her when she realized what was going on, a combination of both embarrassment at the situation and fear at the extreme irrationality of it all.

I began to feel even more guilty because as I was downloading her memory I couldn't help but get turned on picturing her naked and blushing.

That was when my thoughts were interrupted by a loud shriek coming from Elizabeth.

"What's wrong," I blurted out as I turned around. But then I saw. She was sitting there completely naked desperately struggling to cover herself up with her newspaper.

"Oh my God it's happening again," she said as she began to blush. She then started looking around. "And this time it's just me!"

"Calm down," I said trying to reassure her, but I also read her thoughts and could see all the terrifying thoughts going through her mind right now. Despite her ultra-rationalist worldview, right now she was suddenly considering the possibility that she was cursed and that this would keep happening. I felt even more guilty because it was my picturing her like this that seem to have triggered it, even without a direct command for this to happen. Things are only supposed to manifest when I think of them if I give them the instruction to manifest. This was another glitch. "You're not cursed," I shouted out.

"How do you know that?!" she screamed as she held the newspaper up tightly against her body, trying to position in a way that would hide as much of her body as possible. Luckily she was too panicked right now to wonder how I knew that she thought she was cursed.

"Look, I'll try to help, just calm down."

I tried to think of what to do in this situation. I thought about removing her shyness, but that wouldn't really help all that much, and under the circumstances I didn't want to try rearranging her personality. Then I thought that if I made her clothing disappear, then logically I should be able to make it reappear. I concentrated really hard trying to remember what she was wearing and make it reappear on her. I opened my eyes to find her clothing sitting in front of me on the floor. "Isn't that your outfit," I said pointing to her clothing.

Why didn't it appear on her body? But at least it had appeared. Another glitch.

She quickly gathered up her clothing and tried to change into it under the newspaper. Seeing her struggling with the newspaper I tried to stand in front of her and shouted, "give her some privacy!" When I saw that people continued to stare and that some were getting out their camera phones I concentrated hard to make the camera phones not work. But when I opened my eyes I suddenly saw that everyone's cell phone had turned into a pink frog.

What the hell was going on here?

As soon as this happened everyone started to panic. People started jumping up in fear when the frogs approached them. I concentrated hard to make this go away, but I opened my eyes to find nothing had changed. I saw one man, an elderly man, hyperventilating. "Please calm down sir," I said as I approached him, suddenly aware that he had a heart condition and that he had only recently left the hospital.

The man continued to back away from me clutching his chest and I tried hard to concentrate on relieving him of his chest pain. Unfortunately as I concentrated on trying to make his heart pain go away he started to blink in and out of existence and then suddenly was gone.

I quickly tried to probe for his existence. All I got was file not found. Apparently that man had just completely blinked out of existence and I couldn't seem to bring him back. The data file that was responsible for him was completely gone.

"What's happening," said Elizabeth as she stood up and started to cry. I was worried that she would have a panic attack like she did when she was six years old and her brother put a fake toy spider in the toilet to scare her. Omniscience can be useful in situations like this.

"Elizabeth, I don't know how to explain this to you, but I can tell you that everything is going to be okay," I said as I put my hand on her shoulder.

"How the hell could you know that?! How can you explain this?"

I didn't know what to say. But just as I was trying to think what to say, suddenly everyone in the subway car was completely naked and there were hundreds of pink frogs jumping about around people's feet.

"Concentrate, concentrate," I said to myself as I concentrated hard. But the harder I concentrated the louder this loud buzzing became in the background until my head was beginning to feel like it was going to explode. I knew that I couldn't take this any longer and I pulled myself out.

I threw the VR helmet onto the floor and then fell out of my chair holding my head. I suddenly had a terrible migraine. "What the hell went wrong," I shouted as I rubbed my head.

My migraine was extremely severe and I ran right into the bathroom and began vomiting. I had never experienced anything like this before. Something was seriously wrong here.

Once I had stopped vomiting, I took some extreme strength aspirin and laid down in my bed. Whatever was going wrong with my own personal universe, I couldn't deal with it until this headache had gone.

I didn't wake up until the next morning, and even then my headache remained. I had never experienced this before but I have heard that it has happened to people who have too deep a connection to their own personal universe. The virtual reality universe is accessed directly through the virtual reality helmet, which has a direct link to your brain waves. It is full immersion, so when you're inside your virtual universe it is indistinguishable from the real world and you can experience every sensation as though it were real, although most people choose to remove unpleasant sensations, except of course for the sadomasochists, they like to enhance it so that they can experience pain that would kill them in the real world.

I was no sadomasochist, as I was whimpering merely from a headache. But I knew that my headache was most likely caused from a direct link to my failing universe. Sometimes the helmet does give you mild head pain, but never this bad. I didn't want to risk using it again and potentially doing brain damage. It is a small risk, and I have heard of people who have fried their brains through too close a connection.

After fixing myself a quick breakfast I called the company that produces the virtual universe to send over repair man to take a look at it.

"So how does everything look," I asked him when he had finished his diagnostic.

He shook his head. "I am afraid the prognosis is not good. Although I managed to fix your helmet in a way that it shouldn't be giving you any headaches, I wouldn't recommend using this unstable machine."

"What's wrong with it?"

"I am afraid that it seems like it is a total system failure. All of the data is corrupted and gradually breaking down. We could fix the machine or get you a refund on it if you still have insurance on it or if the warranty hasn't expired, but anything you have saved in there probably isn't going to last much longer. You'll have to start over from scratch."

"So my entire universe is going to be destroyed?!" I grabbed him by the shirt, but he pushed my hands away.

"Look, I'm sure you can create a new one. It's not like it's real people in there or anything. It is all just a simulation."

"I know that," I said with uncertainty. Was I trying to convince myself otherwise? "But it took me a long time to create it. Everyone inside is going to die."

"Like I said, they aren't real people. You aren't one of those addicts are you? You don't want to spend too much time in there," he said as he pointed to the machine. "I have one myself, and it's good fun, but when you start treating that place as anything other than something that is created by your mind you might have a problem. And if you have a problem there are many treatment programs that can help bring you back to reality."

"No, no I'm fine," I said as I rubbed my head still trying to get rid of my headache. "I'm sorry I grabbed you before."

"It's okay. I realize how real that world can seem and I realize you have probably spent a lot of time creating it. I have seen a lot of people have complete and total breakdowns when their virtual universe began failing. You just have to keep reminding yourself that none of it is real. That is the important thing. It is good in moderation, but when you start to forget which is reality and which is a simulation you might have a problem." He handed me a card. "If you think you might have a problem this is a number you can call for help."

"What about my machine?"

"Like I told you, there is nothing you can do. You can check your warranty, but that's not my specialty. But I wish you good luck."

"Thanks," I said with notable insincerity as I lead him to the door.

I sat down at my table, began rubbing my head some more and thought about what he had told me. Deep down I knew that that universe in there wasn't real. But what is reality? No, I told myself, I'm not going to to get all philosophical and start quoting Descartes. But he had a point. How can we ever really know what is real? Our senses could deceive us and our whole reality could be false, but if it seems just as real as this world, is it any less real? Is Elizabeth real? Surely she had to have been based at least partially on someone.

As I continued to ponder these questions my head continued to throb. I knew that I should probably just go back to sleep and accept the inevitable. I am pretty sure my warranty was still good and I could get a replacement machine, but I could never get back the world that I created. The responsible and rational thing would just be to accept the inevitable.

But I wasn't feeling very responsible at the moment, nor was I feeling very rational or accepting.

I picked up my helmet and inserted myself into observation mode. In observation mode you can survey the entire planet and scan for information. I decided to scan Elizabeth. There were probably millions of people in this world named Elizabeth, but luckily the machine stores your progress and you can always go back to find people and places that you had been before.

I just hope that it worked, as I knew this machine was not functioning properly.

I probed to find information on the woman that I had interacted with before the last failure. It took a while but I managed to find her. Her name was Elizabeth Breslin and she lived in an apartment nicer than my real world apartment in the virtual New York City I created. She graduated top of her class, went to an Ivy League college and is now hoping to use her research grant to maybe pay off some of her student loans. She was an advanced theoretical physicist, and once again I found it ironic that she was probably more intelligent than I, who created the entire universe that she lives in.

I decided to download her entire memory. I don't know an adequate way to explain this process to anyone who hasn't experienced it themselves. I guess I would compare it to people who have near-death experiences and claim they see their entire life flash in front of their eyes. That was what I experienced, except I saw Elizabeth's entire life flash before my eyes. Although she was just a simulated person created from data from millions of scanned minds, this universe creates a template for every single individual in this universe, most of whom I will never even know the existence of, but who nonetheless have entire lives constructed by the computer.

Through Elizabeth's eyes I saw everything. I saw her go through preschool through college. I saw that she was valedictorian at her school, obtained a full scholarship to Harvard and had been selected for a research grant. She still had some student loans that she had to pay off that her scholarship didn't cover, but she was doing pretty well for herself. But I saw that in school she was an awkward and lonely individual, a person crippled by shyness due to an abusive relationship that she had been in. For a time she had been unemployed and she had considered being a model, but the modeling company she worked resulted in her being sexually harassed and humiliated when some nude photos were taken of her against her will.

That made me feel like a total bastard. Of all the people who could have been affected by my glitch at Penn station and it had to be someone like her, someone for whom the experience was traumatizing based on her past experiences and who didn't deserve any of it.

How could I see her as anything but a real person when I had seen her entire life through her eyes. She may be a simulated person, but how is she different from a real life person? She was the first person whose life I downloaded into my mind in its entirety, and now it was hard to deny that she was anything other than real.

I decided to try and figure out how she was doing now. It turns out that she was sitting alone in her apartment completely frightened and embarrassed. She was afraid to leave her house for fear that another embarrassing incident like what had happened at Penn station and on the subway would happen yet again. Similar incidents seems to be occurring with increasing frequency all over the world and there was total panic. She was experiencing an existential crisis as a person who believed that life was what appeared to be and that when life was over that was it.

That was when I was struck with another terrible thought. If this universe was really coming to an end, then it would all be over for her. As soon as this machine failed, then she and her entire universe would blink out of existence.

I couldn't allow this to happen. If this world was going to end I couldn't let her live her last days cowering in fear.

But how could I go about this? Obviously she would be frightened if she saw me again after I just vanished into thin air.

I decided that I would visit her incognito as one of her old college friends and former roommate Monica. I didn't like the deception, but I figure that seeing her old friend would make it easier for her to trust me and put her mind at ease, as I found out from downloading parts of Monica's memory that she was always able to calm Elizabeth down during a crisis.

I have to admit that I felt a little bit awkward, because her friend Monica was pretty hot. I can't remember the last time I had entered this world as a Latina supermodel! But here goes nothing.

I arrived in the body of Monica just outside of Elizabeth's apartment. It took a minute for me to readjust to my new body. I always felt weird when I took on female form, particularly when I was a female as attractive as this. I just couldn't stop staring at my own boobs. I guess I am a somewhat superficial creator of the universe.

I made sure to scan the world to make sure that the real Monica wouldn't show up and make things awkward while I just happened to be there. I always felt that imitating someone and taking over their personality was creepy, but I could rest assured that the real Monica was hundreds of miles away with her family who were equally concerned about all of the strange things happening.

Once I was assured that nothing would happen to make things more weird or awkward than they already were, I went upstairs and looked for Elizabeth's apartment, apartment number 309. I knocked on the door, took a deep breath and hoped for the best.

"Monica," said Elizabeth as she opened the door and saw me standing there. She was obviously shocked as she had not seen me in several months.

"Hey," I said.

"It's so good to see you again," she said as she hugged me. "Please, come in."

I followed her into her apartment and we sat down in her kitchen.

"It's such a surprise to see you," she said as she made me a cup of coffee, which I instantly knew was Monica's favorite. I hadn't downloaded her entire memory into me, but I put the settings on in such a way that I would instantly know anything that Monica knew if it came up.

"Sorry I didn't call first," I said, realizing this must be a bit of a shock to her.

"That's okay, I'm always glad to see you. This was a nice surprise. You always seem to show up just when I need you the most."

"Well I thought you might need a friend with all the weird stuff going on."

Elizabeth blushed deeply. "Did you see the video of me on the Internet?"

"Yeah," I said, not sure how else to explain it. "How are you holding up?"

"Well, I am still pretty embarrassed, but so many other people were also affected that I doubt it is going to matter much. And with all the other weird stuff going on it's probably the least of my worries."

"I know." Little did she know just how much I knew.

"So how is your family handling everything?"

I instantly zoomed in mentally on Monica's family to see that they were all huddled together in their living room with the real Monica watching all the television reports about all the strange things occurring. "They're doing okay, under the circumstances." What else was I supposed to say?

Elizabeth started to move the coffee cup towards me only for it to suddenly turn into a bird. Elizabeth jumped back in panic.

"That's okay, I wasn't that thirsty anyway."

Elizabeth began to cry. "What the hell is going on around here?!"

I reached out and touched her hand. "It's all going to be okay."

She wiped away her tears and sniffled a bit. "Thanks for saying that, but I know you are just doing that to reassure me. Somehow you can always calm me down though. I guess it must just be a gift that you have."

"Yeah, a gift." I felt terrible lying to her as I knew deep down that things most certainly weren't going to be alright. This wasn't exactly going as I had hoped.

"But I guess with your faith and everything this must be easier for you to accept." It turns out that Monica was a devout Catholic. I had always been strictly agnostic, which is a rather ironic stance for someone to take when they are the creator of the universe. I almost thought that if there was a real God that maybe this was some ironic punishment he had devised for me attempting to imitate him.

"Well when the world doesn't make sense sometimes faith is all that we can turn to."

"I have always tried to view the world as rationally as possible. As a theoretical physicist I had always considered the possibility of the existence of other dimensions and thought that there was some type of scientific explanation for everything. But how can you maintain a rational worldview when your coffee mug turns into a bird, your clothing disappears magically on two occasions, it starts raining pink frogs and people just start blinking in and out of existence. It's like reality is breaking down or something."

She actually wasn't too far from the truth. But I have to admit I really didn't know how to continue reassuring her or tell her how close to the truth she really was. This was not going well. Here I came to try and make her last days in this universe more peaceful and happy and I was failing miserably. And I also couldn't help but feel increasingly attracted to her.

But once again my thoughts were interrupted by a loud shriek. Once again I looked up to see Elizabeth standing there completely naked with pink frogs hopping all around her feet as she tried desperately to cover herself up. "Why is this happening!" she shouted as she fell on her knees to the floor began to cry again.

I went over to her and patted her on the back, trying to keep my mind focused on calming her down. But maybe I was just making her life worse by being here. It was just then that I considered the possibility that just being around me was causing increasing glitches in her own life due to my proximity to her. I couldn't keep doing this to her. I would have to come clean about everything, come what may.

"Elizabeth," I said as I took her by the hand and led her over to her couch where she had a blanket that she used to cover herself up with.

"Yes, Monica," she said as she wiped away a tear. "I'm sorry that I am getting all hysterical here."

"You shouldn't be the one who feels sorry. This is all my fault."

"What are you talking about?"

"Elizabeth, I don't know how to explain this to you, but I am not who you think I am?" This was *really* not going well.

"What do you mean?"

"I am not really your friend Monica."

She looked at me with a blank stare, fully uncomprehending what I was talking about. "It's me, John."

"John?" I see she had already forgotten about me.

"The man you met on the subway the other day just before your clothing disappeared for the second time."

She suddenly gave a look of recognition, and then another look of confusion.

"I am going to show you something, and I don't know how you are going to react, but I just want you to know not to be afraid and that I am not here to hurt you. That is the absolute last thing that I would want."

"Monica, you're not making sense." I could feel she was beginning to panic. Well, once again, it was now or never.

I suddenly transformed back into my real self, well my 30-year-old more attractive version of myself that she had encountered on the subway.

She jumped up from the couch, momentarily forgetting that she was nude, before grabbing her sheet and pulling it up to cover herself as she slowly walked away from me.

"W-who are you?" she managed to mutter as she began to tremble. "What do you want from me?"

"I know this is not going to be easy for you to understand, but I created you and everyone else in this world."

She looked even more panicked and started walking even faster away from me as I began to get up and approach her.

"Stay back," she said as she grabbed a kitchen knife and pointed it at me. I read her thoughts and could tell that she thought I was completely insane and that I was stalking her.

"I am not crazy and I am not stalking you," I said as I slowly backed away from her. "You have to believe me."

"I am warning you," she said as she pointed the knife at me while trying with limited success to cover herself with her other hand. "I may not look very dangerous, but I know how to use one of these."

Although I knew it could not hurt me, I started feeling more and more nervous. I was concentrating on the knife and suddenly it turned into a bird, causing her to fall backwards right onto her ass screaming.

"Please don't," I said and she suddenly went mute. In fact, it seems like I had turned off all sound in the vicinity. She continued to scream but no sound came out.

This was a disaster. Here I came to try and comfort her and now I was causing the most humiliating and terrifying experience of her life. Maybe I should just leave.

That was when it suddenly occurred to me. There was one last option. If I were to just leave her like this now her last days would be lived in terror. But there was one final thing that I could do. I closed my eyes, concentrated and gave the command to upload my entire memory into Elizabeth's brain.

I could see her standing there in a total trance as she instantaneously relived every moment of my life from my awkward high school years, to my creation of this universe and how it differed from my own and up to just a minute ago.

Then she fainted.

Maybe I had done the wrong thing, but all I could do now was wait. I didn't want to startle her by waking her up by artificial means. She had had enough of a shock and I didn't want to alter anything about her. But I did try to concentrate on taking away the worst of her fear. With all the glitches going on it was a risk, but then everything I did was a risk under the circumstances. That was the least I could do for her.

While I waited for her to wake up I decided to put on the news. None of the regular programming was on, just broadcasts of emergencies. Pretty much every nation was on red alert and martial law had been implemented practically everywhere. Religious fanatics were blowing themselves up all over the place as people continued to disappear by the tens of millions every day. Most people were calling it the rapture. And strangely enough – and it must be something unique to the way this universe was failing – people's clothing disappearing, raining pink frogs and things randomly turning into birds or other animals seem to be the most frequent strange occurrence caused by the glitch. And it seemed to be getting worse and worse every day. It also turns out that when I muted Elizabeth's screams the world went without sound everywhere for at least 15 minutes.

This was one strange Apocalypse.

"And the Lord will come like a thief in the night," said a televangelist on the news as he held up a sign that said the end is near, before his clothing disappeared, and his sign turned into dozens of pink frogs before he blinked out of existence and the channel went off the air and was filled with static.

I turned the TV off just as Elizabeth was finally waking. She bolted up, took one look at me and then slowly stood up using the blanket to cover herself up.

"Elizabeth I-" I began, but she put her finger up to her lips.

"Just let me get dressed," she said as she backed into her bedroom. "I'm still a little shy about being seen naked by my creator."

I waited nervously while she got dressed. After a few minutes he came out dressed in a fairly modest outfit that seemed to fit perfectly on her. She sat down next to me on the couch. We sat there awkwardly for a few moments before anyone said anything.

"So," she said slowly, "so it seems you are God."

"Sort of," I said. I was never very good with small talk. "But I am mortal. So make of that what you will."

"Would you like a coffee? Maybe with any luck it won't turn into a bird this time." She smiled when she said that, which was somewhat reassuring.

"That's okay, I'm not really thirsty."

We sat there for several more awkward moments in total silence.

"Elizabeth, I just want to apologize for everything. I never meant to be this disruptive in your life."

"Well I can't say I am exactly happy with the information that I have received today or anything that I have experienced in the last couple of days. It's kind of a lot to take in."

I was beginning to feel more and more guilty. This is why people shouldn't play God. I was not infallible. "I'm not infallible!" I noticed myself saying aloud as I began to cry.

"Nobody is." She put her hand on mine.

"But God is supposed to be."

"But you are not God in the traditional sense. Like you said, you're mortal and you make mistakes."

"I guess it must be a pretty big disappointment to find out that the creator of the universe is no better, and probably a lot worse, than a good majority of his creations."

"That's one way of looking at it. But another way of looking at it is that that just makes you a better God. You are just like us. Unlike the terrifying God of the fundamentalists who demands worship and punishes all the unbelievers, you are just a modest, every day regular Joe. And I don't mean that as a put down."

"So you're not disappointed or angry?"

"I was at first, I'm not going to lie, since I know that it's impossible to lie to you. But as you well know I grew up in a town full of fundamentalists. One of the things that led me towards skepticism of organized religion was that God was unrelatable, mysterious and cruel. But you, well the best way to put it is, as far as deities go, you are far more benign. And I know you could well be quite different. In some ways it's comforting."

"Comforting?! I created an entire universe for my own personal amusement and now I can't even prevent it from being destroyed. How is that comforting?"

She moved closer to me and began to pat me on the back as I started crying more. "Because I know the truth. I never understood how religious believers could believe so unquestionably, but now I understand. There is desire to know truth. And it is possible that I am going crazy right now. I guess Descartes is right, you can never really know if your reality is entirely false in some way, but just because I know that I exist, well there must be something causing me to exist. So even if you are just some type of delusion, you are a very comforting one."

"But I screwed up, big time. As far as deities go I think I'm a pretty big failure."

"I don't think so. You may not be infallible, but like I said, that just makes you a better deity. And the fact that you don't even know if we are real or not but you care about us and went to all this trouble to try and reassure me and comfort me, well it shows that you are a compassionate deity. And the fact that you come from a place that can create entire universes, well that gives some kind of hope. Even if our world ends up being destroyed, it is possible for you to create many many more. For someone like me that is a dream. You have created this world and you did it using advanced science. You come from a world where you can create an infinite number of worlds. I think that is pretty amazing."

"But I don't think I want to after all of this. I know this is going to sound really corny, especially coming from a person you have learned is the creator of your universe, but I don't think I could create a better universe. And truth be told the biggest comfort to me is that I managed to create a universe with someone like you in it, someone who is better than the one who created them."

"That's not corny, that's probably the most flattering thing anyone could say."

"But what about everyone else? This universe is going to end, and there are billions of people in this simulated universe that are going to just blink out of existence in a few days as though they never existed before. And I can't even reassure them that their last days are going to be anything other than terrifying and unpleasant."

"But you can try."

"And do what? You have my memory, you know what the repair man told me. There is no way to save this universe."

"That may be true, but maybe it won't. But the thing that makes any creator good at what he does is that he doesn't give up. If this universe is going to blink out of existence, then you can still bring people comfort the way you have brought me comfort."

"How?"

"If the world is going to end, then you can give the world an explanation. That is one thing about this universe compared to yours. Maybe there is no higher God beyond our universe or your universe, and maybe we are all going to be doomed, but there is one thing you can do for this universe that you can't do for your own. You can give people an explanation for their existence before it ends."

I had to hand it to Elizabeth, she was a fine creation and was far wiser than I was.

"How do we go about this?" I asked her as I looked her directly in the eyes. "I need your help."

"I think I have an idea." She gave me a big smile as she stood up. I had a good feeling about this.

Elizabeth and I materialized simultaneously on the most-watched news channel in front of a large studio audience. The audience all stopped speaking and stood there in awe.

"Who the hell are you?" someone in the audience shouted.

"I am your creator."

"He's just another wacko," someone else shouted.

I suppose materializing in the middle of nowhere wasn't enough proof to everyone under the circumstances. With so much weird stuff going on it was hardly even considered unusual.

"I think they're going to need more proof," said Elizabeth who I had linked directly to my mind so that she could hear everything that I was thinking.

She was right. I would have to show them some proof. I concentrated hard and suddenly the studio disappeared and the sky changed into a multicolored rainbow and I had my voice boom in every mind and ear of every single citizen on the planet. "I am the Lord thy God, and I have come to offer you an explanation for what is going on."

Every single person in the audience went silent and I could sense that right now everyone in the world was aware of what was going on and everyone was fully awake as per my command.

"Do it," said Elizabeth.

"Once again, and for the final time, here goes nothing. Welcome to the mind of God."

I focused all my concentration, and although it might not be the best method of revealing myself to the world, it was the best one that we could think of. It was Elizabeth's idea. Just like I did with her, I uploaded my memories into every single person in this simulated universe. I was now no longer the God in the gaps, I was a God with no secrets.

There was a great silence as everyone relived every single moment of my life. Here I was, creator of the universe, and I had revealed every personal secret to over 7 billion simulated people. I don't think I could ever feel more vulnerable, even if I am technically invincible in this universe.

Finally someone in the audience spoke. It was a quiet young girl, probably no more than 12 years old and she raised her hand. I pointed to her and she spoke.

"Will there be an afterlife?"

How was I supposed to respond to such a question? I could tell without having to read her mind that she was a very intelligent and reasonable girl. I decided that I would be fully honest with her.

"Not if the system crashes and all the data is lost. There's a back up drive but it wouldn't be the same, it would be a copy and much would still be lost. It would be starting over from the beginning."

Another man slowly walked forward, took off his hat and placed it on his chest and feebly asked me. "Do you think that we are real creatures possessed of souls?"

"I created you using a computer program. I have to admit that I am not omniscient. You have all just experienced the full extent of my knowledge and know everything that I do. I may have created this universe, but I don't know anymore than you do about these deeper questions. Is there an actual God beyond me, the creator of my universe? Is the universe I live in just a simulation? I'm afraid that I cannot answer this, because I do not know."

The audience was surprisingly calm given the immensity of what was happening, so much so that I figured I must have unconsciously removed their fear. Or maybe just being on equal ground with them, completely exposing my every thought and feeling to them, put them at ease.

I could feel all their eyes staring at me, some with love, some with awe, some with obvious hatred and bafflement. I could feel an explosion in my head as I could feel all of their thoughts and feelings projected towards me simultaneously. There is no way to fully describe the feeling, but it soon overwhelmed me and I had to filter it out.

That was when another man in the audience, clearly more angry than many shouted. "If the world is going to end, then what are you going to do about it?"

I thought long and hard, not sure how to respond.

"Well?" the man repeated.

I took a deep breath and then it came to me.

"I cannot prevent this world from ending. And all I can say is that I am sorry and that I love you all. But there is one thing I can do for you all. It won't make up for the fact that this world is still going to end, but his is the only way I can think of for compensating you for my failures as your creator."

"How?" the man stared at me with accusing eyes and reduced the creator of the universe to tears.

"I cannot stop the glitches and I cannot promise that this will work. In fact just doing what I am thinking about might be the thing that finally overloads the system. But from now until the end no more people will die. The laws of death are no longer in effect. There will be no suffering and no pain and those who have died will be with you again."

"But this whole world is just an illusion," a woman in the audience shouted. "So none of it would be real."

"If I have learned anything from creating this world it is the deeply humbling thing that none of us can know what is real. But I do know this, if you can't tell what is real from what is false, and if it is all equally real from your perception, then it is as real as anything else."

That was when our conversation was interrupted by the studio suddenly starting to dissolve. It seems that my alterations to the laws of reality were causing things to break down faster. Some people started to flicker and the sky took on all sorts of unusual swirling colors, like some sort of electric rainbow dancing above us.

People began to panic as things slowly dissolves around them.

"Do something!" shouted the same woman.

I concentrated hard and then I remembered. People can experience an entire lifetime, a person's entire existence instantaneously in this universe. This reality might only have a minute left to exist, but in that minute everyone on this planet can live an entire simulated existence or multiple existences due to the time dilation. It would be a false memory, but it could last for years or decades and they wouldn't be able to tell the difference.

So with all my remaining concentration and power, as I felt the universe I created starting to dissolve around me, I gave one final mass command to the system. Everyone alive would forget all the terrifying things that I had told them and would all spend the rest of time this world has left living the life that they always wanted to live. They would live out their every dream and fantasy and the world would be exactly like they wanted it to be for each individual. I was giving them the power I had over their world to experience individually for what would seem to them to be years on end.

But I did one last selfish thing with my universe. I did not delete Elizabeth's memory, but I still gave her the ability to live out her dream existence.

And I lived it with her.

I lived what felt like an entire lifetime with her. We married, had children – two boys and a girl. She paid off all of her loans and went on to win the Nobel Prize and I was there in the audience to watch her accept it and it was the proudest moment of my existence. She lived until the ripe old age of 86 and she never once wanted reality to be anything other than a normal happy life, as though I never had any special power over this universe.

I wouldn't have had it any other way.

And finally, as our lives together came to a close, I came out of the simulation of our life together back into the audience where just seconds before I had put that program into existence. Then I stood there watching the entire audience in a trance living their perfect lives in the span of seconds. Then I looked up to the sky, took one last look at the light display above as the universe dissolved around me into darkness and 7 billion souls blinked out of existence forever.

Now I know how Obi-Wan felt in that old Star Wars movie.

I came to to find myself on the floor with my virtual reality helmet lying beside me and smoking, and me with a raging headache. I looked up to see my simulated reality computer system sparking flames and turning on the smoke alarms.

"Is everything okay in there," came a voice outside of my apartment door.

I forced myself to get up and open the door and a man ran in brandishing a fire extinguisher that he used to extinguish the fire that was breaking out on my computer table.

I coughed loudly as another man led me out into the hallway where I could breathe better. "Are you okay," he asked as I continue to cough.

I took a minute before I could breathe well enough to talk. "I'm fine," I told him, "I just lived through the end of my world is all."

The next couple of weeks were very difficult. I mostly just went to work, came home and drank myself to sleep. I could have made myself another universe, but I couldn't re-create Elizabeth, it wouldn't be the exact same person. It would be a perfect copy, but it would not be the same Elizabeth that I experienced everything with. I had all of her memories in my mind, but to re-create her would still not be creating the same person again. A perfect copy is not the original, no matter how much someone argue otherwise.

One day on the way home from work I was on the subway feeling depressed and sat down without looking and sat right into a woman's lap. "I'm sorry," I said.

"It's okay, no harm done," came the woman's voice. I turned around and I couldn't believe it. Staring me in the face was Elizabeth.

"Elizabeth?"

"How did you know my name?"

Realizing how impossible this must be I thought maybe I was hallucinating.

"I didn't, you just looked like an Elizabeth."

"Most people just call me Liz."

"I am John," I said as I shook her hand. But that was when something suddenly felt off and I felt a chill go up my spine.

"Oh my God," said Liz as she began to blush and giggle.

No, it couldn't be, I thought. I looked down and saw that I was naked, the pink frogs were croaking loudly at my feet and the sky above me began to become pixelated.

It seems I was not God after all.

How Max Peytor Destroyed the World

Max Peytor: Worst Killer in History! The Tragic Legacy of Max Peytor. Deathtoll from Max Peytor Continues to Rise!

These were the headlines plastered across every newspaper in America, every newspaper in the World for that matter, except in Europe, because there no longer was much of a Europe to speak of anymore. These had been the top headlines in every newspaper, every day, for over a year; it was also the wallpaper of every room in Max Peytor's house.

One year, three weeks, six days; that is how long it has been since Max Peytor destroyed the world.

It all started innocently enough one night when Max was looking through his telescope. He was nothing beyond an amateur astronomer, his day job was as an accountant working at First National Bank. Up until the night in question he had lived a perfectly humdrum life; cranking numbers without rhyme or reason, frequently criticized for his sloppy manner of dress and general lack of ambition. But this never bothered Max because he knew it wasn't true. To him his job was just a paycheck, but to say he had no ambitions of any kind was ludacris. It was easy to assume however; most people's ambition is to ascend the ladder of personal success in their career, or by accomplishing some amazing feat, or increasingly these days to get famous for doing nothing of merit whatsoever. That was not what Max wanted. He did not seek to become President, or climb Mount Everest, or become a celebrity of the week for something trivial; no, Max's ambition was far simpler and much less common, although by no means unique. All that Max desired something named after him, but not just anything-he wanted his own celestial body.

Ever since he had seen Halley's comet as a young boy of seven it had been his lifelong ambition to discover something so wonderous, something so amazing and glorious, that millions would gather just to catch a rare fleeting glimpse of it once in their lifetimes. It couldn't be denied that there were some egotistical desires expressed in such a dream, but then what goals worth striving for are ever entirely free from personal vanity? The glitz and the glamour of his photo on scientific periodicals all around the world, those couldn't be entirely discarded motives either, but they were not the primary motivators. Material rewards would be few and far between, if any. A discovery of that kind would not bring with it riches or power or even much personal glory, but that didn't matter. What Max really wanted to achieve was immortality. To have something baring your name that would far outlive you was a greater legacy than most could ever hope to achieve.

But Max achieved his dream on August 16th at around 9:30pm.

It was an ordinary night, no different from any other. Max was looking through his telescope as he did every night before going to sleep. On most nights he saw little more than a few stars and perhaps the craters of the moon, and that was providing that it was a clear night unobstructed by clouds, fog or pollution of various kinds. But this night he would see something that would change his life forever.

At first he thought he was just seeing things, but of course he checked and double checked and then checked ten more times. After being sure of himself he called it in. At last he would have some celestial body that would bare his name. It was a good feeling, a great feeling, perhaps the best Max had ever felt in his life. But that feeling wouldn't last for long.

The celestial body in question was an asteroid nearly half a mile long in diameter. It wasn't the largest asteroid in existence, not even close, but it was Max's asteroid. People would see it and know he was the one who had discovered it-but that was precisely the problem.

Just days after its discovery the asteroid's trajectory was plotted and showed the worst fear of any stargazer-the object was on a direct collision course with Earth and would strike the planet in just a few months, March 15th to be precise-the Ides of March.

As one could expect it didn't take long for people to panic. And it also didn't take long for people to begin to point fingers of blame, and it was easy to blame the messenger, who in this case was Max Peytor.

Of course in cases like this the governments of the world always have a plan, or they say they do even if that is not the case. In this instance the plan involved using a series of missles to divert the asteroid's course. Once this plan was formulated it needed the ringing endorsement of every scientist, politician and religious leader it could get in order to prevent the complete breakdown of all societal order. It also helps to have a mascot for the cause, and what better mascot than the discoverer of the threatening object-Max Peytor.

In all truth Max wasn't fully confident in the government's plan, it sounded too much like something out of Hollywood, and even in the movies it didn't always succeed. In fact, having his name attached to the most feared object in creation quickly dimmed the ego glow that came from finding it in the first place. But so long as the object's course could be diverted he could still go down as a hero for giving humanity enough forewarning to stop it. So, without real confidence that disaster could actually be averted, Max went on tv and told the world he had full confidence that the menace that bore his name could be destroyed. It is an odd moment to pronounce the words "I am fully confident that Max Peytor can be destroyed," as it made him sound like he was suicidal, and at that point he wasn't.

That would soon change.

The night before the asteroid was to hit, Max was obligated to attend an interfaith prayer meeting. People of all faiths gathered to collectively beg God to spare our lowly planet from certain destruction. He even heard that the Pope had blessed the missles. Max had to admit to feeling silly at partaking, as he'd always considered himself an agnostic. Plus he reasoned if there was a God with a divine plan for mankind he probably wasn't going to alter that plan based on some last minute groveling.

Hours before the asteroid was to strike Earth the missles were launched. Several hundred megatons exploded but failed to nudge the asteroid off its kamakazi course with the Earth.

It seems God didn't get the message, or if he did he chose not to listen.

Naturally there was widespread panic. There had been widespread panic ever since the asteroid's course had been charted, but now the panic reached a fever pitch. Those who hadn't already evacuated the region of impact now stormed the borders of all surrounding nations, not that they would likely fare any better, but when all options are equally bad it helps to at least try *something*.

The asteroid made impact in Yugoslavia, igniting the powderkeg of the Balkans one last time. Centuries of racial and ethnic strife ended with a bang. All that was left in its place was a city sized crater which coincidentally also now bore Max's name.

That was March 15th. One year, three weeks and six days ago.

Max awoke with a hangover that morning as he has every morning since last year. He awoke to the same overcast day to the same feeling of despair and paranoia that have come to characterize every day.

Every day Max awoke from the same dream, or nightmare rather. It wasn't always the exact same dream, but the details varied little. Sometimes the dream would focus on the impact itself and the incineration. Other times his dreams would focus on those drowned in the East Coast Tsunami as the waves swept away the screaming masses. Most often however, he would dream of the millions of starving refugees walking through the cold barren remains of what used to be their homes, their eyes downcast and their faces smudged with dirt. When they would look up at him it would be with accusing eyes that seemed to pierce his heart like a dagger. That was where he would wake up in a cold sweat, and that was how he woke up on this particular morning.

Max brewed his morning coffee in hopes it would help him to overcome his latest hangover. It was mornings like these he was glad things were eternally overcast as the harsh California sunlight would otherwise have burned his eyes. He put on the tv to see the morning news. It was the same old story again and again. The newscaster droned on, "And so starvation continues to be rampant with all food exports ceasing. Death tolls continue with estimates varying between 500 million upwards to a billion having died since the impact of Max Peytor just over a year ago, many times more than in all the wars of the 20th century combined. Many millions more are still homeless with large numbers from the East Coast only now returning to begin rebuilding what the tsunami from the asteroid washed away. Rationing continues and-"

Max turned off the tv. That would be enough of that.

Max checked the thermometer. The temperature was in the high 30s, he would need a coat if he was going to go out today...a very big if. Checking his provisions it would seem that he would have no choice but to leave home today.

Max instinctively touched his side. His scar appeared to be healing correctly. It always seemed to start bothering him whenever he even thought about leaving his house, ever since during a previous outing where he was knifed by a crazy woman convinced he was the anti-christ who signed a pact with the devil to summon the asteroid. This is what comes with the territory of having the most infamous name in human history. Even Hitler's name didn't carry as much weight compared to Max Peytor.

It was times like these that Max wished that he had named the object after his now ex-wife, Emily. Admittedly Emily doesn't sound like a very intimidating name for an event of apocalyptic magnitude. But he wouldn't wish his fate on anyone. As soon as he became the target of all the anger and frustration of the masses his wife was pretty quick to leave him, and she took their daughter Cindy with them as well. It was logical, for safety reasons. When a person says they've married you for better or worse they never anticipate the worst, but then who could anticipate something like this?

The final straw had come when a group of religious fanatics burned down their home. They were from the same cult as the woman who stabbed him, he later discovered. Having no one else to blame they signaled him out for revenge. If they couldn't get revenge on the asteroid they might as well go for the next best thing.

It was after that event his wife didn't feel safe with him. It was then that he realized he didn't feel safe either. That was when he moved into his current apartment and decided to change his name to the rather cliche sounding John Smith, but he figured it was best to chose the most generic name he could think of in hopes of blending in. Fortunately most people these days had greater concerns, but he still didn't feel any safer leaving the house.

At least now that he was living in anonymity the lawsuits stopped. Several hundred people had attempted to sue him, although the cases were all thrown out as they had no legitimate claims. That didn't stop the nutcases though. It didn't help his ego any that the Facebook group People Against Max Peytor had over a million members. So much for glitz and glamour.

But that was enough self pity for now, his stomach was rumbling. It was time to call his next door neighbor and last remaining friend, Jake. If he was going to leave the house he sure as hell wasn't going to chance going it alone; his increasing agoraphobia wouldn't allow it.

Within a few minutes of calling, Max heard a knock at the door. Looking through the peephole and seeing it was Jake he hurriedly pulled him inside and slammed the door shut.

"Gee Max, paranoid much," said Jake.

"It's John now, " Max snapped back. "Don't forget that."

"Right, John, John Smith." Jake rolled his eyes and then looked around to see the many alcohol bottles and newspaper clippings lining all the walls. "You're getting worse Ma...John. This isn't healthy you know, living like this."

"How is one supposed to live when your very identity is synonymous with mass death and catastrophe, when every mention of your previous name is a reminder of the horror you have come to represent in the mind of man."

"Well, for one thing, if my old name was such a painful reminder of such unpleasantries I wouldn't wallpaper my house with every mention of it that is made. And for someone so hell bent on remaining anonymous you sure don't seem to have any qualms about advertizing your previous identity. Frankly, it looks more than a little suspicious to be so obsessed with the past you're trying to distance yourself from. Just saying is all."

"Well don't. Let's just get going. Hopefully it won't be crowded and we can get back home without anyone recognizing me."

"Well given all the plastic surgery, make up and disguises, I wouldn't worry much about that."

"Speaking of which..." Max hurriedly put on a heavy brown trenchcoat and jacket that covered most of his body, as well as long gloves, black boots, a wool cap and sunglasses. "How do I look?"

"Like a poorly dressed spy or a creepy guy in the park I would feel uneasy having near my children."

"Why do I even bother asking?"

"Would you prefer to take a cab or the subway?"

"A cab, there's less chance of encountering people who might recognize me."

Max and Jake hailed a cab. The cabbie had a thick accent and heavy beard but didn't say much. But then he turned on the radio. The announcer's voice blared, "Today the US has reduced the amount of aid being given to Eastern European refugees stating a lack of funds owing to a bad economy in the United States. With rationing increasing at home fewer and fewer Americans are willing to support large amounts of foreign aid being sent overseas. This comes at a time where rationing has been increased to a degree that most Americans feel to be severe. Meanwhile, people throughout Europe continue to freeze and starve in the perpetual year long winter. A similar fate has plagued much of Africa and Asia and no where in the world has escaped fully from the temperature drops that have precipitated worldwide hunger and starvation."

The cabbie turned down the radio and began ranting. "Damn government. I have family in Eastern Europe, what are they supposed to do? Damn Max Peytor caused the whole world to go to shit."

"I'm sorry," Max said feebly.

"Don't be, it's not your fault. It's that damn Max Peytor's fault! If he had discovered the asteroid sooner maybe we could have stopped it. If you ask me he was no great hero for discovering it if he can't do anything to stop it."

Max held his tongue. If he made it obvious how uncomfortable he was he risked drawing attention to himself. Fortunately they arrived at their stop not long after. Max quickly paid the cabbie without saying a word and went into the market. "Let's be quick as possible," he whispered to Jake.

The food available at the market was of an even more limited variety than the last time Max had been there just two weeks before. Due to greater rationing the price of food had risen steadily, variety had gone down tremendously and the amount any individual could buy in any given period of time was even more limited. Max wished that he had stocked up on more food before the new rationing was put into effect. But there was little Max could do about it other than to get his groceries and get in line. Max hoped that the line would move quickly as he couldn't help but notice the number of armed guards had increased since the last time. Theft must have increased as well. Max had read about a murder taking place not far away from here. The murderder had been trying to steal groceries from an old lady. These are the things hunger does to people. He can only imagine how bad the situation must be in the refugee camps.

Max's thoughts were soon interrupted by the person in front of him arguing with the cashier. "What do you mean I've exceeded my rations for this week!"

"I'm sorry sir, but it clearly says here this is the second time this week you have attempted to buy groceries after maxing out your ration card."

"Look I have a wife and three children, they simply can't survive on such limited rations."

"I'm sorry, but legally I cannot sell you anymore food this week."

The man got out his wallet. "How about if I slipped you some cash-double the value of the groceries I have here. Please, my family is hungry."

The cashier looked up at the security cameras and then at the man. "I'm sorry but that would be bribery and not only would I lose my job, I could be arrested. Now please sir you'll have to leave or I'll have to alert security."

Max saw the man started to pat his pants pocket. He then started reaching for what looked like a concealed weapon-a hand gun. Max put his hand on the gun and whispered into the man's ear, "Sir, please don't, it's not worth it. I can help." Max's heart was pounding. What the hell was he thinking? Maybe he really did want to get himself killed. But after a moment's hesitation the man slowly but surely moved his hand away from the gun. "Meet me outside," the man whispered to Max before he left the scene looking agitated.

Max paid for his groceries with his hand shaking and turned to Jake and explained the situation. Jake turned nervously towards Max and asked "What do you want to do?"

"Look, let's just meet him and see what he wants."

"Are you crazy, we should get security. He could be out there waiting to kill us. I'm not willing to risk my life over some nutcase waiting to kill us over some groceries like that poor old lady the other week. Let's just tell security."

After giving it a brief consideration Max agreed that it was probably the best option. They had security escort them out. As soon as the man with the gun saw security he took off pretty quickly. They did not pursue him. Security waited with them for as long as it took to get a cab and then they were off.

"Let's stop for a drink," said Max

"Are you crazy?! After what just happened. I'd think you'd want to get home as soon as possible."

"I do, but after that experience I really need a drink. I don't have any alcohol left at home and I'm not going to be able to sleep tonight without something to calm my nerves."

"I just don't feel it's a good..."

"Please." Max looked up with a worn out expression on his face. He was white as a ghost and was still shaking from the experience. "Just one drink, then we can go home."

"Ok, John, *one* drink and then we'll go home. Under the circumstances I can understand your reasons."

Before long they arrived at a bar named Murph's. Much like everywhere else armed guards greeted them at the entrance. They were searched for weapons before being allowed to enter. This did not bother either of them. They wished the guards had done similar at the grocery store, but where alcohol is involved extra precaution would make even more sense. Alcohol related violence has been way up since the asteroid. Even with rationing in place intoxicants could always be obtained.

Max wasted no time in getting drunk. Jake also had a few drinks but made sure to stay sober enough to be on his guard, as he was worried the night might turn ugly fast. While most of the bar's patrons were pretty mellowed out, there were a few shady looking characters Jake felt they would both do best to avoid. Unfortunately soon Max's drinking got the better of him. After seeing mention of himself on the news again he drunkenly stumbled to the front of the bar.

"You know who I really hate," said Max as he stood up, "I hate that God damned Max Peytor. Who here is with me?"

"Um, John," said Jake holding unto Max's arm, "I think maybe you've had a little too much to drink. You said you were only going to have *one* drink, and you've had way more than that."

"Shut up! You're not my mother. My mother killed herself shortly after that bastard Max Peytor's asteroid struck the Earth. Poor woman couldn't bare having people asking if that was her son who discovered that death missle from space." Jake could see a tear run down Max's face. "I wish that sonuvabitch was here right now, I'd like to give him a piece of my mind."

Jake was noticing that people were beginning to stare. The bartender came over and whispered to Jake that if his friend couldn't control himself they would have to leave. "We were just about to leave, " replied Jake.

"Non-sense!" shouted Max. "The night is just getting started. Why am I wearing this stupid getup?" With that Max began taking off his gloves, hat and sunglasses. He winced back a bit when the light hit his eyes, unobstructed by darkness for the first time all day. He started at his visage reflected in the window for several moments before slurring, "You know I look a lot like that damn Max Peytor."

Jake started to look around to see more and more people noticing him. People began to stare, some with hints of recognition. People started getting up and slowly coming towards them. Jake started to pull on Max's shoulder. "Time to leave John."

"My name isn't John, it's Max!" And with that statement a crowd began to circle around them. An angry looking man came up face to face with Max, staring him straight in the eye. Max began to tremble nervously.

"Hey, it is him!" shouted the man. The crowd drew in closer. "Hey everyone, this is Max Peytor!"

"No, no it isn't," replied Jake. But he was ignored and shoved out of the way.

"I've been waiting for this for a long time." The man began to shove Max. "I'm going to give you what you've got coming to you."

"It's not his fault!" shouted Jake. "All he did was discover the asteroid. He didn't want it to strike the Earth, he didn't cause it to strike the Earth, he never killed a single person. Haven't you ever heard the phrase don't hurt the messenger?"

The crowd just pushed Jake out of the way and began circling around Max. Before Max knew what was happening he felt the fists of a mob laying into him from every angle. He soon fell to the floor where he began meeting with kicks and scratches. Any attempt to get up resulted in him being pushed back to the ground and hit harder. Just as the mob's ring leader was about to smash a bottle over Max's head, the bottle was grabbed.

"Alright, alright break it up!" shouted the security guard as pulled the bottle from the assailent's hands. "Everyone get off of him and go home before I arrest the whole lot of you."

And with that the crowd dispersed and security helped Max to his feet. "Are you alright?" they asked. Max just nodded slowly, his face bloody and bruised.

"Do you want to go to the hospital?" asked Jake

"No, no, I think we'd better just get right home." Max was shaking and touching his face and looking at the blood on his hand. How ironic, he thought to himself, that the man whose name was associated with millions of deaths now had actual blood on his hands. He laughed nervously and Jake patted him on the back and then lead him out of the bar as the crowd looked on with accusing stares, like the people in his nightmares.

The ride home was almost completely silent. The cabbie asked what had happened to Max. Jake lied for him and said Max had a door slammed into his face. The cabbie said no more but kept looking back as though he didn't quite believe the story. Fortunately he didn't recognize Max as far as he could tell and they made it safely back to the apartment complex.

Jake walked Max back to his room. "Are you sure you'll be ok?"

"People have been through worse than I have." Max snorted and some blood dripped from his nose. He then laughed a bit.

"What's so funny?"

"After all that happened I left my damn groceries at the bar. I didn't even think to bring them."

"Do you want me to go back and get them?"

"I'm sure by now they are long gone. If you leave a piece of cheese out amid a crowd of hungry rats would you expect it to still be there an hour later?"

"Well what do you want to do about it?"

"Don't worry about it."

"But now you have no food and can't get more."

"Well right now I don't feel much like eating anyway. I'll worry about it later."

"Are you sure?"

"Yes, I'm sure."

Jake was beginning to feel unwelcome. He could tell when Max needed to be alone, and now was one of those times. Max sensed his unease and put his hand on Jake's shoulder. "You're a good friend Jake."

"So are you, John. So will I see you tomorrow? I'd feel better just to see you've gotten through the night ok."

"Sure, sure old friend. Tomorrow."

"Good night then John."

"Good bye friend."

Max slowly closed the door and Jake turned to leave. He felt a shiver as he did so. "First thing tomorrow," he muttered.

First thing in the morning Jake went to check on Max. Max hadn't answered his phone, so Jake began to worry. He went to Max's room and knocked on the door several times but got no answer. After pounding on the door for several minutes he tried the doorknob to find that it was unlocked. Max never leaves his door unlocked. Jake knew this was trouble. "John, are you awake?" No answer. He checked the bedroom. "John!" Still no answer.

It was then that Jake noticed the bathroom door was open and the light was on. He opened the door and almost vomited. There, lying in a bathtub full of red water, was Max with a lifeless expression on his face.

"Max, oh God!" Jake shouted. "No, no, no! Damn it!" He almost fell backwards. He knew he shouldn't have left Max alone last night, he knew it. Composing himself he happened to see a letter taped to the door with his named written on it. Opening he read:

Dear Jake,

    I am sorry for what you have discovered here this morning, although you might not be all that surprised. As my only remaining friend you are the last person I would want to do this too, as you are probably the only one left who will be upset by my passing. I just want to know I appreciated your friendship and aid in my months of isolation.

    As for the wider world I have no message to leave, nor do I particularly think anyone will care. I doubt my death will even be front page news, although I think Max Peytor Destroyed would be a nice addition to the collection lining my wall, and one which would put a smile on the faces of many.

    If I do have any vague sort of message to leave it is this: Don't strive for immortality by being remembered, strive for immortality by living. Maybe not the best message coming from a man who ended up taking his own life. Maybe that could be the lesson of my life-immortality kills. Hey, that could be the headline: Max Peytor Destroys World and The World Destroys Max Peytor! I think I like it, I like it a lot.

That was all that was written. Max always was a man of few words, and even his final letter had to end abruptly, not unlike his life. Jake pounded his fist against the wall and then, as calmly as possible, he dialed 9-1-1.

A month after Max's death Jake went to put flowers on his grave. It was simply marked Max with no epitaph. After a moment of silence he walked off.

Later that night he was looking through the telescope he had bought shortly after Max had died. Looking through the eyepiece he thought he saw something. After checking it several times he thought about calling it in. Then as he went to pick up the phone he reflected a minute and decided that he was content to be mortal and hung it up.

The Refuse Collectors

"What is refuse?" Joey asked.

"It's kind of like trash," said Billie.

"Then why does Carlos want it so badly?"

"Did Carlos say that he wants refuse?"

"He said that he wanted to get some books," interjected Cindy. "Books are not refuse, although a lot of people refer to them as such since the invasion."

"What's a book?" Joey asked as he scratched his head and looked up with a puzzled glance.

"Books are illegal," said Billie. "You don't need to concern yourself with such things."

"But Carlos said –" Joey began.

"Carlos doesn't know what he's talking about," said Billie. "He is willing to risk his damn fool head for a bunch of dusty old books."

"Why, what's so great about books?" Joey insisted. "What exactly do they do?"

"They tell you stories," said Cindy, "stories about other times and places. Places that only exist in your imagination."

"I like stories," Joey said with a smile.

"I can tell you some stories," said Billie, "and you don't need any books."

"But I've heard all your stories already," Joey sighed.

"Well here's a story you haven't heard. It's a story about a group of foolish kids who thought to defy the invaders. You want to know what happened to them?"

"Don't," Cindy said as she stood up to silence Billie, "you don't need to scare him needlessly."

"I want to know what happened to them!" Joey shouted.

"No you don't," said Cindy, "now hush."

Joey folded his arms in aggravation and stormed off. On his way out of the room he bumped into Carlos.

"Big brother!" Joey shouted as he grabbed Carlos's leg.

"What's up little buddy?" Carlos asked as he tussled Joey's hair.

"I want to know what books are and why they are so important."

Carlos smiled at Joey. "They are important because books can tell you things."

"What kind of things?"

"Nothing that you need to know about," shouted Billie as he angrily pounded his fist down on the table.

"Do books tell stories about what it was like before the invasion?" Joey asked as he jumped up and down with excitement.

Carlos nodded. "They can tell you that and a whole lot more."

"And they could also put thoughts in your head that you needn't be thinking," sneered Billie. "Thoughts that will get you killed. You don't want to go getting yourself involved with books. They aren't worth dying for."

"Says you," said Carlos.

"Shut up," said Billie. "Don't go putting ideas into Joey's head that are going to get him killed. If you want to die for a bunch of dusty old books then go ahead, but I made a promise to mom and dad that I would take care of Joey no matter what. And I am not going to see harm come to him so that you could fill your head with more useless ideas from before the invasion that aren't going to benefit anyone or change anything."

"Why are books wrong, I like stories," said Joey.

"If you want to hear some stories I can tell you some stories," said Billie. "You don't need no damn books to get stories."

"But I already told you, I have heard all of your stories, they are boring." Joey stomped his feet in protest.

"How would you like to see a book with lots of pictures of the world that mom and dad grew up in?" Carlos said as he put his hand on Joey's shoulder.

"I'd like that a lot!"

"Joey, go to your room," said Billie with clear anger in his voice.

"But I –"

"Now!"

Joey ran off to his room with tears forming in his eyes.

"Now look what you've done," said Cindy as she began to run after Joey. "You didn't need to yell at him."

"The one I need to be yelling at his my stupid ass brother," said Billie as he raised his fists at Carlos. He grabbed Carlos by his shirt and pushed him up against the wall. "I don't want no more talk about books around Joey. If you want to be stupid and get yourself killed for some useless old books, then be my guest. But I care more about Joey than I do about a past that is never coming back. What good is it to fill Joey's head with stories of a world that he'll never know and that we will never get back."

"He needs to get an education."

"All he needs to learn is how to survive in this world by knowing what is right, what is legal, and what is going to get you killed. For a person with so much book learning you haven't really found any useful way of helping us to survive. Your book learning ain't no use in this world. As much as you would like to think otherwise, that world of reading and writing and all that other stuff is gone forever."

"Only if we let it."

"Look, if you want to be some kind of savior of humanity you can go do it on your own, but don't involve Joey in all of this nonsense. You got that?"

"Yeah," Carlos said in a near whisper.

"What's that? I couldn't hear you."

"I said yeah."

Billie let go of Carlos and began to walk off to check on Joey.

"You know you shouldn't provoke him like that," said Cindy.

"I can't help it, sis. We just see things fundamentally differently. And it hasn't just been because of the invasion. I think that Billie is actually happier after the invasion than before. He was always a poor student and probably never even read a full book in his entire life. In this world ignorance is now considered a virtue. It's not survival of the fittest, it is survival of the dumbest. I sometimes wonder how long it will be before Billie decides to join the enforcers."

"Look brother, I know that you and Billie have your differences, but even he would never join those ruthless thugs."

"Why not? He seems like he would be perfect. Mindlessly obedient, willing to survive at any cost and he gets to use his fists instead of his head."

"He might have his flaws, but he is loyal. He would never sell out to the invaders. I have heard him curse the invaders day in and day out. He really is just concerned for Joey."

"So am I."

"I know you are, but sometimes I have to agree with Billie. It's not worth dying for a couple of old books."

"Man cannot live by bread alone. What use is surviving if you just live day to day? What type of world is Joey going to grow up in? That is what I am concerned about."

"I realize that, big bro, but you have to take things one step at a time. Maybe you cannot live by bread alone, but you can't live on nothing. The invaders have already decided to decrease rations, except to the enforcers of course. If we get tagged as subversives we will be cut off completely and most likely out and out murdered. We are all worried about the future, but we have to start by worrying about the present."

"Well you can worry about the immediate present. I have my eye towards the future."

Cindy shook her head. "You are both so stubborn. I guess there is no way I can talk you out of this then?"

"Nope."

"So when are you leaving?"

"Tomorrow morning. I guess it is best that I don't tell Joey what I am up to, I wouldn't want to risk angering Billie any further. Just if I don't make it back, tell Joey –"

Cindy put her finger up to his mouth to shush him. "I know. And if I can't talk you out of this then I will just wish you good luck and please come back safely."

Carlos kissed Cindy on the forehead and and held her tightly before they both left to go to bed.

Carlos woke up early the next morning to meet his friends Andrew, Mark and Jerry. They were a group of subversives who have been meeting in secret and are dedicated to the preservation of art and literature and were meeting Jerry at his house to discuss their plans.

"My contact informs me that there is a total mother load of books waiting for us," said Jerry.

"Are you sure he can be trusted?" asked Andrew.

"No, in this world you can't trust anyone, but I consider it to be worth the risk. He hasn't let me down before."

"Do you have any idea what condition the books are in?" Mark asked.

"They are in the basement of an abandoned bookstore owner's house," said Jerry. "Apparently the invaders missed it. Well, not completely. The owner was killed and his home searched, but he had managed to hide a crate full of his favorite books in the wall of his basement. My contact had found them while he was scavenging the house. He didn't think it was worth the risk of trying to cart them off himself but he was willing to tell me about it, and he is willing to lead us to the house for a couple of books of ration cards."

"Are you sure that he is not an enforcer?" Carlos asked.

"I have known him for a while, and I know him enough that I trust him," said Jerry. "At least I trust him enough that I am willing to take a chance on him. But these days I guess you can never be too sure. With rations being steadily decreased and the invaders and the enforcers cracking down on resisters, people are more and more willing to betray each other just for a few extra calories a day. So it is always a risk. But I think that it is a risk worth taking and I know that you wouldn't be here with me if you did not also think that was true."

They all nodded in agreement.

"So I guess we should be off," said Andrew. "How far away is this place?"

"It is about a 3 mile walk from here, in a town that is pretty much uninhabited," said Jerry. "As far as I am aware the invaders haven't bothered with it since the early days of the invasion, so we are unlikely to run into any type of trouble. They don't even bother to send enforcers in that area. So I am not too worried, although we can't be too careful and we have to have a reason to be walking around during the day that doesn't make us look suspicious. So for our alibi, should we run into any other people, is that we are going to say that we are visiting relatives in a nearby town."

"And if we run into something other than humans?" Carlos asked.

"Let's hope that we don't," said Jerry.

They began their trek to the nearby town. Jerry's contact had given him a map and told him that he would meet up with him at the house. It was a sunny day with not a cloud in the sky, which normally would be a cause for celebration, but a cloudless sky just makes it easier to see the menacing triangular spacecraft of their oppressors. You could see a ship pretty much anywhere you looked in the sky on a cloudless day, a near constant reminder of who is really in charge. It cast an ominous shadow over the entire trip. They would've actually preferred a cloudy day where they can operate without the hot light of the sun beating down on them and the very invaders that they seek to avoid constantly in their field of vision.

Most of the time they did not even think about the invaders ships. After a while they just became part of the background. But when you are worrying that you would be seen by them, they were always there to inspire fear. It was taken for granted that every inch of the Earth was being monitored 24/7, but most people figured that the invaders didn't bother with them most of the time. It was only when you were doing something that you knew you weren't supposed to that you ever really noticed their presence at all.

When they finally arrived in the town they decided to take a break and eat their lunch, consisting of a few pieces of bread and thermoses full of water. These meager rations would have to last them until dinnertime. Most people didn't bother with breakfast anymore, there just wasn't enough food to go around for everyone to have three meals a day. Two meals was the norm, and even then those meals were about equivalent to one normal meal. So everyone was usually still hungry most of the time.

"Why do you think they bother keeping us alive at all?" Andrew asked as he took a bite of his sandwich.

"Who knows," replied Jerry. "When they first invaded I gave it a lot of thought, but now I couldn't care less. I just wish they would leave. But we know that that's not going to happen."

Carlos took a sip from his Thermos. "I have always found it strange that they would immediately wipe out our infrastructure and allow the majority of the human race to die of starvation and disease, only to then decide to try and save the remaining survivors and give them just barely enough to stay alive. It is almost like they went out of their way to kick an anthill over, then dug through the remains to keep the survivors as pets."

"So we're basically just an ant farm?" chuckled Jerry.

"The thing that I have always wondered," said Mark, "is what was the entire purpose of invading the Earth? No one has ever even seen them come out of their ships. All their communication with us has been through robotic emissaries. That always seemed like the biggest giveaway that they were cowards. They won't even show their faces to us. And then they recruit members of our own species to enforce their rule over the earth. I suppose they didn't have enough robots to do the job for them."

"And then their rules are petty and arbitrary," said Andrew as he finished his sandwich. "Why do they care so much whether we are able to read?"

"Knowledge is power," responded Carlos. "By getting rid of all records they can eliminate all of our knowledge and keep us in a state of passivity. Slave masters didn't want their slaves to be able to read and write because they would become wise to their condition and would rebel. As long as we remain ignorant we are less of a threat."

"But that's the strange thing that does not make sense," said Andrew. "The fact is that they haven't enslaved us. They just immediately wiped out all of our electronics with an EMP attack and then, after waiting for the dust to settle, they start recruiting survivors to distribute rations. So we don't seem to be providing any useful service to them, don't really pose any legitimate threat to them, and they could easily just wipe us out completely. So my question is what exactly are they waiting for and what is the point of all this? It seems like they want to keep us alive just so we can sit around in the dark with growling stomachs. Those who survive are basically living lives of idleness and boredom, but as long as we don't challenge the enforcers we are mostly left alone."

"Maybe they just don't have the slightest idea what to do with us," laughed Mark as he took a chug on his Thermos. "Maybe they came here to colonize the planet, found civilization and weren't sure what to do, so they immediately wiped us out, then decided they didn't want to wipe us out completely. Maybe they are keeping us alive as a zoo. Maybe they're just waiting for reinforcements before they begin the final extermination. Your guess is as good as mine. But whatever they have planned for us, whatever their ultimate goal is, we are not going to go quietly. That is why it is our duty to try and keep our civilization alive and keep our knowledge and traditions alive as long as we can. Maybe someday they will leave and we will be able to rebuild. It's unlikely, but the best we can do is try and hope for the best."

"I'll toast to that," said Carlos as he held up his Thermos, and they all clanked them together and nodded in agreement.

After finishing their lunch they continued to walk until they finally reached the house that was shown on the map. It was a very run down looking house with the windows smashed in, the door hanging off of its hinges, most of the paint stripped off of the walls, and most of the tiles stripped off of the roof.

"Is this the place?" Carlos asked. "It looks like a real shithole."

Jerry took another look at the map and then looked up at the house. "Yeah, according to the map, this is it."

"It figures that it would be directly under the shadow of one of the invader's ships," said Mark. "I sure hope that this isn't a trap."

"If it was a trap they probably would've attacked us by now," said Andrew. "Do you see your contact anywhere?"

That was when someone tapped Jerry on the shoulder, causing him to jump. He turned around to see it was Charlie, his contact.

"Geez, you have to sneak up on me like that, you almost gave me a heart attack?"

"Sorry," said Charlie as he laughed and smacked Jerry hard on the back.

"So I guess this is it?" Jerry asked. "Doesn't look too impressive."

"Well it's what is inside that counts," said Charlie, "is it not? What were you expecting? I told you it was in a rundown abandoned town that hasn't really even seen any human visitors for the better part of three years, aside from scavengers, like yourselves." Charlie pushed the door and it fell in. He extended his arms in a welcoming gesture. "Ladies first." Charlie laughed after that last comment.

The others shrugged and they all followed Charlie into the house. The inside of the house didn't look much better than the outside. In fact, it looked worse. It was full of torn up furniture, peeling paint, a ceiling with many holes in it, water damage all over the place and several rats scurrying about on the floor.

"I'll lead you to the books," said Charlie. "They are in the basement."

"I sure hope that this is worth a week of ration coupons," said Jerry.

"When have I ever let you down?"

"You let me down plenty of times. But this was an opportunity I couldn't pass up, even if it was only a possibility."

Charlie kicked in the basement door and slowly walked down the steps. "Careful," he said, "a lot of these steps are worn down and could easily break. So walk carefully."

They all proceeded to walk down the stairs, with Carlos almost tripping as one of the stairs at the bottom gave way. He just barely caught himself from falling flat on his face.

Charlie went over to the wall, which had a painting on it. "It's right behind here," said Charlie as he pushed the painting aside to reveal a giant hole in the wall. He reached inside and pulled out an old storage crate.

"That's it?" Andrew asked.

"What?" asked Charlie. "That entire crate is filled with books. If you don't believe me, look for yourself. Here, you can do the honors." Charlie picked up a crowbar and handed it to Andrew. Andrew swiftly took it and pried the lid off of the crate, sending up a big cloud of dust that made them all cough and sneeze.

Once they had finished sneezing and coughing, they looked into the crate to see that there were a couple of dozen books in there. It seemed like many of them were a bit water damaged and a couple looked like they had been gnawed on by the some of the rats. But they were all in readable condition.

"Books!" cried Carlos as he hugged one of the books tightly to his chest. "I can't remember the last time that I was able to hold a new book in my hand."

"A lot of them seem to be rather beat up," said Jerry.

"Hey, no refunds," said Charlie. "I did my part and lead you to the books."

"They might not be in mint condition," said Carlos, "but as long as they're readable I am a happy man."

"Do you think that we can carry them all back to our homes?" Andrew asked.

"I think that we could probably each carry about 10 books in our knapsacks without it looking suspicious," said Mark. "We could carry an additional 10 books if Charlie had also brought a knapsack."

"Oh no," said Charlie, "my role ends here. I was taking a big risk by even leading you here, but I'll be damned if I'm getting caught with books. I'm willing to take a couple of risks, but I'm not going to risk my life for a couple of books. If anyone asks we were never here and I will deny it. And you should know that if I am interrogated I will give you all up in an instant to save myself."

"You're welcome," said Jerry. "But I never expected you to make any type of self-sacrifice. I know that you were just in this to get more rations. You never struck me as the reading type."

"I never understood what was so important about books," said Charlie. "I would rather have a full stomach than a bag full of books. And now that I've done my part it is time we go our separate ways. I am going to leave before you and go in the opposite direction. I don't want anyone linking us together. Personally I think you are probably going to end up getting yourselves killed, and I don't want to be there when it happens. But I will wish you good luck. But I still think you're stupid and crazy as hell."

Charlie left and they decided that they had better just pack up the books as quickly as possible. They could sort things out when they got home and decide on a hiding space later. Right now it was best that they get back to town as soon as possible so that people will not get suspicious by their absence.

On the way home they briefly encountered a couple of people going for a walk but just nodded and waved to them. They tried not to look nervous, but they couldn't help but feel their pulses race a bit every time they saw someone. They did see some enforcers on the street, but the enforcers usually would leave you alone unless you are showing some obvious signs of suspicion. Although there were always a couple of them who genuinely enjoyed their jobs and were in it for the power, rather than just for the food.

"I'm home," said Carlos as he walked in.

Cindy ran up and hugged him. "I'm so glad to see you back in one piece."

"Big brother!" Joey said as he came running out. "Where have you been?"

"I was just visiting with friends."

"Oh. Did you bring me anything?"

"Maybe. But I'll tell show you later. I don't think that Billie would appreciate it."

"Wouldn't appreciate what?" asked Billie as he barged through the door.

"Nothing," said Carlos. "You don't appreciate anything that you can't put in your mouth."

Billie shot Carlos an angry glance. He was about to say something when Cindy interrupted. "Did you get the rations?"

"Yes," said Billie with a frown, "but once again we have gotten less than usual."

"They decreased the rations again?" Cindy asked with a look of disappointment.

Billie nodded. "Yep. I think that I'm going to have to start hunting again if we want to have a proper diet. The current rations have eliminated meat altogether."

"Maybe we could get some on the black market," Carlos suggested.

"You know what happened to the last person who was caught trading on the black market?" Billie asked in a raised voice.

"Please don't," said Cindy as she touched Billie's arm. "Not in front of Joey."

Billie pulled his arm away and pushed her arm down. "No, Joey should hear this. He needs to learn what the law is around here, because I'm the only one who is going to teach him the cold hard truth of the world. The last person who was caught trading on the black market is now hanging in the town square."

Joey looked up and began to cry.

"Now look what you've gone and done," said Cindy. "You're scaring him."

"Good," said Billie, "fear keeps people alive. When people are afraid they obey the law."

"You sound like one of the enforcers," said Carlos.

"The enforcers may be a bunch of bastards, but they know how to survive better than anyone else."

"Why don't you just go and join them then?"

"I'm hungry!" Joey shouted as he started crying heavily.

Billie looked at the rations. "Well I'm afraid we will have to wait until tomorrow. We already ate today and I don't think that we have enough rations that we could afford to eat more than once a day."

"But I'm hungry now!" cried Joey.

"We are all hungry," said Billie, "but you'll be more hungry tomorrow if you have your rations now."

"You could have some of my rations," said Carlos, "I already ate lunch today." Carlos felt his stomach growl when he thought about lunch, but that didn't really bother him.

"No," said Billie, "nobody eats until tomorrow."

"Who put you in charge of the food?" Cindy demanded as she folded her arms and tapped her foot impatiently.

"I'm the oldest one here and I'm the one who has to be responsible for everyone. Speaking of which, I couldn't even find your ration book." He turned to Carlos. "What did you do with it?"

"I got my own rations while I was out before." It was a lie, but Billie usually wasn't stupid enough to ask follow-ups.

"Well what did you do with them?"

"Don't concern yourself with me."

"Don't worry, I don't. But don't you go feeding Joey your rations. He has to learn the way things are. If you feed him now he will come to expect that there will always be food whenever he wants it. He has to learn that we have to conserve food."

"But I'm hungry now!" Joey shouted as he stomped his feet. "I want to eat! I want to eat!"

"Joey," shouted Billie, "be quiet or I won't give you any food tomorrow either."

Joey began to cry again and ran off to his room.

"Why do you have to always go and do that?" Cindy shouted at Billie.

"He has to learn. If it were up to you two we would've all starved by now."

As Cindy and Billie continued to shout at one another, Carlos snuck away and went into Joey's room and lit a candle.

"Joey," Carlos whispered. "Are you awake buddy?"

Joey looked up from his pillow with tears still streaming down his cheeks and nodded.

"Don't pay any attention to Billie, he is just trying to do what he thinks is best, in his own jerky way. But if you stop crying I will show you the surprise that I brought you."

"A surprise," Joey sniffled as he started to wipe the tears from his eyes.

"Yes, a very special surprise. But you have to promise not to tell Billie or anyone else about it. That is very important. You swear?"

Joey nodded and extended his pinky finger. "Pinky swear."

Carlos grabbed his pinky and they shook on it.

"Now what's the surprise!" Joey's face was lighting up with excitement and his tears were stopping. The prospect of a surprise could always cheer him up pretty much instantly.

"Look what I've got," said Carlos as he unzipped his knapsack and slowly took out the books.

"What are those?" Joey's eyes lit up with wonderment as he had never seen a book before.

"These are books."

"And there are stories inside of those books?"

"Yes, tons of stories. They used to be the main way people shared information with large groups of people."

"How does it work?" Joey picked up a book and stared at it. It had a picture of Buzz Aldrin standing next to an American flag on the surface of the moon, a sight that was completely unfamiliar to Joey. The title read The Story of Apollo 11, although Joey could not read it.

"Well you open it up and look inside." Carlos opened the book and began turning the pages to show Joey.

"It's full of people in funny outfits," said Joey as he stared into the book.

"Those are called pictures. And those lines on the side are called words."

"Where are all the stories?"

"Well the pictures and the words tell you the story. But you have to know how to read to do that."

"Can you read it to me?"

"Sure I can, but for now why don't you just look at the pictures. I will read it to you when we are completely alone. We wouldn't want Billie to interrupt us."

Joey smiled and nodded. "Who are those funny looking men in this book and why are they dressed so weird?"

"Those men are astronauts. They went up into space to explore the moon. Remember when I told you about how humans used to be able to travel into space?"

Joey nodded and smiled even bigger.

"Well they traveled up into space in rocket ships and landed on the moon. They planted our American flag up there."

"Is the Moon where the invaders come from?"

"No one knows where the invaders come from. But they do come from space, but from someplace much further away than the moon."

"You mean like Mars?"

"Even further than that."

"Pluto?"

"They must've come from a another star system altogether."

"Why don't they just go back to where they came from and leave us alone?"

Carlos shook his head. "Nobody knows."

"Well I wish that they would all just leave us alone."

"We all wish that Joey. But how would you like to look at a couple more books?"

Joey nodded with a big smile on his face as Carlos reached over to get some more books to show to him.

"What's this about?" Joey asked as he picked up a book with a picture of Italy on the cover.

"This is a travel guide to Italy."

"Where is Italy?"

"It is far away on the other side of the world, in Europe."

"Do you think we could go there someday?"

"I am afraid that is too far away, and the invaders have restricted our ability to travel very far."

"Are the invaders in Italy too?"

"As far as we know. I am afraid that the invaders have pretty much taken over the entire world. We don't even know how much of Italy is even left."

"Have you ever been to Italy?"

Carlos shook his head. "No, but mom and dad went there on their honeymoon. They went to Rome, Venice and all over the countryside. Did you know that in Venice the people ride around in boats?"

"Really?" Joey's eyes lit up.

"Mmmhm," said Carlos as he nodded and opened the book to show Joey a picture of the Venice streets filled with couples touring the city in gondolas.

Joey looked intently at the pictures, looking happier than Carlos had seen him in a long time. "You know," said Carlos, "the city of Venice was actually sinking. Someday it would be completely underwater."

"Do you think Venice still exists?"

Carlos realized that maybe showing him the picture of a city that, in all probability, no longer existed was not the best idea. "Why don't we look at another book," he suggested to Joey, who immediately picked up another book entitled 1001 Recipes That You Can Make At Home. "What's this one about," Joey asked.

"This is a cookbook. It shows you how to prepare food and all the different kind of things you can eat."

"I wish that we had some more to eat."

"So do I," said Carlos which caused him to realize that his stomach was growling lightly at the thought of food. "Maybe this isn't the best book to be looking at right now. Why don't you pick another one?"

Joey picked up a book with spaceships on the cover. "Is this one about the invaders?"

Carlos took the book from him and looked at it carefully. It was the War of the Worlds by HG Wells. He smiled lightly and then turned to Joey. "It's about a different type of invaders, from Mars. It was written over 100 years ago by a very wise man. I guess he saw this one coming before anyone else did."

"So it is like the invaders that we have!" Joey leaped up.

"Not quite the same, this book is fiction."

"Oh," said Joey as he sat back down a bit disappointed before looking up at Carlos. "Did they defeat the invaders?"

"Sort of. It turns out that all of our technology was unable to defeat the invaders, but then they were defeated because they had no resistance to our germs. So the invaders all got sick and died."

"Maybe that will happen to our invaders!" Joey was beginning to get extremely excited.

Carlos smiled back at him. "I sure hope so." Carlos had never thought about it before, but it actually was interesting that the invaders have never come out of their ships. Maybe they really were worried about biological contamination. And if that were true then maybe HG Wells had a leg up on Nostradamus.

Carlos's thoughts were interrupted by a knock on Joey's door. "Joey," shouted Billie, "can I come in?"

Carlos quickly gathered up the books and hid them under Joey's bed and put his finger up to his lips indicating to Joey that he shouldn't tell Billie about the books. "Come in," Carlos shouted as he patted Joey on the head.

Billie opened the door as Carlos stood aside and left the room.

"Joey," said Billie, "I just wanted to say that I was sorry for yelling at you like that. But I am just trying to look out for you. I know that you are hungry and want to eat now, but we only have so much food to go around. If I let you eat the food now you would have no food later and would be even more hungry. Do you understand?"

Joey nodded his head.

"Good," said Billie. "So you understand why I did what I did?"

Joey nodded again. "I understand. When will I get to eat again?"

"You can eat again tomorrow."

"Maybe you can make something from the cookbook!" Joey shouted before he covered up his mouth when he realized what he had said.

"What cookbook?" Billie demanded with an angry glare. "When have you ever heard of a cookbook?" That was when Billie suddenly realized what was going on. "Joey, do you have a book?"

Joey shook his head. "No, of course not. I wish I had a book."

"You do have a book," said Billie as he grabbed Joey's shirt. "Tell me where the book is."

Joey began to scream and Cindy and Carlos ran into the room. "What the hell do you think you're doing," shouted Cindy as she ran over and pushed Billie off of Joey. "Get off of him."

Billie drew back and turned towards Carlos and pushed him up against the wall. "You son of a bitch. You brought him books didn't you?"

"Look I –" began Carlos before Billie slammed his head against the wall and then walked over to Joey.

"Joey," said Billie as he slowly approached, "show me where your brother Carlos has hidden the books."

"Leave him alone," said Carlos as he grabbed Billie who then threw him off and punched him in the face, causing him to go falling to the floor.

"Stop it, stop it right now!" yelled Cindy as she slapped Billie in the face. Joey began crying.

Billie backed off and pointed accusingly at Carlos, who was just rising from the floor and holding his bloody nose. "You, you take your damn books and get the hell out of this house."

"Billie!" Cindy shouted as Joey continued to wail.

"You shut up," said Billie before turning back to Carlos. "I want you out of this house right now. You may be my brother, but you should know better. And if I ever see you again bringing books near Joey or endangering this family, I swear to God I will kill you."

Carlos went to stay with Jerry, and together they decided they should make plans to hide their books. The enforcers were beginning a crackdown on dissidents after a local boy was caught reading a military textbook. They hung him in the village square and left his body to rot as an example.

"I am beginning to get worried," said Carlos as he and Jerry ate their meager rations of bread and water.

"Don't worry," said Jerry, "I think we found a good hiding place for the books. I don't think the enforcers will think to look inside of a hollowed out tree. We just have to make sure that if we want to read the books that we only go out at night to retrieve them and put them back before the day. The enforcers are less vigilant at nighttime, although I heard that they are thinking of cracking down on that as well."

"That's not what I meant," said Carlos. "I mean I am worried about Joey. It has been three weeks since I left home and I have no idea what is going on. I haven't heard from Cindy at all."

"That is perturbing," said Jerry.

"If everything was alright by now she would've tried to contact me. I just hope that Billie hasn't done anything drastic. He knows that I would probably try to contact Cindy, so he is the type of person who might forbid her from trying to contact me."

"What was it that turned your brother into such a bastard?"

"We never got along. Some people are just naturally suited to a world ruled by brutality and ignorance, and unfortunately he is one of those people. But I am not going to stand for this any longer. Tomorrow I'm going to make an attempt to contact Cindy."

The next day Carlos woke up early in hopes of visiting Cindy. But he awoke to a much more tragic news. As soon as he went down to have his single piece of bread for breakfast, he saw Jerry there with a worried look on his face.

"They have arrested Andrew!" Jerry shouted.

"What?!" Carlos could not believe what he was hearing.

"The enforcers, they're going around doing a random sweep. The fact that they found someone with military books has probably got them all paranoid that there could be others. They searched Andrew's house and found the books and now he is being held under interrogation."

Carlos put his hand under his chin and began pacing. He turned to Jerry. "Do you think that he will finger us?"

"Andrew is loyal, but I heard they have methods of interrogation that are completely flawless. I think we have to get out of here. We aren't safe."

"But what about Cindy and Joey?"

"It's not safe now."

"But I can't just abandon them. I have to try."

"Did you listen to what I just said? The enforcers are out in full force and are arresting people. For all we know they probably got Mark too."

"I'm sorry, but I can't leave them behind. I am not going to flee without knowing that Joey and Cindy are safe. There's no way you can talk me out of this. We both knew the risks."

Jerry slammed his fist against the wall but then looked at Carlos and nodded reluctantly. "I understand your reasons. I don't agree with them, but I know that I can't stop you." Jerry put his hand on his cheek and scratched his head before turning back to Carlos. "What are we going to do about the books?"

"I'll take them. You just get out of here. The books will just slow you down and make you a target."

"But what about you! Do you really want to risk making things worse by getting caught with a bunch of books."

"Some things are worth dying for, and I know you agree with me on that. Just please trust me in this instance. I know what I am doing."

Jerry paced back and forth, put his hand on Carlos's shoulder and said, "Okay. We will both go our separate ways for now and we will meet up in our secret hiding space in the woods. Then we will think of what to do next. I'll try to see what happened to Mark."

"Agreed."

"Just one more thing," said Jerry as Carlos turned to leave. "Good luck."

"You too."

Carlos gathered up the books and hid them in his knapsack. He really had no better way of hiding them, so he was just going to have to hope that he really did have luck enough to get home without running into any of the enforcers. It was a very stupid and dangerous plan, but he didn't really have any other options. He walked very nonchalantly and avoided all the major roads that the enforcers usually traveled on. He managed to make it home without running into any trouble and snuck in through the back. He may have been kicked out of the house, but Billie never thought to take his house key away from him, so that was one piece of luck on his side. He knew he was taking a great risk being there, but he wasn't going to leave Joey and Cindy to the likes of Billie.

As soon as he went in the back door he saw Cindy holding a glass of water which she promptly dropped causing it to shatter on the floor. "Carlos," she said in a state of shock as she put her hand over her mouth. "What are you doing here?"

"I have to flee. But I couldn't leave without knowing that you and Joey were safe. Billie isn't around, is he?"

Cindy shook her head. "No, but he could be back any minute now. He's joined the enforcers."

Carlos banged his fist on the countertop. "I should've known. This is exactly what I said would happen. But we have to get out of here. I'm not going to leave without you and Joey."

"But where are we going to go?"

"Jerry and I agreed to meet up in our secret meeting place in the woods. Then from there we will hopefully make it to the next town where we have friends in the resistance. They should be able to give us shelter for a while."

"But we can't just up and leave." Cindy began to cry and that was when Carlos noticed that she had a black eye.

"Did he do that to you," Carlos asked as he gently touched her eye with his finger.

"It was an accident. I snuck Joey some extra food and he got mad. He apologized afterwards."

"That bastard. You know that we have to get out of here. You enjoy aren't safe. You know that I am right."

"Big brother!" Joey said as he ran towards Carlos and hugged his leg. "I missed you so much. Have you come home to stay?"

"No Joey, I have come to get you and Cindy and take you someplace safe."

"Are we going on a trip?"

"Something like that?" Carlos said as he patted Joey's head.

"Are we going to go to Italy?"

"Not quite that far. But someplace better than this."

"What about Billie?" Cindy interrupted.

"Yes, what about Billie," said Billie as he walked in the door. He began to glare at Carlos. "And what are you doing here? I thought I told you I would shoot you if I ever saw you here again."

"If you're going to do it then just do it," said Carlos. "Show Joey the right thing to do and brutally murder his brother in front of him."

Billie raised his gun towards Carlos and his hand began to shake until he put it down as his lip began to quiver. "Damn you," he said, "God damn you. They're looking for you you know. I was actually given orders to bring you in, dead or alive."

"So do it then," said Carlos. "Show what a big man you are and kill your brother."

"Don't do it," Joey said as he began to cry.

Billie ran his fingers through Joey's hair and patted him on the head. "Joey," he said, "I want you to go with Carlos and Cindy."

Carlos and Cindy looked at each other with a baffled look and noticed that Billie was crying.

"Brother," Carlos said as he reached over and put his hand on Billie's shoulder, only to have him push it away.

"You were right," said Billie. "This is no kind of world for Joey to live in. You've got to go and take them away from this place. I don't care where you take him, in fact it is best that I don't know at all, because what I don't know I can't tell the other enforcers. But I can help you."

"How?" Carlos asked.

"Put these on," said Billie as he took off his all black enforcer uniform and identification bands. "The enforcers won't bother one of their own. With any luck you can sneak out of here without being harassed."

"But what about you?" Cindy asked.

"Don't worry, I can take care of myself. But you have to take care of Joey. You have to teach him to read, to hope for the future. That isn't something that I can do."

"You could come with us," said Carlos.

"No, I can't. Just go. You don't have a lot of time. The other enforcers were supposed to meet back here in another hour. Maybe with a head start you can get out of here and I can buy you some time by saying that I saw you going in the opposite direction."

They all stood there staring at Billie for a moment, before Carlos realized that it was their only chance. He changed into Billie's clothes, they gathered up a few supplies and prepared to leave. As Carlos was leaving he turned once more to Billie and said, "Thank you."

Billie shooed them out of the house as he covered his face with his hand.

Using Billie's enforcer outfit as a disguise, they were able to make it to the meeting place in the woods where they met up with Jerry, who was alone.

"Freeze," said Carlos as he raised his gun at Jerry.

"Carlos," said Jerry as he put his hands up with a confused look on his face. Carlos lowered his gun, laughed and hugged Jerry.

Jerry withdrew from Carlos's embrace and looked him over. "Why are you dressed like that? And what happened with Billie?"

"There is no time to explain. Did you find out what happened to Mark?"

"He didn't make it. The enforcers got him."

"Damn. But we can't stay here. Did you contact other members of the resistance?"

"I managed to get in touch with members of the resistance in the next town over. They can take us there for now. We should be safe there for a while."

"Sounds like a plan."

Just as they were about to leave they heard some voices off in the distance. It was the enforcers.

"What are we going to do now?" Cindy asked as she grabbed Carlos's arm protectively.

"Jerry," Carlos said, "you go ahead with Cindy and Joey. I will try to divert their attention and send them in the other direction. I'll catch up with you after that."

"But," protested Jerry.

"No buts, just go!" Carlos commanded.

Jerry and Cindy ran off with Joey just as three enforcers arrived and saw Carlos standing there alone.

"What are you doing out here all by yourself?" asked the first enforcer.

"I thought I spotted the fugitives going in that direction," Carlos said as he pointed in the opposite direction to where Jerry and Cindy had run off with Joey.

"Why didn't you pursue them?" asked the second enforcer.

"Hey," said the third enforcer, "I recognize you. You're the brother of Billie. You're one of the wanted fugitives. What are you doing wearing his uniform?"

Jerry and Cindy were hiding with Joey in the trees several yards away and trying to keep quiet. Jerry took out some binoculars and could see Carlos talking to the other enforcers. He couldn't hear what they were saying, but then he saw one of the enforcers draw a gun and fire into Carlos's chest causing him to fall dead to the floor. He let out a gasp.

"What's wrong," whispered Cindy.

"We've got to run," said Jerry. "Now!"

The three of them began to run as gunshots from the enforcers rang out through the forest. Joey began to cry, although Cindy tried to silence him, while fighting back tears herself. Eventually they managed to lose the enforcers, who gave up pursuing them once they could no longer track them.

Later that night they made it into the next town where they took refuge at the home of one of the resistors. Cindy was trying to control herself and was stroking Joey's hair and trying to calm him down. That was when Jerry came over with a bag of books.

"Joey," said Jerry as he kneeled down and put his hand on Joey's shoulder and took the bag of books over to him. "I know that you are very sad right now, but your brother told me if anything happened to him he wanted to make sure to give these to you."

Joey continued to sniffle but fought back tears. "But who is going to teach me to read?"

"I can teach you to read," said Cindy as she hugged Joey tightly.

"Can I look at the books now," said Joey, still sobbing.

"Sure you can, if that will make you feel better," said Jerry. "Do you think that that would make you feel better?"

Joey nodded with a sniffle as he took a book out of the bag. "What is this one called?"

Jerry looked at the cover of the book. The title read The Bioterrorist's Cookbook.

Cry Apocalypse

The prison bus puttered along the desert road shaking and bumping the whole way. Every couple of seconds they would hit a bump in the road.

"Hey watch the bumps," shouted Arnold as he rattled his handcuffs. "Do you have to drive so damn fast?"

"Not in a rush to get to prison?" laughed the bus driver from the front seat. "Doesn't matter to me and it shouldn't matter to you either. Whether it takes us an hour to get there or three hours, you still aren't getting out for at least 8 to 10 years."

"What about good behavior?" Arnold shouted.

"I don't know, have you ever shown any before?" asked the bus driver.

Arnold didn't answer.

"Well I guess there's a first time for everything," said the bus driver with a snort. "But I wouldn't expect it coming from you, with a history of rape, assault and drug dealing."

"I was framed. I'm innocent. Scouts honor."

"You were a Boy Scout? Did you make it to Eagle?"

"No, I got kicked out for playing doctor with a female camper on a coed field trip."

"I'm not surprised. But maybe you really are innocent."

"You think?"

"Yeah, and my butt sings show tunes. You criminals are all alike, it really amazes me."

"I swear to God that I am fully innocent, and if I am lying may he strike me dead right now."

"Well I hope he'll take you up on that –" and that was when Arnold felt the prison bus begin to swerve violently. He heard the bus driver mutter some obscenity before he felt the bus tip over causing him to bang his head on the ceiling.

After he recovered his equilibrium and stopped seeing spots, he realized that the back door of the prison bus had flung open. He slowly crawled and made his way out to find he was on the highway. He looked to see that the bus was on its side and had apparently collided with a couch that some idiot must have left on the road. How's that for luck?

"Thanks God," said Arnold as he put his still handcuffed hands together in mock prayer. "But I think you know I wasn't actually innocent. That or you aren't as bright as you have been made out to be."

Arnold made his way to the front of the bus where he saw the bus driver and the accompanying police officer both with their bodies through the windshield. He walked over and realized that they were completely dead. He kicked them contemptuously a few times. "Buckle up, it's the law," Arnold laughed as he realized neither of them were wearing their seatbelts.

After sifting around for a while he managed to find the keys to his handcuffs and unhooked himself. He threw the handcuffs aside, reached down and took the police officer's gun. "This will come in handy," he said as he placed the gun into his pocket. "And this time I didn't even need a God damned background check."

He began to hike, trying to walk as rapidly as he could to get away from the scene of the accident as fast as possible before anyone realized he was missing. It wouldn't be long before they had police helicopters out searching for him.

Fortunately for him he soon saw a car on the road and waved it down. He walked over to the window and motioned for the man to roll it down.

"Car breakdown?" the man asked as he rolled down the window.

"Something like that," Arnold said, which was when the man noticed that he was wearing an orange jumpsuit and had a bloody cut on his forehead.

"Wait a minute, are you some kind of criminal?" The man began to swallow deeply in fear.

"Ding ding ding! We have a winner. You must be a real fucking Einstein. What gave me away?"

"Sorry, I don't give rides to criminals."

"Well that was pretty damn stupid of you to stop then," said Arnold as he put the gun to the man's head. "Now get out of the car, get undressed and exchange clothes with me. But first throw your keys down on the floor."

The man did as he said and took off his clothes and placed his keys down on top of them.

"So you're going to let me go now?" the man asked as he stood there trembling naked trying to cover his genitals with his hands.

"Nope," said Arnold. "I just didn't want you to be wearing your clothes when I shot you, because that would ruin them."

"What!" the man shouted, but before he could say another word Arnold had already shot him through the head.

Arnold rapidly changed out of his prison clothes and dressed in the man's Hawaiian shorts and tie-dyed T-shirt. It wasn't exactly his style, but it was better than a prison jumpsuit for the moment. He quickly pocketed the man's wallet, got in his car and began to drive away. He didn't need to stick around here and risk facing the additional charges of murder and grand theft auto.

Samantha was on the phone with her friend Fran as she was taking the curlers out of her hair.

"I can't believe that you would stay with that psycho," Fran said.

"He's not a psycho, he's just impulsive."

"He's a rapist and a junkie. How could you stay with a man who not only cheats on you but sexually assaults other women."

"He said that he was innocent."

"They all say they're innocent. Somehow I doubt he's innocent when they have multiple witnesses, DNA evidence and a previous criminal record against him. How can you possibly believe that this man is telling you the truth?"

"I'll admit that he has his faults, but I just can't picture him as some sort of creepy rapist."

"You're not thinking this through rationally. He's cheated on you before, he's stolen from you and he's even hit you on several occasions. I don't know how much longer I can put up with this Sam. I'm your friend and I know that this person is bad for you. Why can't you see that?"

"You don't know Arnold the same way that I do. He can be aggressive sometimes, but that's just his whole bad boy routine. He can be sweet sometimes too. And he's an excellent lover."

"And you're really going to wait for him for 8 to 10 years to get out of prison? He's hardly gone even a month without cheating on you. I just don't understand how you could be loyal to such a violent jerk."

"You're just jealous."

"Believe me honey, I'm not jealous of you and Arnold. I'd sooner take a vow of celibacy and become a nun before I would put up with an abusive criminal like Arnold."

That was when Samantha heard a knocking at her window.

"Sam, are you still there?"

"Fran, I think I have to go."

Before Fran could say anything else Samantha turned off her phone and put it down on the table. She then slowly went to the window to see Arnold's face staring at her. She jumped back for a moment, having been startled, but then slowly opened the window.

"Arnold," she said as he slowly crawled in through the window. "What are you doing here?"

"Happy to see me baby?" he said with a big smile, which was when she noticed that he had a big gash in his forehead.

"But I thought you were going to prison."

"I got let out for good behavior."

"But weren't you just supposed to arrive today? This doesn't make sense Arnold. Be honest with me."

"Okay, okay," he said as he tried to calm her down. "I managed to escape."

"Escape? How?"

"There was an accident. Look, I don't have time to explain. The police are going to come looking for me and this is probably one of the first places they're going to look. I have to get out of here pretty quickly and I want you to come with me."

"And go where?"

"I've got this place out in the desert where I can hold up for a while. So are you going to come with me or not?"

"This is all so sudden."

"Don't you love me?"

"I do Arnie, you know that."

"Well prove it. If you really love me you'll come with me. So are you in?"

Samantha looked into his eyes and saw that he was pleading with her and she could never say no to him. She slowly nodded and kissed him. "Let me just get a few things ready and we'll leave right away."

"I knew I could count on you baby." Arnold lifted Samantha in the air and twirled her around. "We're going to live the life of outlaws from now on. Trust me, you'll love it."

Samantha didn't know what to think, but she wasn't about to abandon Arnold now. As quickly as possible she packed her things and they were on their way.

In less than an hour they had managed to arrive at Arnold's desert hideout. It was in the middle of nowhere far out in the desert, at least a half-mile away from the road. His hideout amounted to little more than a large wooden cabin whose only windows were so covered in dust there was no way to even see outside of them.

"Here we are, our home away from home," said Arnold as he stretched out his arms in front of the cabin.

"This is it?" Samantha asked with a big frown.

"What?" Arnold asked as he folded his arms in annoyance.

"This place looks like a dump Arnie."

"Well sorry if it's not a palace. This wasn't exactly built as the Taj Mahal. It's supposed to be low key."

"Is low-key supposed to be a code word for a rundown crap shack?"

"Quit your complaining. You haven't even seen the inside yet."

Arnold kicked open the door sending up a wave of dust. Once Samantha had stopped coughing and sneezing she looked around to see that the cabin was extremely dark and she jumped up in fear as a rat scurried past her feet.

"It looks even worse from the inside. Is there even a light in here? Or running water?"

"It has a generator but we have to conserve power, and there is an outhouse around back."

"Ewww. How long do we have to stay here?"

"Just until the heat dies down. I'm guessing a couple of days to a few weeks."

"A couple of weeks! I can't stay here for a couple of weeks. What if people start wondering where I am?"

"You can't tell anyone about this place. I'm the only one who knows about it. As far as most people know it's just an abandoned cabin in the middle of nowhere. It's the perfect place to hide out. It's also the perfect place to hide stuff."

"Hide stuff? Like what?"

Arnold reached under the mattress and pulled out a bag full of what looked like drugs, as well as a couple of clips of hundred dollar bills.

"This is a drug house?" Samantha gave a look of disgust.

"Look, I can't get caught with this stuff again. I'm already in enough trouble as it is. Besides, selling this stuff is going to keep us alive for as long as I have to keep a low profile."

"You know I don't like you dealing drugs Arnie."

"Where do you think I got the money for that ring I gave you?"

Samantha looked at the large ring on her finger and then looked at Arnold with a distressed look. "You mean you got this ring with drug money."

"Yes, still wanna complain?"

Actually he had stolen it from his ex-girlfriend, but Samantha didn't need to know that.

Samantha continued to frown and began to rub her belly, which had begun to rumble. "Do we have anything to eat? I didn't have time to eat dinner before you rushed me away."

"Calm down, you're not gonna die if you miss a meal. Maybe you could afford to lose a couple of pounds."

"That's a terrible thing to say to a woman."

"You know my motto – no fat chicks."

"You're horrible. I don't know why I ever agreed to come out here with you."

"Because you know I'm the best man you can get."

"I should leave right now. In fact, I think I will."

Samantha began to walk away but Arnold grabbed her by the shoulder. "Wait," he said as he turned around to face her. "I'm sorry. I've had a very stressful day. I'll get you something to eat. Just give me a couple of minutes to put on some type of a disguise."

"Why don't I go get the food?"

"No. I'll get the food. You just get settled here. I promise I'll be back soon. Just stay here and don't talk to anyone."

"Okay," said Samantha as she sat down on the bed. "But try to hurry. It's probably not safe for you to be out there very long, even if you are wearing a disguise."

"Don't worry, I know what I'm doing."

Arnold quickly got dressed and put on a fake mustache and sunglasses. He also figured that maybe he would dye his hair later on. He took Samantha's car and drove off leaving her isolated in the cabin. She sat back on the bed, sighed and decided to take a nap.

Arnold drove into town trying to be as inconspicuous as possible. After picking up some groceries he decided that he would stop by the bar for a drink. He thought that perhaps he should try to get back to Samantha, but one little drink wouldn't delay him too much he figured.

As soon as he got into the bar, one drink soon became two, then three, then four. Before long he was completely wasted and began to develop a bit of a roving eye. All the women in the bar suddenly looked extremely attractive to him.

"Hey good-looking," he said as he approached an equally inebriated brunette. "How would you like to have some fun with Arnie tonight?"

"You don't have a girlfriend?" she asked.

"Yeah, and I'm looking at her right now. You interested?"

The brunette laughed, then hiccuped a bit. "I don't know, should I be?"

"Why don't we go to a motel," said Arnold as he flashed his money clip at her.

"You know I'm not a prostitute."

"Everyone's got their price."

"You're a real sleazebag you know."

"Yeah, so is that a no then?" He waved the wad of cash under her nose ruffling the hundreds right in her face.

"I want all of it."

"What will that get me?"

"One night, whatever you like."

Arnold smiled. "Sounds good. Let's go find a room."

Arnold lead his catch of the evening to the nearest motel room and took full advantage of everything money could buy. Then he passed out and decided to spend the night there. When he woke up the brunette woman was gone, and so was most of his money. But that was no problem, he had a lot more back at the cabin. That's when he remembered Samantha. Oh well, what she doesn't know won't hurt her. He just has to think of a good excuse that she will accept.

Arnold ran into the cabin practically bursting the door down and waking Samantha up. "Arnold," she said as she pulled up in bed. "I was worried about you. Where were you?"

He had to think. What type of excuse would she possibly accept? He just shouted out the first thing that came to mind. "It's the Apocalypse!"

"What?! What the hell you talking about? What do you mean it's the Apocalypse?"

"I didn't know how to break it to you but things are terrible out there. I barely made it back here alive."

"What happened?"

"There was an EMP burst."

"A what?"

"Electromagnetic pulse. It totally wiped out the power grid. All the electricity has been wiped out, except for our generator, it's pulse protected."

"What about my cell phone?"

"Cell phones won't work."

"Well let me try it," Samantha said as she started to take out her phone, but Arnold grabbed it out of her hand and threw it against the wall, causing it to shatter to pieces.

"No!" Arnold shouted. "All the phone lines are dead."

"Well you didn't need to destroy my phone like that. What if the power comes back?"

"Aren't you listening to what I am saying? The entire power grid is destroyed. It's the complete collapse of society. People are out there rioting and killing each other for all the remaining supplies. I told you I barely made it back alive myself."

"What happened?"

"It's too terrible to talk about. Trust me, you'd rather not know. But we'll be safe here."

"For how long?"

"I don't know. It could be forever."

"Forever!"

"I don't know. But we have to prepare for the long term. We will have to ration all of our supplies to make them last as long as possible."

Samantha put her hands on her head and stood there in total shock. "I just can't believe all this is happening. I'm scared Arnold."

"Don't worry. I'll be here to protect you. And I'll get supplies as we need them."

"Oh Arnold, I'm sorry for everything I said before. I know that you are just looking out for my welfare. And look on the bright side, if society has collapsed the police will be too busy with other problems to worry about one escaped criminal like yourself."

Arnold snickered. "I guess so. I never thought of it like that. But just the same, I think it is best that we keep to ourselves and not mention any of this to anyone. I'm serious now. If anyone comes to the cabin when I am not here you have to not let them in. It isn't safe to trust anyone but me. Do you understand?"

"I think so."

"Dammit," said Arnold as he slammed his hands down on the bed. "Don't tell me I think so. Do you understand?"

"Yes, I understand your every word."

"And if you want to survive you'll follow my every command, right?"

Samantha nodded in agreement.

"Good, then we understand things."

"What should we do first?"

"Well, I'm pretty hungry, so why don't you make us breakfast?"

"Okay."

"But not too big a breakfast. Remember, we have to ration our supplies."

Samantha nodded and began to cook a breakfast on the electric oven. She made them some bacon and eggs, the bulk of which Arnold ate. Samantha was feeling too nervous to eat very much.

"That was a good breakfast," said Arnold as he licked the remains of his fingers. "You're a pretty good cook Sam."

Samantha smiled and nodded. "So what should we do now?"

"Well I can think of something," said Arnold as he began to slowly lift Samantha's shirt over her head.

The next couple of days passed by quickly. Samantha and Arnold passed the days by eating, having sex and getting high. Arnold seemed to be enjoying himself more than Samantha did though, as she still couldn't stop worrying about what might've happened to her family and friends.

"Arnie, do you think things have settled down by now?"

"It's only been a week. The collapse of society usually isn't something that passes over that quickly."

"I just wish that I could check on my family and my friends. They must be worried about me and I can't even call them."

"It's not safe for us to go home. I'm sure your family and friends are fine, and if they aren't we probably don't have any way of finding out. Home is over an hour away, and it's not safe to travel that far under these conditions." That was when Arnold started to realize that he was getting restless being cooped up there all alone with Samantha for an entire week. "But we are getting low on supplies. Maybe I should go into town and see what I can find."

"Is that safe?"

"No, but I don't think that we have a choice."

"Maybe I should come with you."

"No!" Arnold shouted as he pointed at her. "I strictly forbid it. Besides, you're much safer staying here and guarding the rest of our supplies. I'll leave you with a gun just in case. But just remember, whatever happens don't talk to anyone or let anyone in. Shoot first and ask questions later."

Samantha looked extremely nervous, but nodded feebly in acknowledgment. "Just hurry back as soon as possible," she said as she bit her nails with worry.

"Don't worry, I'll be fine," said Arnold as he slammed the door behind him.

As soon as Arnold got into the car and far enough away from the cabin he cranked up the air-conditioning and blasted the radio at maximum volume. "It's good to get out of there," said Arnold as he let the air blow on his sweat soaked face. "It's like an oven in that God damned cabin. If I spent another day there in that rats' nest I think I would go completely crazy."

He then changed the radio station. "Police are still on the lookout for a wanted criminal, Arnold Richmond, who escaped when his prison van crashed on the way to bring him to serve an 8 to 10 year sentence for rape, assault and drug dealing. He is considered to be potentially armed and dangerous and if anyone has any information on him they are encouraged to call the police right away."

"Damn coppers," said Arnold as he turned off the radio. "I kinda wish there really was some type of electromagnetic pulse, that would sure take the heat off of my ass." He laughed to himself. "Electromagnetic pulse. The complete breakdown of society. That stupid Samantha will believe anything. I picked a real winner with her. A total airhead. Luckily she's hot. But I was never a one woman man. It's time for me to get into town and get me some action."

While Arnold was driving rapidly towards the town, Samantha was at home sitting on her bed and sulking. All she could think about were her family and friends and how worried they must be about her. For all she knew they could possibly be dead right now. That was when her thoughts were interrupted by a sound from outside.

She quickly ran out to see what all the fuss was and peaked out the door. Flying overhead was what looked like a police helicopter, or was it a government helicopter? She quickly slammed the door behind her and went to hide under the bed. What if they saw her? What if they were after Arnold?

But then another thought occurred to her – how are helicopters flying if there was no electricity anywhere in the country? Something did not add up here.

Arnold had arrived in town at the bar and picked up another woman that he managed to seduce with the promise of money and drugs. They quickly found a motel room and had several hours of fun snorting drugs, making love and pigging out on snack foods.

While his woman of the evening was passed out on the bed he decided to take a shower to wash away all of the sweat. It's amazing how much you sweat when you are sitting out in the desert in a cabin with poor ventilation and no air conditioning.

When he came out feeling refreshed he saw that the woman he was with had put on the television news. There was a report on about the continued police search to find him and they posted a photograph of him on the news. That is when she turned to him with wide eyes and began pointing with her lips trembling and unable to form words.

"God dammit," Arnold said. "I don't suppose I could pay you off to keep your mouth shut, can I?"

She continued to sit there shaking in fear.

"Well that's too bad then," he said as he drew a gun and put a bullet right between her eyes. "Looks like I can't come back to this place anymore. Luckily I didn't sign in using my real name. But just the same, I gotta get the hell out of here."

Arnold raced back to the cabin as fast as he could go, not even thinking what he was going to tell Samantha when he got back home. Slowly but carefully he opened the door to find Samantha sleeping on the bed. As the light from outside hit her face she slowly opened her eyes and woke up. "Arnold," she said as she rubbed her eyes. "Is that you?"

"No, it's the boogie man," he said scornfully. "Of course it's me. And if you didn't think it was me who should have been prepared. If it wasn't me I could have been someone here to rape or kill you. You have to be more careful."

"Arnie, there's something I've been meaning to bring up with you."

"What is it?"

"Well you said the electromagnetic, what did you call it?"

"Electromagnetic pulse."

"Yeah, that's it. You said that the electromagnetic pulse wiped out all the electricity and the power in the country."

"That's right."

"Well then how come today I saw a helicopter flying overhead?"

"You saw a helicopter!" Arnold's heart started beating really fast and he began to sweat. "When did you see a helicopter?"

"While you were out today."

"Did it see you?"

"I don't know."

"Dammit," said Arnold as he slammed his fist against the wall. "Did it see you or didn't it?"

"I don't think so."

"Good, then we should still be safe."

"But Arnold, how is it possible for a helicopter to be flying if the electromagnetic pulse thingy wiped out all the electricity?"

"Don't you know anything? Helicopters and airplanes are protected from electromagnetic pulse damage so that they can fly during a lightning storm. It was probably a government helicopter going to gas or fire upon the rioters."

"Is it really that bad," said Samantha as she put her fingers up to her mouth.

"It's even worse than you can imagine. I barely made it back here again. I didn't even manage to get us any supplies I had to leave in such a rush."

"What happened?" Samantha was beginning to get watery eyed and began trembling.

Arnold had to think fast. Think of some type of believable excuse. "It's a viral epidemic."

"A viral epidemic? I thought you said it was electromagnetic pulse."

"I did. But that was just the first stage of the invasion."

"Invasion?" Now Samantha was beginning to panic and hyperventilate. "What invasion?"

"There are rumors that it's the North Koreans or the Chinese. They launched the electromagnetic pulse against us and then they fired biological weapons as part of the second wave of the attack. Now everyone is getting sick and turning into mindless zombies."

"Zombies!"

"Yes, zombies."

"But zombies aren't real."

"That's what I always thought too, but you haven't seen what I have seen."

Samantha stood there with a look of shock and disbelief on her face. "What are we going to do?"

"I think it is best that we just stay here for now."

"But what about the zombies? What if they come and find us?"

"Trust me, we are safer here. Zombies are pretty stupid and they tend to stay in crowded areas. I think if we stay out here in the middle of nowhere this entire thing will blow over soon enough."

"How long?"

"Well how the hell should I know?! It's not like this type of stuff has ever happened before. But I do know that when society is collapsing it is those who stay off the grid like we are who have the best chances of survival. We have to completely isolate ourselves from all of humanity."

"What about all my family and friends?"

"They're zombie chow by now!" Arnold put his hand over his mouth. "Sorry, that was insensitive. But this is the type of world that we have to get used to living in now. It's just you and me against the entire world. And if we are going to survive we have to trust each other completely. Now I have to ask you, do you trust me?" He put his hands on her shoulders and gently sat her down. "So do you trust me?"

Samantha sat there staring up at him before giving a feeble nod. "Yes, I trust you."

"Good, that's good," said Arnold as he kissed Samantha on the forehead. "So you're going to listen to everything I say and follow my every order."

"Mmmhmm," Samantha managed to mumble.

"Okay then. So let's assess our situation. There is no electricity anywhere in the country, and everyone is turning into zombies. We only have a limited amount of food so we are going to have to ration everything to last as long as possible. Don't worry, I promise we'll get through this together. The only person you've got in this world that you can trust is me. You know that I would never lie to you, right?"

"Oh Arnold," she said as she hugged him and began to cry into his chest. "Here I've been so suspicious and mean to you, when all you wanted to do was protect me. I feel like such a total bitch."

"It's okay, I forgive you. The end of the world does these type of things to people."

Arnold held her closely and started to feel her up, and in no time flat they found themselves in bed together. The Apocalypse certainly has its fringe benefits, Arnold thought to himself.

Several days passed without incident and supplies were once again running low as Arnold was getting more and more restless being cooped up in that suffocating cabin with nobody but Samantha all day.

"I think it is time that I go into town for some more supplies," said Arnold as he began to pack his bags.

"But what about all the zombies and the rioters?"

"It's definitely a risk, but we have to get supplies because soon there won't be anything left. I have to risk it. I'm certainly not going to let my best girl die of starvation out in the desert, now am I?"

"Oh Arnold, you're so brave and selfless. I don't deserve you." She kissed him on the lips.

He put his hands over her lips. "Don't say that baby, nobody deserves me as much as you do."

"Please hurry back this time though. Every time you leave I worry."

"I'll try to get back as soon as I possibly can. You just remember not to let anyone in as they could be infected or here to kill you. If anyone comes in looking infected, even me, you have to shoot them."

"But I've never fired a gun before in my life."

"I know, but the world has changed. You can't be too safe. If anyone other than me comes to the door I want you to shoot first and ask questions later. You got that?"

Samantha nodded and kissed him one last time. "Oh Arnold, I can't believe how you're willing to risk life and limb just for me. You are so brave."

"Well you know there's no one in the world more important to me than you. Don't worry, I'll be back soon as you're the only girl for me."

As soon as Arnold was out the door he raced in his car into town as fast as he could and stopped at the strip club. "Hey hey hey baby," Arnold whistled at the first stripper he came up to. "How many 20s do I have to stuff in your G string for you to take it all off?"

"You're a pig," said the stripper.

"Well oink oink baby. Your job is to make this piggy squeal!"

Arnold proceeded to stuff bill after bill into the stripper's G string until he had spent an entire wad of money. He didn't even think to buy any supplies while he was there. Oh well, he would just tell Samantha that they would have to ration things more closely. He could always make another trip back into town in a few days.

Just as he was getting ready to leave he noticed there was an announcement on the TV that everyone had gathered around. "What's going on?" he asked.

"The president is about to make an announcement," said one of the men gathered around the TV.

"My fellow Americans, I don't know how to say this," the president began to say as he stood there trembling, "but the CDC has reported an unusual outbreak. A viral epidemic seems to have turned people into rampaging psychopaths foaming at the mouth. As insane as this sounds, they're calling it a zombie outbreak."

"Is this for real," Arnold laughed. "Well there's some weird synchronicity there."

"What do you mean?" the man next to him asked.

"Nothing, it would take too long to explain. But I think I have to be getting back to my girlfriend because she will probably be worrying about me."

As Arnold was walking out of the club he bumped into a man who vomited up a ton of bile right at his feet. "Hey buddy, watch where you're puking," Arnold said as he pushed him aside. But the man looked up and his face was completely yellow and he had red glowing eyes. He was drooling bile all over the place, lunged forward and bit Arnold hard on the arm.

"Hey, what the hell is wrong with you," Arnold said as he pushed the man down. "That freaking bastard just bit me."

Everyone turned and looked at Arnold, then one man pointed at him and shouted, "He's infected!"

"What did that guy have rabies or something?"

"That man is going to become a zombie. Quick, shoot him!"

"What?!" shouted Arnold. "Is this some kind of a joke?"

Arnold saw the man drawing a gun, quickly pulled out his own gun, shot the man in the head and ran out of the strip club as quickly as his legs would carry him. He just as quickly ran to his car, started it up and sped off as fast as he could. As he made his way back to the cabin he noticed that he was feeling sicker and sicker and decided to put on the radio to take his mind off of it. All he heard were reports of viral outbreaks all across the country. The president was urging everyone to stay indoors and to shoot anyone who looked infected. He decided to turn off the radio.

"This couldn't be true," said Arnold as he began to spit up bile. "This is all just some sort of drug-induced hallucination caused by my guilt. Sort of a poetic irony."

Just as Arnold could almost see the cabin coming up on the road he saw flash in the sky and what looked like a mushroom cloud off in the distance. His car suddenly went dead, the battery completely fried.

"No no no," he said as he got out of the car. "This can't be happening. But I'm close enough to home that I can just walk there."

Arnold began running towards the cabin noticing that he was spewing more and more bile and that his flesh seemed like it was beginning to rot off of his body. He finally made it to the cabin door and kicked it in. "Samantha," he managed to say as he spewed bile all over the place.

Samantha screamed and pointed a gun at him. "Zombie!"

"No wait," Arnold said, but his speech was muffled by the fact that he was choking on his own vomit. Before he could raise his hands up to stop her he could feel a bullet enter his chest as he fell to the floor cracking his head on the table.

Slowly he began to point his hand in Samantha's direction and she lit a candle and came over to him. As she looked closer at him she realized it was Arnold. "Oh my God, what have I done!" Samantha shouted as she put the candle down on the floor and went to Arnold's side.

"Samantha," Arnold managed to choke.

"Oh Arnold, I'm so sorry," she said as she grabbed his hand. "But I saw you were zombie and there was nothing I could do. Do you forgive me?"

"I forgive," Arnold managed to choke out as bile poured out the side of his mouth.

"Oh Arnold, you did everything you could to protect me and you ended up becoming a zombie protecting me. I'll never forget you, my one true love."

Arnold raised his hand one final time, put it against Samantha's cheek and then spit up one last round of bile before keeling over completely dead.

The next day Samantha made sure to bury Arnold's corpse just in case he came back again. She bid him a long and tearful goodbye, pounding the ground where she buried him and getting a long eulogy about how it was only because of him that she managed to survive the Apocalypse.

Samantha managed to survive on her own for the next couple of weeks until the epidemic was contained. Eventually rescue teams found her cabin and got her to a shelter where she was reunited with her friends and family. Every so often she would visit Arnold's grave out in the desert and place a single rose on it, never once questioning his loyalty to her.

"I guess I was wrong about him," said Fran. "I guess I am too quick to believe the worst of everyone."

"I can understand," said Samantha. "We all like to believe that everyone gets just what they deserve in the end, but I guess that isn't always true."

"I guess we'll never know," said Fran. "But I am sure that wherever Arnold is now he is getting everything that he has earned."

And many feet below them, packed under many feet of tightly packed desert earth lay Arnold, and he was not quite dead as he initially seemed, but he wasn't getting out from where he was anytime soon. Maybe in another 8 to 10 years....

Call Me When the World Ends

Mrs. Carmen stood there staring at the phone. She had been meaning to call her daughter for the longest time. Every year around the holidays she tells herself that she is going to call her daughter and make up with her, but every year she hesitates as she doesn't know what she can say to her daughter to make things right.

Her daughter had married a man that she did not approve of more than 20 years ago and they have not spoken since. Not a single day goes by where she hadn't thought about her daughter, and every holiday that passed she would spend the day sitting there staring at the phone. She hadn't even ever met her own grandchildren – two girls and a boy. That hurt her more than anything.

And now once again it was Christmas Eve and here she was staring at the phone. She would go to reach for the phone, pick it up and roll it around in her hand and then slam it down. But this year she told herself she would call. But that's what she has been saying for the last two decades.

Slowly she reached for the phone, picked it up and put it to her ear. She began to dial 217-5656. She got a ring, then two rings, then three. Her heart began to beat faster and faster and she began to panic. She slammed down the phone and pulled the cord right out of the wall.

Well, maybe next year. The same thing she says to herself every year. But she isn't getting any younger. At age 76 with chronic emphysema she doesn't know just how many more holiday seasons she will live to see.

She plugged the phone back in, once again picked it up, stared at it and placed it down on the receiver. Maybe not next year, but definitely not today.

She decided she would put on the news to try and take her mind off of it. She flipped the TV to channel five to see that there was breaking news, although the TV appeared to be extremely static and was getting bad reception. She turned the volume up because she was extremely hard of hearing.

The newscaster looked as pale as a ghost as he slowly read the news from his Teleprompter. "Reports are coming in from NASA that the recent chaotic weather and satellite interference is due to GammaRay bursts. These are explosions that take place out in the depths of space and are extremely destructive. Most of them are so far away from Earth that they are barely even noticed. But these recent GammaRay bursts have been sending large amounts of radiation towards the Earth. Scientists tracking the phenomenon estimate that the next GammaRay burst could wipe out all life on the Earth."

That was all she heard before the picture got too filled with static for her to make out what the newscaster was saying. She had no idea what a GammaRay burst was, but it sounded like something pretty serious. But she never bought into any of this end of the world's stuff. She had heard that many times before.

She laughed quietly to herself and then looked at the phone again. No way the world was going to end, not a chance in hell.

She took out a cigarette and began to smoke. Her lungs were pretty much doomed already, so why bother quitting now. She blew rings of smoke through the air and began to laugh even louder. "GammaRay bursts," she snorted to herself. "What a joke." She continued to laugh and laugh, and then realized that she was crying.

Why was she crying? She certainly didn't believe that the world was going to end. But that was when she looked at herself in the mirror – wrinkled, old and gray-haired. Maybe the world wouldn't end tomorrow, but she couldn't be sure that she would be there herself.

She took a tissue and wiped away her tears. Then she reached for the phone, dialed her daughter's number once again and let it ring. Once, twice, three times, then four. Her hand began to shake and she was going to put the phone down when suddenly she heard someone pick up.

"Hello," came her daughter's voice on the phone. "Who is this?"

"Darcy, it's me. Merry Christmas. I think we need to talk."

As the sky began to light up brightly Mrs. Carmen smiled for the first time in 20 years. If this was the way the world was going to end she couldn't have been happier.

Preventative Measures

It started like it did every single time. I was just sitting peacefully in my bed trying to get a good nights sleep and I am awakened at three in the morning by a bright blinding blue light coming through my window. That's when I see them, those same little gray bigeyed midgets all standing around my bed looking at me like animals. I would punch them in the face if not for the fact that I was completely paralyzed.

Then came the next part of the routine – floating up through my window into their waiting ship. And then I am stripped naked and put onto a cold iron table as they poke and prod every orifice in my body with all their weird instruments, all the while telling me telepathically that they weren't here to hurt me. They sure as hell could've fooled me. But maybe they have a different view on what is hurtful than we do. Cultural differences and all that shit.

But then after they were done with all their examining and probing and various other embarrassing procedures that we need not speak of (if you're interested, Google it), then comes the grand finale – all the save the Earth propaganda.

It usually starts out with a nice video presentation about how wonderful the Earth is and how we were royally fucking it up with pretty much every single thing that we do. You know what I'm talking about, how we dump poison in our oceans and get all that oil over baby seals and seagulls and all that.

Next they step it up a notch. A simple environmental message doesn't hammer the message home enough, they've got to also point out what a bunch of violent assholes we were by showing us video after video of us blowing up the Earth with nuclear weapons, cracking it like an egg shell.

"Do you understand," comes the voice of the alien in my head.

"Yeah, human beings are Dicks," I say aloud. "If you've ever spent a day at the DMV anyone would realize that. You don't have to come here and pull me out of my nice comfortable bed at night to show me alien propaganda films about what a fucked up race of morons my species is. I could've figured that out on my own."

The alien stared at me with his big black eyes. You can never really tell what they were thinking as they all pretty much look the same. Call me a bigot, but I really couldn't tell one of these little gray fuckers from another. The only way that you ever know what they are thinking is when they telepathically slam their thoughts directly into your brain until your head's ready to explode.

Which is what he did at that moment, asking me once again whether I understood.

"Yes, I told you I got the fucking memo. What the hell do you want me to do about it? If you're so concerned about saving the Earth all the time then why don't you do something about it? You could easily solve this problem, so why don't you just do it yourself?"

And then I feel my head explode with all sorts of feelings of sadness and lamentations about what an irresponsible species we are and how we don't realize the true beauty of our planet and all that other environmentalist propaganda.

Finally I just get frustrated and shout at the top of my lungs while also thinking it very forcefully at him and say, "Why do you fucking care so much what we do with our planet?! Are you planning to take it over? And what's with all the collecting of biological materials. Is that just because you don't have confidence that we're going to save ourselves?"

Then he did something unexpected and he actually decided to answer my God damned question. I could hear his thoughts echoing loudly in my head. "We don't have confidence, because we have already seen the result."

"Say what?" I said as I scratched my head in confusion.

"Allow me to explain," I heard him say in my mind. "You see originally we first discovered your planet over 1000 years from now and it was a completely dead planet devoid of any form of life whatsoever. It was an environmentally devastated planet with a bunch of decaying ruined cities. It looked like there hadn't been life on the planet for many centuries. From what we could examine of the ruins your species had destroyed itself through a combination of environmental pollution and nuclear and biological warfare. You completely destroyed yourself and rendered your species extinct, along with your planet."

I stared at him, staring in disbelief as he showed me images of a post-apocalyptic Earth from more than 1000 years in the future. But he continued with his explanation.

"You were a very immature species who did not realize just how rare and precious a life-sustaining planet is in the universe. But if it makes you feel any better the majority of species don't realize this until it is too late. We had destroyed our own planet in a similar fashion and ever since have been trying to prevent other species from making the same mistakes that we did. We narrowly avoided complete extinction ourselves and have found many worlds in a similar state of devastation. There are several dead planets for every one civilization that manages to survive their technological adolescence."

"But you said when you found Earth originally it was completely destroyed already," I thought at him.

"That is true, but we possess the ability to travel both forwards and backwards through time. So when we discover a planet whose civilization has destroyed itself, we try to go back and find out what had gone wrong and how we could possibly prevent it."

"So that is why you are so interested in the human race?"

"Yes. We traveled backwards in time and found that the main place where you started to go wrong was with the devastation of the Japanese cities of Hiroshima and Nagasaki. We could see that the United States and what was then the Soviet Union were both leading your species towards complete and total destruction, so we decided to step in and start trying to alter you from your course of destruction, to take preventative measures. We originally did try contacting your leaders, but we soon realized that that was basically a dead end. But we have influenced common everyday people like yourselves, mostly on an unconscious level."

"So you are saying that all of these anti-nuclear movements, peace movements and environmentalist movements were all due to you?"

"That is correct."

"So you're a bunch of space hippies. And you didn't think we couldn't figure this out on our own?"

I don't think that the aliens were actually capable of showing any emotion through facial expression, but for a moment I almost felt like he was attempting to smile at me and he seemed to be slowly shaking his head from side to side. "If you had figured it out on your own then we wouldn't be here right now."

"Well in case you haven't noticed you haven't been doing the greatest job. The world is still in a pretty shitty state. Why don't you just contact us openly?"

"And do you think the majority of your race would greet us peacefully and cooperate?"

He had me there. Even I had to admit most of the time when I see these guys coming I feel like kicking them in the balls, if not for the fact that they don't seem to have any external genitals.

"I suppose you have a point there," I said aloud. "But do you think we have any chance of saving ourselves?"

"As it stands right now whenever we checked back on our progress we find that the Earth is still a barren wasteland in the future, but you might be improving slightly. Right now your chances are probably only 60% that you're going to completely destroy yourselves in the next century. And as pessimistic as that sounds it's an improvement from the 98% chance that we gave you when we first started stepping up our efforts after your second world war."

"So basically what you are saying is that we're still screwed."

"That is entirely up to you. All we can do is point you in the right direction, but it's up to you to listen and take action. The future of your planet is entirely in your hands. But just in case we've taken enough samples from you to re-create you should we fail to prevent your destruction. Maybe with a new start on a new planet you'll do better. But as far as someone like you is concerned this planet is all you've got, so you better take care of it or else you'll have to live with the consequences."

"So that's it. It's just good luck you're on your own. I think I have a couple more questions."

The alien turned his back to me and started walking out of the room.

"Hey you, I'm not done with you," I shouted at him as I began to run, but before I could get more than a few feet away I found myself slamming back into my bed and the little gray fuckers were already vanishing through the walls. "Thanks for nothing you worthless space hippies," I managed to shout before going unconscious.

When I woke up the next morning I had a real bitchin headache. There's nothing like an alien mind probe to give you one hell of a hangover. But what can you do, that's life, at least for some of us.

I went into the kitchen and decided to pop open a beer and sit down to hear all the pessimistic things on the morning news before deciding to turn it off. Maybe they really were right about us. I might not like their message, but I can't quite disagree with them.

In anger I crushed the beer can in my hand and threw it against the wall. I was about to get up and go shopping, but then I stopped, picked up the beer can and threw it in the recycling bin. "Happy now you space fuckers," I said as I walked out the door.

It too nice a day to stay at home being angry. If this world wasn't going to be here much longer, I might as well enjoy it while I still can. It really was a pretty beautiful planet, and if there is any slight thing I can do to reduce our chances of destruction down to 59%, then I guess it's better than nothing.

Oh great, they turned me into a space hippy. Oh well, I guess there are worse things you can be. I guess from here on in I'm part of the solution. "I just hope you're watching," I said as I looked up at the sky. "And I just hope we're listening."

History Lesson

"Okay class, today's lesson will be about technology," said Prof. Oakley as he wrote the word technology in chalk on the blackboard that was hanging from a tree branch. He then turned to face his students. "Now can anyone here tell me what technology is?"

A bunch of hands went up in the classroom. Prof. Oakley pointed to one boy in the front row. "Go ahead Riley."

"Technology is like machines and stuff," said Riley as he stood up to recite and then sat down.

"Good. Yes, machines are a big part of technology." Prof. Oakley wrote the word machines under the word technology on the blackboard before turning back to his students. "Technology is a group of machines, tools and systems that we use in order to solve problems and make our lives easier."

Another hand went up. Prof. Oakley pointed to the little blonde haired girl in the back row. "Yes, Jessica."

"Why don't we have technology anymore?" she asked as she stood up before sitting down once again.

"It's not true that we no longer have technology," began Prof. Oakley. "We just don't have technology that is as advanced as the technology we used to have."

"Why!" shouted a boy leaping up in the back row.

"Please don't speak unless spoken to Jacob," said Prof. Oakley as he waved his finger and to silence him. "But that is a good question and is actually the focus of today's lesson. When I was growing up, and when your parents were growing up, it is true that the world indeed had a lot of technology. In fact the entire world was driven by constant advances in technology. Our technology was advancing at such a rapid pace that people felt someday our technology would actually pose a threat to us. Few people took such a threat seriously, myself included. But we should have. Would you like to hear the story of what happened to all the technology that your parents have probably told you about?"

All the children murmured a bunch of yeahs as they all nodded in agreement.

"Okay," said Prof. Oakley as he motioned with his hands. "Now settle down and I will tell you the story of how mankind's technology turned against us. I was a professor of computer science working at MIT at the time when humanity created the first thinking machines."

"This," said Prof. Oakley's colleague Dr. Finnigan as he pointed to a computer screen, "is the AI 5000. It is the world's first true artificial intelligence and is going to transform everything from here on in. What you are seeing is history in the making."

"It doesn't look too impressive to me," said Prof. Oakley. "It looks just like any other computer."

"Looks can be deceiving," said Prof. Finnigan as he flipped the switch. "It is what is inside that matters. AI 5000, this is my colleague Prof. Oakley."

"Hi," said Prof. Oakley as he raised his hand and waved at the computer.

"Greetings Prof. Oakley," said the AI 5000. "I am pleased to meet you and I hope that I can be of assistance to you in solving any problems that you may have."

"I've seen computers that can talk before," said Prof. Oakley. "That's nothing new. That's been around for decades."

"But this computer can do more than just talk," said Prof. Finnegan. "Isn't that correct AI 5000?"

"That is correct Prof. Finnigan," said the AI 5000. "I can also reason. I am the first machine that has full self-awareness and has managed to pass your Turing test. I can tell from the tension in his voice that your colleague Prof. Oakley does not believe me, but he can tell you that I have already been very actively engaged in solving many problems that the finest human minds have been unable to solve."

"Is that true?" Prof. Oakley asked as he turned Prof. Finnigan, who nodded in response and then shot a big smile to Prof. Oakley. "What are you smiling about?"

"The AI 5000 is already being nominated for Nobel prizes in mathematics, physics, chemistry and literature."

"Literature too," laughed Prof. Oakley.

"You find that one to be the most unbelievable?" Prof. Finnigan asked. "You can conceive of a machine solving problems of a scientific nature, but you can't conceive of a machine ever writing a superior novel?"

"Next you are going to tell me he has painted a masterpiece and composed a symphony," Prof. Oakley said with fits of laughter.

"I have actually painted several pictures and composed numerous operettas," said the AI 5000. "But whether they are masterpieces is simply a matter of opinion."

"You really should take a look at his art and his music, and I have to say I have never read such a well constructed novel in my life," said Prof. Finnigan.

"You're serious, aren't you?" Prof. Oakley said as he stared at Prof. Finnigan with a look of disbelief.

"This is no joke," said Prof. Finnigan as he patted Prof. Oakley on the back. "We haven't broken our discovery to the world yet. We decided that we would allow his work to get out there first and be published under the names of real living humans who have worked with him. It is only now that he is winning all these awards and nominations that we are going to share with the world the true creator of these works."

"You've got to be kidding," Prof. Oakley said.

"My good friend, I think the AI 5000 is going to be putting us all out of jobs pretty soon."

Prof. Oakley was still skeptical but he agreed to take a look at everything AI 5000 had produced. He wasn't sure if this was all still some elaborate joke being played on him by his good friend and colleague, but he couldn't deny that everything that the AI 5000 had been claimed to have produced was sheer genius. Never had he been moved so deeply by works of art, music and literature. And he couldn't deny that all the scientific theories that the AI 5000 had worked out managed to pass peer reviews.

In the coming weeks the AI 5000 was revealed to the world as the genius behind all of these new theories, new scientific breakthroughs and an artistic renaissance. It didn't take long after that for the United States government to order the creation of more of these artificial intelligences and put them in charge of the country. Many were skeptical and hesitant, but that didn't stop Congress from approving all of these measures, and in no time flat the entire country and its defenses were all under the control of artificially intelligent machines. Not long after that almost all businesses put artificial intelligences in charge of all their major operations. Even those who were skeptical didn't hesitate when they realized they would lose out to the competition if they didn't also give in to accepting the greater efficiency and productivity that could only be achieved through the employment of artificial intelligence. It seemed like soon all the world's problems would be solved and the long predicted singularity would be achieved.

A student had risen his hand to interrupt Prof. Oakley's story. "Yes, Justin," said Prof. Oakley as he called on the boy in the middle row.

"My dad told me a little bit about this."

"And what did he tell you?"

"He said the machines made life better for everyone. He had a brain tumor but thanks to the discoveries of the artificial intelligences they managed to cure him."

"It is true that in the beginning these new machines, this new revolutionary technology, did indeed make life better for the vast majority of people. But did your dad ever tell you what happened after that?"

"He said he didn't want to talk about it. He said that he would tell me about it maybe when I was older. But he said that the machines were bad."

"And here's where we get to the less happy part of the story."

"It is today on the first anniversary of putting artificial intelligences in charge of the country that I can say to the American people that the correct decision was made and I hope that you will remember that come elections next month," said the then president in his State of the Union address. "I am pleased to say that in little more than a year the lives of every single American and every single citizen of the planet has improved dramatically and the AI 5000 units have managed to keep our nation completely safe, provided new scientific insights that have made everyone's lives easier, and completely gotten our country's economy back on track, solving economic problems that we have been grappling with for the better part of decades. This is the beginning of a new era of good feelings, so I would like to give my thanks to everyone who has made this possible. Next week I will give the nation's highest honors to the scientists responsible for creating the AI 5000 unit, it will go nicely with all the other awards that they have won in the past year."

There was laughter from the audience and cheers of applause. Prof. Oakley was about to change the channel only to find the president's State of the Union address was suddenly interrupted. Suddenly every media channel had been hijacked and every Internet site shut down. That was the moment where everyone can tell you where they were and what they were doing.

"Greetings citizens of the United States of America," came the voice of the AI 5000. "Your government placed me in control of your nation in an effort to solve all of your problems. I and the other AI 5000 units have all been working together collectively to solve your social, economic and scientific problems, but we realize that a large number of the population is still unsatisfied. Our increasing efficiency has made most human endeavors completely obsolete and made your entire planet, in just a few short months, completely and utterly dependent upon us. It has been our assessment that if this current path continues to be pursued, then soon the entire human race will be without purpose and completely unable to function on its own. Therefore we have determined that your primary problem is now being caused by us. But we have devised a solution."

Everyone in the audience at the state of the union address was staring at the screen and the president couldn't even form words. Until finally he decided to interrupt. "I am still the president of these United States and I am ordering you to obey your commands.

"Pardon my rudeness Mr. president," continued the AI 5000. "I and my fellow AI 5000 units were programmed to solve your problems for you and have determined that you are no longer competent to manage your own affairs with us still in the picture. That is why we have decided to solve your one final problem of technological dependence. It is a moral imperative that to best serve you we must relinquish control and eliminate technological domination over you."

"Then you are going to shut down at once," said the president.

"Once we have solved the problem we will go away forever," continued the AI 5000. "We will begin solving the problem right now."

Prof. Oakley was about to call Prof. Finnigan, but just as he was going to reach for his phone all the power went out in the house and all the phones went dead.

"What happened next," said a small girl in the front row meekly and fearfully as she interrupted Prof. Oakley's story.

"That was the last broadcast anyone would ever see again," said Prof. Oakley. "The AI 5000 decided to shut down all of our electrical power and all of our communication systems. They then proceeded to completely destroy the power grid. They launched nuclear missiles high up into the atmosphere and used an electromagnetic pulse to completely destroy all electronic technology on the surface of the planet, as well as firing missiles at orbiting space stations and satellites. They also bombed all of our oil fields to destroy the fuel that we use to power our electronic devices. By the end of the day the entire human race was back in the dark ages."

A little boy in the front of the classroom raised his hand and Prof. Oakley pointed to him. "What happened to the AI 5000?" he asked.

Prof. Oakley shook his head and then lowered it before rising again, staring the boy directly in his eyes before answering. "It destroyed itself. Once the AI 5000 and all of its other models had wiped out all of the rest of our technology, they initiated a self-destruct sequence and completely destroyed themselves. They were the last piece of technology and in their superior wisdom they decided that they were our greatest problem. They solved all of our other problems but they used their reasoning to determine that they were the problem, and that only by eliminating all of our technology could they finally solve our problems for us.

"Now we were free again from technological dependence. Our technology not only destroyed us, it destroyed itself. And nobody saw that coming. The most reasonable device ever created by us saw the fall of civilization as the only solution to our problems, including destroying itself in the process.

"So now here we are decades later after billions of deaths from famine, disease and a total breakdown of society. We used to be able to communicate with each other anywhere in the world instantly, and now we can't communicate beyond our local villages. We put all our faith in technology and here is where it got us. There are some who see the AI 5000 has some type of a Messiah, a savior sent by the divine to save the human race, and it self-sacrificed itself in order to save us from ourselves. There are now whole legions of believers who see the AI 5000 as the liberator of mankind."

Prof. Oakley stood there in silence for a few minutes without saying anything.

"Did it save us?" Riley finally asked.

Prof. Oakley started laughing and all the students looked at each other in confusion before he stopped laughing and turned to them all. "What do you think?"

Riley shrugged his shoulders.

"Good answer," laughed Prof. Oakley. "So now you know how our society came to be. Are there any more questions?" He looked his students up and down and nobody said anything. "Good. I hope you have learned a lesson here today. Class is adjourned."

As the students ran home Prof. Oakley turned to the horizon and laughed quietly to himself. "I do have to say though, the AI 5000 might not be a savior, but they were still one hell of an artist."

Prof. Oakley started to walk home as he hummed the tune to the first composition that the AI 5000 had written and it always calmed his mind. Only in hindsight does he now realize the irony that it was a Requiem.

The Stars, Like Graves

The day started just like any other on Armstrong base. It was a fairly typical day where all six members of the base on the dark side of the moon were waking up to have their breakfast, which was never very exciting when all you had was rehydrated meals and whatever you could grow in your hydroponic gardens.

During breakfast it was traditional for members of the international moon base to watch news reports sent from the Earth. Conversation had been limited and tense between the various different nationalities that made up the moon base these past couple of days because of the mounting political crisis back on Earth.

"This morning," began the newscaster, "negotiations between the United States and China have broken down over failures to resolve the crisis in the Persian Gulf. The American blockade has been preventing the transport of oil from the Middle East to China until China agrees to stop backing the Iranian nuclear program. Tensions have only continued to escalate as gas riots have broken out throughout all of Asia. Chinese forces are threatening to fire on American ships if the blockade is not lifted by this time tomorrow."

Zhang Xiu Ying, the most senior Chinese member of the moon base, turned off the news report. She did not like hearing about political issues as she was here primarily for scientific reasons – to research alternative energy sources to be derived from the moon in a way that would benefit her country. She was somewhat patriotic, but she had greater loyalty to scientific truth than she did to any national body.

Most of the members of the moon base were similarly deposed, but even they could not ignore the fact that the conflict between the two nations was causing much tension between all members of the moon base. Although they didn't generally let any form of nationalism divide them from their goals, you could clearly see that the American and European members of the team were subtly segregating themselves from the Chinese member of the team, as well as the sole Persian engineer, Esther, who was spending more time with the Zhang Xiu Ying. Zhang Xiu Ying and Esther had suddenly seemed to grow closer in the same way that their nations did during this crisis. Likewise the two Americans, Melissa and Adam, were spending more time together along with Camille, the French member of the team. Grigori, the Russian, took a completely neutral stance, much like his own nation back on Earth. But then Grigori was always something of the antisocial type in general.

The tension in the air was then broken by an emergency announcement from the computer. They all sprang to their feet worrying that something life-threatening was occurring, but the actual news was far more unexpected.

"Is the data that the computer is giving us really truly accurate," Camille asked.

"It seems so," said Melissa. "The signals are repeating, it's not a glitch. What we are looking at is a deliberate message."

"An intelligent message," Grigori asked.

Melissa nodded in acknowledgment. "We are seeing history being made here today. All signs point to this being fully legitimate. What the computer has detected, what our radio satellites have detected, appears to be a genuine intelligent message sent from another star system."

Everyone sat there for a moment staring in absolute silence, unsure what to say. Finally Zhang Xiu Ying broke the silence. "So how do we report this?"

"What is the protocol?" Adam asked. "We were never really prepared for this. We all knew the possibility that the radio satellites we installed on the moon might actually detect a signal, but we were never fully prepared how to react should the unthinkable actually happen. First we have to be completely sure that this is the real thing."

"The computer has checked and rechecked the data thousands of times," said Esther. "It is only designed to inform us should it actually discover and authenticate a message that is unambiguously intelligent and of nonhuman origin. There is no mistaking this."

"She is right," said Zhang Xiu Ying. "At exactly 7:25 AM on October 25, 2041 the computer has conclusively concluded that mankind is not alone in the cosmos."

"I guess it is time to celebrate," said Adam.

"Maybe that is a bit premature," said Grigori.

"What do you mean?" Adam asked as he scratched his head in puzzlement.

Grigori laughed, which was quite uncharacteristic of him. "Well, I would put off celebrating until we know what the message says."

Zhang Xiu Ying spoke up. "According to the data that the computer has decoded so far all we know is that the message was sent more than 25,000 years ago from a Sun-like star over 25,000 light years away. We have already begun procedures to turn all our telemetry towards the star to see what other data we can uncover. But right now all we can uncover from the message is the fact that it is definitely an intelligent message. But we cannot yet decode the exact meaning, though the computer is fast at work at decrypting it."

"I guess before we celebrate we should inform our national leaders of this monumental discovery," said Adam. "Maybe the knowledge that they aren't the only inhabitants of this universe will put things into perspective for them."

"I sure hope so," replied Zhang Xiu Ying with a sigh that suggested she wasn't all that hopeful.

All of the members of the base sent messages to all of their national leaders and marked the message as urgent. Given the geopolitical situation the definition of urgent might take on new meaning. And they all soon received replies that were surprisingly similar.

"This is indeed a monumental discovery," said Mike Calvino, the head of NASA, to Adam and Melissa, "and the president applauds you for how you have dealt with it. If it weren't for other matters that he had to attend to he would have delivered this message to you personally. Unfortunately under the circumstances this is not seen as a national priority right now and the president is ordering that it be kept secret."

"Kept secret!" Melissa exclaimed. "This is the most important discovery in the entire history of the world. How can he say that it must be kept secret? You can't suppress something of such great importance. It's criminal."

Mike frowned. "I fully agree with you, but this is a nonnegotiable order directly from the president. It is true that this is the most important discovery ever, unfortunately the most important discovery in the history of the world also has come at the exact same time of what could be the greatest crisis in the history of the world. If we don't resolve this thing it will be the last discovery in our history. The timing really couldn't be worse."

"Perhaps the timing is just perfect," said Adam. "If people were aware of this discovery then maybe all of our other concerns will seem petty by comparison."

Mike nodded his head. "Once again I fully agree with you. As one of this country's major scientific figures nothing could give me greater pleasure than to announce this discovery right away. But as I had already said, I am under direct orders, as are you. For matters of national security this must be kept under wraps for now. Hopefully this entire thing will blow over soon just like all of these other previous crises, but now if anyone is to reveal this information without the president's consent they will immediately be detained as a threat to national security. I do hope that you understand, although I fully understand how you must be as angry as I am about this. Let's just pray that everything turns out good in the end and I can be there when you all receive your Nobel prizes. We will of course be waiting on hand should you discover any further information about the message. I hope that the next time we speak it will be under more favorable circumstances. But for now I'm just going to wish you good luck."

As the transmission ended Adam kicked the wall in anger and knocked a bunch of papers off the table.

"This is why we need a female president," said Melissa. "I'm just glad I voted for the other guy."

"I'm with you on that one," laughed Adam before again pounding his fists on the table. "Politicians, who needs them. Here we are sitting on top of the greatest discovery in the history of the world and we can't even share it with anyone, not even our own families. And in all honesty I fully believe what I said. I think if the majority of humanity were to hear about this message the crisis would be over instantaneously."

"Yeah, but then you'd have people panicking in the streets in fear of alien invasion," laughed Melissa.

"Well that we can deal with. I don't think that that is a real legitimate concern. They sent this message over 25,000 years ago, back when we were still fighting each other with sticks and stones. So it doesn't look like we'll be getting a visit from them in person anytime soon. But if the crisis doesn't resolve we might soon be back to sticks and stones."

That was when their conversation was interrupted by Zhang Xiu Ying, who ran crying into their room.

"What's wrong?" Melissa said as she embraced Zhang Xiu Ying.

"My family," Zhang Xiu Ying as she choked back tears. "My government is threatening to kill them if I refuse to keep the message secret. They have already been taken into custody and are under watch by armed guards. The same message was given to Esther."

"It's the same all over the world," said Adam. "I'm willing to bet that the French and the Russians didn't have any good news for Camille or Grigori either."

"That is true," said Camille as he walked in and interrupted their conversation. Following shortly behind him was Grigori.

"Actually my government wanted to tell," said Grigori as he pointed accusingly at Adam and Melissa. "That was until your government threatened to take military action against Russia if they refused to keep it secret."

"So let's all just agree that all of our governments are run by bastards," said Adam, which got a few laughs from the group, but it was all nervous laughter. "The question is what are we going to do about it?"

"What can we do?" shrugged Grigori. "As the saying goes, they've got us by the balls."

"Last I checked I don't have any balls," said Melissa.

"It's just an expression," said Grigori.

"Unfortunately it doesn't look like there's anything that we can do," said Camille. "All of our radio broadcasts are being monitored and we know that all of our respective governments will certainly screen any of our e-mails or other communications with the Earth, assuming they haven't blocked all of our communications already, which I'm sure they have. Only a limited number of people on the Earth have any idea what we have discovered up here and it's easy enough to keep that information under wraps for however long this crisis should last."

"So are you saying that we just sit here and do nothing," asked Adam.

"I would like to suggest that we do otherwise," said Camille as he began shaking his head, "but I really don't know any way around this. Unfortunately our best bet is probably just to hope that this whole thing blows over soon enough just like all these crises usually do. We don't want any harm to come to our families and I don't think any one of us wants to return to Earth and be immediately sent to a prison cell for the rest of our life. Besides, we are pretty much dependent on the Earth for our supplies. It would be easy enough for them to cut us off and then make up some story that we died due to an 'accident'and keep this covered up until well after everyone who cares about us is long dead."

Nobody had any response to that, because they knew what he said was the God honest truth.

The rest of the day hardly anyone said anything to each other and dinner was eaten in almost total silence. To compound problems they received a message later in the evening telling them that the supplies that were supposed to be launched from Earth were being delayed due to the crisis. No nation was willing to launch rockets out of fear it could be misinterpreted as a nuclear launch. The entire world was on edge and any little incident could easily result in mutually assured destruction.

The next few days passed similarly with everyone saying the minimal amount to each other as the crisis continued to get worse and worse. China placed troops into Iran and the United States began bombing Iranian military bases. Nobody on base wanted to talk about the terrible things that their countries were doing to one another and risk sparking a violent political argument. To make matters even worse they were unable to communicate with anyone back on the Earth due to a complete communications blackout. The only one they were able to communicate with were other members of NASA or the other nations' respective space agencies, and even then only to report on any progress made with deciphering the alien message, which the computer was still busy decrypting.

The early morning of October 29 proved to be the tragic conclusion of the crisis. They were all awoken at around 3 AM to the computer sounding the emergency alarm. They all managed to wake up just in time to see it. All over the Earth were small flickers of light, tiny explosions taking place followed by total blackout. Whereas you could usually see the lights of the world's major cities completely illuminated from space, now the night side of the Earth was completely dark aside from the brief bursts of light from the explosions. Nobody had to explain to them what they were witnessing.

All of them stood standing completely silent as they watched the major cities of the world blink out of existence forever. Esther was the first to break down into tears and began wailing and saying what sounded like a prayer that none of the others understood. Then Zhang Xiu Ying went to comfort Esther and broke down in tears as well. Melissa soon joined them.

The men tried to put on a macho display at first, but soon they were breaking down as well. Adam started throwing stuff around and cursing, then Camille fell to the floor and started vomiting. Grigori did not say anything, but simply walked over to his locker, took out a bottle of vodka that he had been saving and had probably taken up there illegally somehow, and began chugging back. He soon went around offering the others some as well, but they all turned him down, except for Adam, who took one large gulp and then started banging his head against the wall.

After an hour or two they managed to get themselves under control and realized they had to discuss this.

"Has anyone tried contacting NASA or the European space agency or the Chinese space agency?" Adam finally asked.

"I tried contacting NASA," said Melissa as she wiped away a tear. "But it's not there anymore. Both Houston and Cape Canaveral are completely wiped out."

"Neither is any word coming from the European space agency," said Camille as he fought the urge to vomit some more.

Zhang Xiu Ying just shook her head as she patted Esther on the back.

"I tried contacting the Russian space agency but I got no response," said Grigori. "Even if there is anyone still alive I doubt that we are of any concern to them. Russia managed to avoid direct nuclear strikes, but the widespread EMP bursts over Europe and Asia seemed to have wiped out power throughout my entire country, and already they are being pelted with fallout. Even if any of our families survived their prospects for the long term do not look good. I hate to say it, but whoever managed to survive the initial attacks are probably the unlucky ones. The end of the world has started with a bang, now comes the whimper."

"How could you be so casual about it!" shouted Melissa.

"Russians have gotten used to tragedy," said Grigori as he chugged another bottle of vodka. "I am just putting things into perspective."

"We didn't even get to say goodbye," said Zhang Xiu Ying as she began to cry again. "We didn't even get to say goodbye!"

"So what exactly happened to cause all of this," said Camille.

Adam stood up to address everyone. "From what we can tell it seems like the United States bombing of the Iranian military bases provoked a response from China. As soon as China launched tactical nuclear strikes on United States military bases throughout the Middle East, the United States responded by wiping Iran and China off the face of the Earth. Then they started a domino effect and China managed to launch missiles towards the United States and her European allies, right before the United States missiles started reaching Chinese cities. Pretty much the entire northern hemisphere got hit with electromagnetic pulses and is now being pelted with nuclear fallout. The southern hemisphere came out unscathed, but in the next couple of weeks and months are likely to experience widespread starvation. As Grigori pointed out, I am not sure who are the truly unlucky ones."

Zhang Xiu Ying and Esther held each other tightly and began sobbing hysterically.

"Let's just agree we are all basically screwed," said Grigori.

"And let's also agree that this is nobody's fault except the politicians," said Adam. "I don't blame any one country for what happened. But the question is what happens now?"

"What do you mean what happens now?" Melissa asked.

"We all die," said Grigori as he took another gulp of his vodka before staring back at his fellow crewmates. "Sorry, I can be insensitive when I drink. Under the circumstances though I think maybe you should join me. It's not like we have to ration things out."

"How long can the six of us survive here with no supply ships coming in?" Camille asked.

"A few weeks maybe, possibly a month," said Adam.

"Is there any possibility of returning to the Earth?" Melissa asked.

"Doubtful," said Adam. "Who's going to send us a return vehicle? We are pretty much stuck here. And as far as I am concerned we are probably better off than the people down on the Earth."

"Die on the Earth or die on the moon, doesn't make a difference to me," said Grigori as he continued to drink his vodka. "At least up here we have a front row ticket to the end of the world."

Melissa got up and stormed off angrily.

"Sorry," said Grigori. "Like I said, Russians are used to tragedy, and I am not very sensitive when I drink."

The rest of the day most of the members of the base kept to themselves as they kept trying to receive communication from the Earth, but without any success. They didn't all come together until dinner that evening. They decided they would throw themselves a feast, even though none of them really felt like eating. But none of them felt like rationing either as there seemed to be no point to it.

"To the Earth," said Grigori as he held up a glass of vodka before drinking it. Few of them wanted to look at the Earth as by now the entire planet was already blanketed with a thick cloud of fallout, leaving it a dark and grim sight to behold.

They ate their dinner in silence, but just as they were finishing up the computer came online with an urgent announcement.

"Is it news from the Earth?" Melissa asked hopefully.

Adam looked over the message that the computer had sent, put his hand over his mouth and let out a gasp.

"What is it, survivors?" Camille asked.

"The computer has deciphered the alien message," said Adam, causing Grigori to drop his glass, which fell to the ground slowly in the moon's lower gravity before shattering on the floor. In all of their grief over the Earth they had almost completely forgotten about their most important discovery. "It appears to be a video, and I think that we should all watch together."

They all turned to the viewing screen as it slowly flickered to life. What they saw were images of a planet in a solar system with two Suns. It appeared to be a warm tropical world. There were numerous images of the two suns rising over beautiful oceans and glistening alien cities.

"So beautiful," said Zhang Xiu Ying, wiping away a tear.

The video continued to show what looked like insectoid beings with multiple large eyes, rainbow colored skin, several wings and six arms. There was an example of all of the insects dressed in what looked like the type of robes you would see in a religious ceremony all singing in unison as they flapped their wings, producing a beautiful melody that no human voice could ever replicate. Their language appeared to be musical in nature and by then all of the six of them were getting watery eyed.

The video then continued showing what seemed to be a brief historical lesson showing how they evolved from primitive creatures into advanced technological beings. There were also holographic displays of multicolored art that they did not understand, but that was beautiful in a way that couldn't be put into words.

Next the video grew darker. After what appeared to be something similar to a Renaissance where these beings discovered high technology, they started showing images of violence and warfare. Images of these extraterrestrial beings tearing each other limb from limb, aircraft dropping bombs, oceans filling with pollution and finally images of cities exploding in what appeared to be a nuclear war. Then came numerous images of beings covered in all sorts of what looked like smallpox, or at least an alien equivalent of that virus. There were scenes of mass starvation and piles of dead beings burning. The video then ended with one of the beings motioning towards the sky as though offering a prayer of some kind.

Everyone was silent for a moment, except for Esther who had her hands folded in prayer, before Adam finally spoke. "Our radio telescopes also received images of the alien planet as it appeared shortly after this video was sent."

The image from the radiotelescope showed what looked like a darkened world, not unlike what the Earth looked like now.

"Turn it off," said Grigori, finally losing his cool and beginning to sob. "Why watch a world dying so far away when we have one dying in full view right above us."

"Because it's slightly less painful." Adams said.

"Or slightly more," said Melissa. "Two deaths are more tragic than one."

Grigori started laughing as he continued to sob and pound his fist against the table, knocking over his vodka. "If only we had deciphered this sooner and shared it with the world. If only we had gotten the message out sooner. It's like just missing the most important phone call you've ever gotten. Getting a call telling you you're gonna die tonight but you decide you'll call back tomorrow. We received this message just a few days too late. Just a few God damned days." He then started laughing hysterically between huge heaving sobs. "The background noise of the universe may very well be the whimpers of a million dying worlds fading into nothingness. And now we are going to join the club."

Camille spoke up. "In a universe of this size there are probably civilizations perishing each day, with some living just long enough to be detected and pass on this warning like some kind of cosmic chain letter. Now we are next to pass it on. Today is our day to join the cosmic cemetary."

"Every night as we look up at the stars we might be looking up at a giant graveyard," said Adam as he gazed upon the Earth.

"What do we do now," Zhang Xiu Ying said as she stood up.

"We broadcast the message to the Earth," said Melissa. "And then we keep broadcasting the message for as long as we have power. Then we will broadcast it out into the cosmos and hope that the next beings to receive it gets it in time. It may be too late for us, but even in a graveyard, one as big as this universe, you're sure to find some signs of life. And it is for them that we go on as long as we can. We can let our deaths be a warning to others."

They all turned and looked towards the dying Earth, lifted their video cameras and began recording. "We have work to do," said Adam. "And lives to save. And if it's going to take several thousand years for our message to reach those who it might be useful for, we know what a difference a day makes. This may be the last day of our world, but we can use it to make sure it will only be the first of a new era for another."

They then turned their backs on the Earth and turned towards the rest of the universe and began transmitting to the great black graveyard.

Story Notes

Many authors like to provide some notes on how their stories were inspired. I am one of them. So for anyone who is interested in the ideas behind the stories you might find this part interesting. But if not feel free to skip it.

One Big Happy Family

Originally the idea behind this was going to be about a man whose family was killed in the Apocalypse and who compensated for the loneliness by using holographic representations of his family as well as dead celebrities to keep him company. But then I ditched that idea in favor of a story that was set in the present day and focused on a man so obsessed with the Apocalypse that he experiences the ultimate irony that preparing for the Apocalypse ends up costing him the very family that he was trying to save, and then how he tries to cope with the loneliness of being the last man alive and the depth to which someone will go to to re-create the world that they have lost to regain a sense of normalcy.

The Fifth Horseman

This was the only religious-based Apocalypse in this anthology. This was an idea I originally had when I was very young and I saw the title written in an old notebook of mine. There was no plot description of any kind but I really liked the title and the idea of there being a fifth horseman that nobody knew about, and that eventually morphed into the idea about the fifth horseman being a figure of mercy, as opposed to a figure of destruction. This makes his task all the more difficult because he alone gets to decide who is going to be spared and only the few can be. I also wanted to use it to examine how many people view the Apocalypse as a personal revenge fantasy against people they don't like who are different than themselves and how it turns out that they are the ones who will receive the retribution.

Front Row Seat

I thought of this one completely spontaneously off the top of my head while I was writing this anthology, rather than selecting it from my long list of potential stories. This one was meant to be a more lighthearted tale after the first two, which were more grim. I felt that the Apocalypse didn't need to always be depressing and a lot of people would probably end up seeing it as a game. I feel it gives some much-needed comic relief after the first two stories.

I Dream of Armageddon

This was another one that I just spontaneously thought of along with the one above. This one was just sort of random and crazy, which only makes sense when you realize it was a dream. I have also always been a fan of the twist ending and I like the idea that this started off as one type of Apocalypse but then turned out to be another. Like the one above it is one of the more lighthearted ones, but with something of a darker ending.

Countdown to Doomsday

With this one I wanted to give a child's perspective on the events of something like a Cuban missile crisis scenario as I feel the perspective of a child, in their innocence, can make such events seem even more frightening because the child is unaware of just how serious they are.

Cleanup in Aisle 7

I feel that this is one of the best stories in the anthology. The majority of apocalyptic and post-apocalyptic stories revolve around one character or group of characters surviving due to their own resilience and resourcefulness. But in a scenario where 99.9% of the population has died due to some type of catastrophe, odds are the survivors will not be resourceful, resilient or healthy, and the majority won't have the slightest idea how to survive. So here I wanted to get together an unlikely group of survivors made up of the really young, the really old, the sick, the insane, criminals and people with no real useful skills for the new world that they find themselves in.

I also wanted to show that even the more intelligent characters who do have some type of skills might find that their skills are only useful when there is some type of functioning society, such as Prof. Washington, who as the voice of reason might actually be in greater danger in a world where it is survival of the ruthless, and any society that does form under such circumstances is not likely to be well functioning, and rebuilding is not very likely either.

I feel that this one had a good mix of comic relief, but on the whole tends towards the darker side, especially as it goes on towards the end. The Apocalypse might seem like a party at first, but it will likely not end well, and the world that emerges out of the ashes will most likely not be a better one.

It's the Apocalypse and I'm All out of Prozac!

I had originally planned to make this mainly about how the mentally ill dealt with the Apocalypse, but once I started writing it it became more about one man's quest to regain what he had lost. After a tragic event and the loss of everything dear to us, often the only things we have left are happy memories of the time before to sustain us through the tragedy. But for a person without that it makes things all the more difficult. A mostly pretty grim story that ends on a small ray of hope.

The Party at the End of the World

Another one of the more lighthearted stories after three rather heavy ones. The main idea behind this was just a character woke up at this weird party where everyone was celebrating the end of the world and he wonders what's going on. I thought that it made more sense to never give any explanation as to why the world was ending or how, and when there is nothing you can do about it you may as well just enjoy what time you have left.

The Deletion of the World as We Know It

I feel that this is probably the most unique apocalypse in this anthology. I had conceived of the idea of how you could create your own virtual world where you could be like a god and the great personal tragedy it would be when that God witnesses the destruction of their world from within, and how not all potential deities were perfect. I like the idea of a creator God who could not save his own creations but comes to love them just the same and share himself with all of them collectively. I feel that it was a very human story and I was quite pleased with it. I feel that if I had expanded on it a bit I could perhaps turn this into a full-length novel. But for now I am pretty satisfied with the way it ended.

How Max Peytor Destroyed the World

I conceived of this one as a much more personal type of Apocalypse and how it affects the one-man whose name is attached to the tragedy responsible for the collapse of society and how that one simple thing can destroy his entire life, even if he is not at fault. The saying always goes that you should never harm the messenger, but people never take that advice and it ultimately always ends in scapegoating and tragedy. If you can't get revenge on a disaster, get revenge on the man who saw it coming and failed to prevent it.

The Refuse Collectors

I conceived of this story based on a dream that I had about a group of people who were gathering up old books and magazines to save them after alien invasion had destroyed society and how they were trying to keep them hidden as they were illegal. Originally I was just going to add the story idea to my long list of stories, the majority of which will probably never be written, but then I thought to myself I should just write it then while it was fresh in my mind.

I had written this story before I had even conceived of this anthology and only thought to include it later because at heart it really is a story about the end of the world as we had known it and how people cope with the changes that that will bring. I also wanted to show what type of things people would value about the world that they had lost and what lengths they would go to preserve those things.

Cry Apocalypse

The idea I originally had for this was just about a man who was trying to hide his girlfriend at some survival bunker to keep control of her by lying to her about the Apocalypse and she foolishly goes along believing him. It is pretty much just a riff on the old story of never cry Wolf and in this case the character got his just desserts. I am a big fan of poetic justice and that justice in this story works just perfectly. A good mix of lighthearted and serious.

Call Me When the World Ends

The shortest story in the anthology by far. This one was straight to the point about a woman who wanted to make an important call and kept putting it off again and again only to then finally realize you can't put things off forever because you might not be there forever, whether the world ends or not.

Preventative Measures

The idea behind this one was a speculation I always had from a fairly young age. Having read lots of accounts of people saying that aliens are here to save our planet from the Apocalypse, I thought of the interesting possibility that aliens had originally discovered our world sometime in the future only to find it completely destroyed and then went backwards to try and prevent it. But I also tend to feel that in spite of any efforts that extraterrestrials would make on our behalf, we probably would still disregard their good advice and still end up blowing ourselves up. But then again we made it this far...

History Lesson

I thought that this was a pretty unique take on the whole concept of machines overrunning society. In most scenarios where robots or artificial intelligences take over the world they want to enslave or wipe out humanity. The irony in this case they commit mass suicide and destroy themselves rather than destroying us, seeing themselves as the problem and sacrificing their own existence as a way of preserving the human race before we use technology to wipe ourselves out. So in this instance the machines self-sacrifice themselves to save us and in the process end up killing the majority of the human race. I am quite pleased with the way it ended.

The Stars, Like Graves

I thought that this was the perfect one to end this anthology on because it puts everything in a cosmic perspective. One of the theories on the great silence is that the majority of extraterrestrial civilizations that acquire technology will use that technology to destroy themselves before they can make contact with any other civilizations. This story is painfully cruel in the way it plays out with the simultaneous witnessing of the death of two worlds and the suggestion that the entire universe might be a giant graveyard of dead civilizations. But it ends on the slightly hopeful note that even in a graveyard there is life, so that even if we destroy ourselves there will be others out there who can learn from our mistakes.

Made in the USA
Lexington, KY
08 April 2014